A HORSE OF A DIFFERENT COLOR . . .

Pounding down out of the scrub came the Iron Horse. Lightning flashed on its metallic flanks. It breathed no smoke and whistled no greeting. Its eyes were the fiery orange of the wood box, and the spirits of the dead kept its engine well stoked. It rattled and banged as it ran, and there was a blind indifference about it that was more terrifying than an overt sense of purpose could have been. Looking at it, you'd think it had no more sense in its iron skull, no more care for what it was trampling underfoot than did a train.

It came crashing into the camp, kicking aside piles of big ties like they were toothpicks, its massive iron hooves making pulp of wheelbarrows and buckets and storage sheds.

Then it came for Malone. He could smell steel breath and squinted against the iron filings that were spat his way. Taking a deep breath, he spoke in a voice as large as any the clouds overhead could produce:

"WHOA!"

By Alan Dean Foster
Published by Ballantine Books:

THE BLACK HOLE
CACHALOT
DARK STAR
THE METROGNOME and Other Stories
MIDWORLD
NOR CRYSTAL TEARS
SENTENCED TO PRISM
SPLINTER OF THE MIND'S EYE
STAR TREK® LOGS ONE–TEN
VOYAGE TO THE CITY OF THE DEAD
... WHO NEEDS ENEMIES?
WITH FRIENDS LIKE THESE ...

The Icerigger Trilogy
  ICERIGGER
  MISSION TO MOULOKIN
  THE DELUGE DRIVERS

The Adventures of Flinx of the Commonwealth
  FOR LOVE OF MOTHER-NOT
  THE TAR-AIYM KRANG
  ORPHAN STAR
  THE END OF THE MATTER
  BLOODHYPE
  FLINX IN FLUX
  MID-FLINX

The Damned
  Book One: A CALL TO ARMS
  Book Two: THE FALSE MIRROR
  Book Three: THE SPOILS OF WAR

MAD AMOS

Alan Dean Foster

A Del Rey® Book
BALLANTINE BOOKS • NEW YORK

A Del Rey® Book
Published by Ballantine Books

Library of Congress Catalog Card Number: 95-92543

ISBN 0-345-39362-7

Manufactured in the United States of America

First Edition: March 1996

10 9 8 7 6 5 4 3 2 1

CONTENTS

Introduction

FACE IT, THE AMERICAN WEST HAS ALWAYS fascinated people. Not just Americans, either. It's a geohistorical iconography familiar to people the world over, usually but not always exclusively in the form of film. So thoroughly has the history of the American West been adopted across the planet that tourists still come from as far away as Japan and India expecting to find laconic cowboys riding the range and wild Indians assaulting their tour bus.

Nowadays they're more likely to encounter laconic Indians and wild cowboys. I speak from contemporary experience because I've lived for the past fifteen years in an "old western town" of some note, where on Saturday nights real cowboys and real Indians mix it up in a couple of dozen bars, with a few bikers thrown in for spice. Prescott was the first territorial capital of Arizona and still retains great pride in its history. To get the feel of the Old West hereabouts you don't have to rent a John Ford video or pick up a book. All that's necessary is to walk down Whiskey Row, with its turn-of-the-century

1

drinking establishments, or wander around the courthouse plaza, featured in dozens of films from *Billy Jack* on.

Numerous old buildings flaunt stone dates from the nineteenth century, and the best restaurant in town is located in Gardner's General Store, one of the oldest mercantile buildings in Arizona. A pair of wooden Indian sculptures sat in the front window of that store from the 1930s until it was converted into a restaurant and the decor appropriately modified. One of them now reposes, comfortable and very much at home, in our den.

The Santa Fe rail depot contains shops now, but Solon Borglun's heroic bronze of roughrider and sheriff Bucky O'Neil still graces the approach to the courthouse, and weekend prospectors and the occasional persistent teenager continue to scoop gold nuggets out of the surrounding creeks. John C. Fremont (he of military accomplishment and thwarted presidential aspirations) would find his original log home still standing and respectfully maintained on the grounds of the Sharlot Hall Museum.

North lies the Grand Canyon, to the east is the grand mining town of Jerome (built on a slope that makes San Francisco look flat), and to the south you are greeted by off-ramps from Interstate 17 with names like Bloody Basin and Dead Dog Road. Immersed in and surrounded by so much western history, I suppose it was inevitable that I would eventually write something set in that era. There was always only one problem.

I don't write westerns.

My interests have generally lain elsewhere on the planet, and frequently off it. Living in a mining town, I've tended to mine the future rather than the past and scrabbled for my nuggets in the pages of *Scientific American*, *The Economist*, and *Australian Geographic*, to name but a few veins of inspiration. I did write the book version of Clint Eastwood's flawed but intriguing western film *Pale Rider* and had fun doing so, but I regarded it only as an isolated diversion. Anyway, the idea wasn't mine.

Then one day (to employ a perhaps overly familiar but still effective lead), my wife and I were coming home from shopping. When you enter our house, it's through the den, a spacious room decorated in western style that's filled with the accoutrements of the Old West. A second-floor landing leads to a single tiny upstairs room. Making exceedingly small talk, I happened to glance up at the empty landing and remark, "You know, we need something up there. A stuffed bear or something."

Whereupon JoAnn responded, "Why a bear? Why not a dragon?"

"Don't be silly. There were no dragons in the Old West."

Eyeing me in her usual prosaic west Texas fashion, my mate then countered, "How do *you* know?"

Which set me to thinking. Which led directly to the first story in this collection, "Wu-Ling's Folly." Which led to the invention of the mountain man who is much more than he seems, Amos Malone, whom some call Mad.

Which proves that stories come from everywhere and anywhere, and often when you least expect it (to quote another Alan). Malone was so much fun, I hated to let him go after only one encounter. I enjoy the experience every time I run into him, and I'm sure he'll be coming around for periodic visits from now on.

The Old West was a fantastical sort of place, anyway. Just ask any fanatic German collector of Old West lore (of which there are hundreds). It keeps reinventing itself in book and film, sometimes truthfully, more often with touches of pure fantasy. It's a bottomless fount of inspiration, and if Amos Malone takes the occasional road less traveled, why, who's to say some predecessor of his hasn't been down the same way before? The West's a mysterious place where anything can and often does happen. It grabs the imagination and won't let go, like the coyotes who've been sneaking back east and setting themselves up in the unlikeliest places.

Among the following tall tales only "Wu-Ling's Folly" has appeared previously in book form. It's nice to have them all together.

WU-LING'S FOLLY

What's a dragon doing in the Old West? The Plains Indians spoke of the great Thunderbird, and tales of gigantic eagles and hawks and buzzards are common enough. But dragons belong to another place and culture.

Most notably, they are common in the folklore of China. Of course, you say, China has nothing to do with the Old West. But if you say that, it only proves that your knowledge of the real West comes primarily from Hollywood's version. And the Hollywood version of the Old West tended to be populated strictly by WASPs ... Indians included.

HUNT AND MACLEISH HAD WORKED FOR THE Butterfield Line for six and seven years, respectively. They'd fought Indians, and been through growler storms that swept down like a cold dream out of the eastern Rockies, and seen rattlers as big around the middle as a horse's leg. All that, they could cope with; they'd seen it all before. The dragon, though, was something new. You couldn't blame 'em much for panicking a little when the dragon hit the stagecoach.

"I'm tellin' ya," Hunt was declaring to the Butterfield agent in Cheyenne, "it were the biggest, ugliest, scariest-lookin' dang bird you ever saw, Mr. Fraser, sir!" He glanced back at his driver for confirmation.

"Yep. S'truth." Archie MacLeish was a man of few words and much tobacco juice. He was tough as pemmican and as hard to handle, but the incident had turned a few more of the brown-stained whiskers in his copious beard gray as an old Confederate uniform.

"It come down on us, Mr. Fraser, sir," Hunt continued emphatically, "like some great winged devil raised up by an angry Boston temperance marcher, a-screamin' and a-hollerin' and a-blowin' fire out of a mouth filled with ugly, snaggled teeth. 'Twere a sight fit t' raise the departed. I gave it both barrels of Evangeline." He indicated the trusty ten-gauge resting in a corner of the office. "And it ne'er even blinked. Ain't that right, Archie?"

"Yep," confirmed the driver, firing accurately into the bronze-inlaid pewter spittoon set at a corner of the big walnut desk.

"I see." The Butterfield agent was a pleasant, sympathetic gentleman in his early fifties. Delicate muttonchop whiskers compensated somewhat for the glow the sun brought forth from his naked forehead. His trousers were supported by overloaded suspenders that made dark tracks across an otherwise immaculate white shirt. "And then what happened?"

"Well, both Archie and me was ready t' meet our maker. You got to understand, Mr. Fraser, sir, this varmint were bigger than coach and team together. Why, them poor horses like t' die afore we coaxed and sweet-talked 'em into town. They're bedded down in the company stable right now, still shakin' at the knees.

"Anyways, this ugly bird just reached down with one claw the size o' my Aunt Molly's Sunday dress and plucked the strongbox right off the top, snappin' the guy ropes like they was made o' straw. Then it flew off, still a-screechin' and a-brayin' like the grandfather of jackasses toward the Medicine Bow Mountains."

"God's Truth," said the driver.

"This is all most interesting," Fraser mumbled. Now, while known as a sympathetic man, the Butterfield agent would have been somewhat disinclined to believe the tale to which his two employees were swearing, save for the fact that MacLeish and Hunt were still standing in front of his desk rather than cavorting drunk and debauched in the fleshpots of Denver, spending free and easy the ten thousand in gold that the missing strongbox had contained.

And, of course, there was also the confirmation afforded by the stage's three passengers, a reputable Mormon rancher from Salt Lake and two of his wives. At the moment the ladies were under the care of a local physician who was treating them for shock.

"Couldn't it have been a williwaw?" he asked hopefully.

"Nope," said MacLeish, striking with unerring accuracy into the spittoon a second time. "'Tweren't the likes o' no wind or beastie I ever seed nor heard tell of, Mr. Fraser. I kinna say more than the truth." He squinted hard at the agent. "D' ye doubt our word?"

"No, no, certainly not. It's only that I have no idea how I am to report the nature of this loss to the company. If you'd been held up, that they would understand. But this . . . you must understand my position, gentlemen. There will be questions."

"And *you* should've been in ours, Mr. Fraser, sir," Hunt told him fervently.

The agent was not by his nature an imaginative man, but he thought for a moment, and his slim store of inventiveness came to his rescue. "I'll put it down as a storm-caused loss," he said brightly.

MacLeish said nothing, though he made a face around his wad of fossil tobacco. Hunt was less restrained. He gaped at the agent and said, "But there weren't no storm where we was comin' through, Mr. . . ."

Fraser favored him with a grave look. Hunt began to nod slowly. Meanwhile, MacLeish had walked to the corner and picked up the ten-gauge. He handed it to his partner. The two of them started for the door. And that was the end of that.

For about a week.

* * *

"Another month, boys, and I think we can call it quits." A bulbous nose made a show of sniffing the air. "Snow's in the wind already."

"Damned if you ain't right, there, Emery," said one of the other men.

There were four of them gathered around the rough-hewn table that dominated the center of the cabin. They were spooning up pork, beans, jerky, dark bread, and some fresh fowl. It was a veritable feast compared to their normal cold meals, but they had reason to celebrate.

Johnny Sutter was an eighteen-year-old from Chicago who'd matured ten years in the twelve-month past. "I," he announced, "am goin' to get me a room in the finest whorehouse in Denver and stay stinkin' drunk for a whole month!"

Loud guffaws came from the rest of the men. "Hell, Johnny," said one of them, "if'n yer goin' t' do that, don't waste your time doin' it in a fancy place. Do it in the streets and let me have your room."

"Dang right," said another. "You'll get yourself too stiff t' do what you'll want t' be doin'."

"Not stiff enough, mos' likely," corrected the mulatto, One-Thumb Washington. He laughed louder than any of them, showing a dark gap where his front teeth ought to have been. He'd lost those two teeth and four fingers of his left hand at Shiloh and never regretted it. Two teeth and four fingers were a fair enough trade for a lifetime of freedom.

Wonder Charlie, the oldest of the four, made quieting motions with his hands. His head was cocked to one side, and he was listening intently with his best ear.

"What's wrong with you, old man?" asked Johnny, grinning at all the good-natured ribbing he was taking. "Ain't you got no suggestions for how a man's to spend his money?"

"It ain't thet, Johnny. I think somethin's after the mules."

"Well, hellfire!" Emery Shanks was up from his chair and reaching for his rifle. "If them thievin' Utes think they can sneak in here the day afore we're set t'—"

Wonder Charlie cut him off sharply. "'Tain't Utes. Ol' Com-it-tan promised me personal two springs ago when I sighted out this creek bed thet we wouldn't have no trouble with his people, and Com-it-tan's a man o' his word. Must be grizzly. Listen."

The men did. In truth, the mules did sound unnaturally hoarse instead of skittish as they would if it were only strange men prowling about the camp. It if were a grizzly, it sure would explain the fear in their throats. A big male could carry off a mule alive.

The miners poured out the cabin door, hastily donning boots and pulling up suspenders over their dirty long johns. One-Thumb and Emery fanned out to search the forest behind the hitch-and-rail corral. The moon was swollen near to full, and they could see a fair piece into the trees. There was no sign or sound of a marauding grizzly. One-Thumb kept an eye on the dark palisade of pines as he moved to the corral and tried to calm the lead mule. The poor creature was rolling its eyes and stamping nervously at the ground.

"Whoa, dere, General Grant! Take it easy, mule . . . Wonder what the blazes got into dese mu—"

He broke off as the mule gave a convulsive jerk and pulled away from him. There was something between the camp and the moon. It wasn't a storm cloud, and it certainly wasn't a grizzly. It had huge, curving wings like those of a bat, and wild, glowing red eyes, and a tail like a lizard's. Thin tendrils protruded from its lips and head, and curved teeth flashed like Arapaho ponies running through a moonlit meadow.

"Sweet Lord," Johnny Sutter murmured softly, "wouldja look at that?"

The massive yet elegant shape dropped closer. The mules went into a frenzy. Wonder Charlie, who'd been at Bull Run as well as Shiloh and had emerged from those man-made infernos with his skin intact, didn't hesitate. He fired at that toothy, alien face, a rifle *kaboom*ing through the still mountain air.

The aerial damnation didn't so much as blink. It settled down on wings the size of clipper ship toproyals and began digging with pitchfork-size claws at the watering trough just inside the corral. The mules pawed at the earth, at each other, at the

railing in a frantic desire to crowd as far away from
the intruder as possible.

One-Thumb ducked under the sweep of a great
translucent wing and shouted in sudden realization,
"Curse me for a massa, I think the monster's after
our gold!"

Sure enough, several moments of excavation
turned up a small wooden box. Inside lay the labor
of four men sweating out the riches of a mountain
for a year and a half, a glittering horde of dust and
nuggets large enough to ensure each of them com-
fort for the rest of his life.

Monster bird or no, they'd worked too damn hard
for any of them to give up so easily that pile they'd
wrested from the icy river. They fired and fired, and
when it was clear to see that guns weren't doing any
good, they went after the intruder with picks and
shovels.

When it was all over, a somber moon beamed
down on a scene of theft and carnage. The gold was
gone, and so were the bodies of young Johnny
Sutter and One-Thumb Washington and a mule
named General Grant . . .

There were not many physicians residing in
Cheyenne at the time and fewer still who knew anything about medicine, so it was not entirely coinci-
dental that the one who treated the Mormon
rancher's wives would also become conversant with
the story related by the unfortunate survivors of the
Willow Creek claim. He brought the information to

the attention of Mr. Fraser, the local Butterfield Line agent who had seen to the care of the distraught passengers. Now these two comparatively learned men discussed the events of the week past over sherry in the dining room of the Hotel Paris.

"I am at a loss as to what to do now, Dr. Waxman," the agent confessed. "My superiors in Denver accepted the report I sent to them which described the loss of the strongbox on a mountain road during a violent, freak storm, but I suspect they are not without lingering suspicions. My worry is what to do if this should occur a second time. Not only would the cargo be lost, I should be lost as well. I have a wife and children, Doctor. I have no desire to be sent to a prison . . . or to an asylum. You are the only other educated citizen who has been apprised of this peculiar situation. I believe it is incumbent upon the two of us to do something to rectify the problem. I feel a certain responsibility, as an important member of the community, to do something to ensure the safety of my fellow citizens, and I am sure you feel similarly."

"I agree. Something must be done."

"Well, then. You are positive these two men you treated yesterday were confronted by the same phenomenon?"

"There seems to be no doubt of that." The doctor sipped at his sherry as he peered over thick spectacles at the agent. "With two of their companions carried off by this creature, I should ordinarily have suspected some sort of foul play, were it not for the unique nature of their wounds. Also, they are Christians and swore to the truth of their story quite vociferously to the farmer who found them wandering dazed and bleeding in the mountains, invoking the name of the savior repeatedly."

The agent folded his hands on the clean tablecloth. "More than citizen safety is at stake in this. There is a growing economy to consider. It is clear that this creature has an affinity, nay, a fondness for gold. Why, I cannot imagine. What matters is that next time it may strike at a bank in Cheyenne or some smaller community when there are women and children on the streets.

"But how are we to combat it? We do not even know what we face, save that it surely is not some creature native to this land. I suspect a manifestation of the Devil. Perhaps it would be efficacious for me to have a talk with Pastor Hunnicutt of the—"

The doctor waved the suggestion down. "I think we must seek remedies of a more earthly nature before we proceed to the final and uncertain decision of throwing ourselves on the mercy of the Creator. God helps those who help themselves, whether the Devil is involved or not.

"I have had occasion in my work, sir, to deal with certain individuals whose business it is to travel extensively in this still-wild country. Certain acquaintances sometimes impress themselves most forcefully on these bucolic travelers, who are usually commonsensible if not always hygienic.

"In connection with unusual occurrences and happenings, with unexplained incidents and strange manifestations, one name recurs several times and is uttered with respect by everyone from simple farmers to soldiers to educated citizens such as ourselves. I have been reliably informed that this person, a certain Amos Malone, is presently in the Cheyenne region. I believe we should seek his counsel in this matter."

The Butterfield agent stared across at the doctor, who, having finished his sherry, was tamping tobacco into a battered old pipe. "Amos Malone? Mad Amos Malone? I have heard tell of him. He is a relic, a throwback to the heyday of the mountain man and the beaver hat. Besides which, he is rumored to be quite insane."

"So is half of Congress," the doctor replied imperturbably. "Yet I believe we need him."

The agent let out a long sigh. "I shall defer to your judgment in this matter, sir, but I confess that I am less than sanguine as to its eventual outcome."

"I am not too hopeful myself," the physician admitted, "but we have to try."

"Very well. How are we to get in touch with him? These mountain men do not subscribe to civilized means of communication, nor do they usually remain in one place long enough for contact to be made."

"As to that, I am not concerned." The doctor lit his pipe. "We will put out the word that we require his presence and that it involves a matter of great

urgency and most unusual circumstance. I believe
he will come. As to precisely how he will learn of
our need, I leave that to the unknown and ungover-
nable means by which the breed of man to which he
belongs has always learned of such things."

They waited in the doctor's office. Just before
dawn a light snow had salted the town. Now the
morning sun, hesitantly glimpsed through muddy-
dark clouds, threatened to melt the serenely pale
flakes and turn the streets into a quagmire.

Sitting in the office next to a nickel and iron
stove were the Butterfield Line agent and a distraught, angry, and bandaged-up Wonder Charlie.
Wonder Charlie wasn't feeling too well—his
splinted right arm in particular was giving him
hell—but he insisted on being present, and the doctor thought the presence of an eyewitness would be
vital to give verisimilitude to their story.

The clock on the high shelf chimed six-thirty.

"And that's for your mountain man," snapped
Fraser. He was not in a good mood. His wife, an un-
forgiving woman, had badgered him relentlessly
about risking an attack of colic by tramping outside
so early in the morning.

Dr. Waxman gazed unconcernedly at the clock.
"Give him a little time. The weather is bad."

There was a knock at the door. Waxman glanced
over at the agent and smiled.

"Punctual enough," Fraser admitted reluctantly.
"Unusual for these backwoodsmen."

The doctor rose from his seat and moved to open the door, admitting a man who stood in height somewhere between six feet and heaven. He was clad in dirty buckskin and wet Colorado. Two bandoliers of enormous cartridges crisscrossed his expansive chest. In his belt were secured a bowie knife and a LeMat pistol, the latter an eccentric weapon favored for a time by Confederate cavalry officers. It fit the arrival, Fraser thought.

The man's beard was not nearly as gray-speckled as Wonder Charlie's, but there were a few white wires scattered among the black. His eyes were dark as Quantrill's heart, and what one could see of his actual flesh looked cured as tough as the goatskin boots he wore.

"Cold out there this morning," he said, striding over to the potbellied stove. He rubbed his hands in front of it gratefully, then turned to warm his backside.

The doctor closed the door against the cold and proceeded to make formal introductions. Fraser surrendered his uncallused palm to that massive grip gingerly. Wonder Charlie took it firmly, his age and infirmities notwithstanding.

"Now then, gentlemens, word's out that you folk have got yourselves a little gold problem."

"Bird problem, ye mean," Charlie said promptly, before Fraser or the doctor could slip a word in. "Biggest goddamn bird ye ever saw, mister. Killed two o' my partners and stole our poke. Took off with m' best mule, too. Out o' spite, I thinks, for surely One-Thumb and Johnny would've made the beast a good enough supper."

"Easy there, old-timer," Mad Amos said gently. "It don't do to make your head hurt when the rest of you already does. Now, y'all tell me more about this gold-lovin' bird of yours. I admit to being more than a mite curious about it, or I wouldn't be here."

"And just why *are* you here, Mr. Malone?" Fraser asked curiously. "You have no assurance we are able to pay you for your services or even what extremes of exertion those services might entail."

"Why, I don't care much about that right now, friend." He smiled, showing more teeth than men of his profession usually possessed. "I'm here because I'm curious. Like the cat."

"Curiosity," commented Fraser, still sizing up the new arrival, "killed the cat, if you will remember."

The mountain man turned and stared at him out of eyes so black that the agent shrank a little inside. "Way I figure it, Mr. Fraser, in the long run we're *all* dead."

With the doctor and the agent nearby to assist his memory, Wonder Charlie related his story of the devil-thing that had attacked his camp and killed two of his partners. Then Fraser repeated what his set-upon driving team had told him. He and Charlie argued a little over details of the creature's appearance, picayune disagreements involving color and size, but basically they and their respective stories were in agreement.

When they'd finished, Mad Amos leaned back in

the rocking chair into which he'd settled himself. It creaked with his weight as he clasped both hands around a knee. "Shoot, that ain't no bird you're describing, gentlemens. I thought it weren't when I first heard about it, but I weren't sure. Now I am. What came down on you, old-timer," he told Charlie, "and what lit into your stage, Mr. Fraser, weren't nothin' but a full-blood, gen-u-wine, honest-to-goshen member of the dragon tribe."

"Your pardon, Mr. Malone," said the doctor skeptically, "but a dragon is a mythical creature, an invention of our less enlightened ancestors. This is the nineteenth century, sir. We no longer cotton to such superstitions. I myself once had an encounter with a snake-oil salesman who guaranteed to supply me with some powdered unicorn horn. I am not unskilled in basic chemistry and was able to prove it was nothing more than powder from the common steer."

"Well, y'all better readjust your heads a mite, 'cause that's what got your gold, and those stealings ain't no myth."

"He's right, there," Wonder Charlie said sharply.

"I had thought perhaps a large eagle that normally resides only among the highest and most inaccessible peaks . . ." the doctor began.

"Haw!" Mad Amos slapped his knee a blow that would've felled most men. His laugh echoed around the room. "Ain't no eagle in this world big enough to carry off a full-grown mule, let alone twenty pounds of gold in a Butterfield steel strongbox!

Ain't no eagle got bat wings instead of feathers. Ain't no eagle colored red and yellow and blue and pink and black and everything else. No, it's a true dragon we're dealing with here, gentlemens. By Solomon's seal it is!"

The Butterfield agent spoke up. "I cannot pretend to argue with either of you gentlemen. I have not your scientific knowledge, sir," he told the doctor, "nor your reputed experience in matters arcane, Mr. Malone. The question before us, however, is not what we are dealing with but how we are to be rid of it. I care not what its proper name be, only that I should not have to set eyes upon it." He eyed the mountain man expectantly.

Some said Malone had once been a doctor himself. Others said he had been captain of a great clipper. Still others thought he'd been a learned professor at the Sorbonne in France. General opinion, however, held to it that he was merely full of what the squirrels put away for the Colorado winter. Fraser didn't much care. All he wanted was not to have to explain away the loss of another strongbox filled with gold, and there was a shipment of coin coming up from Denver the very next week.

"That's surely the crux, ain't it? Now, you tell me, old-timer," Malone said to Wonder Charlie, "how many appendages did your visitor have streamin' from his mouth? Did he spit any fire at you? Was his howling high-pitched like a band of attacking Sioux or low like buffalo in the distance?

How did he look at you ... straight on or by twisting his head from one side to the other?"

And so on into the late morning, until the old miner's head ached from the labor of recollection. But Charlie persisted. He'd liked Johnny Sutter and One-Thumb Washington, not to mention poor ole General Grant.

Canvas tents pockmarked the sides of the little canyon, their sides billowing in the wind. Piles of rails and ties were stacked neatly nearby, along with kegs of spikes, extra hammers, and other equipment. Thick smells rose from a single larger tent, while others rose from the far side of the railroad camp. One indicated the kitchen, the other the end product.

The line from Denver to Cheyenne was comparatively new and in need of regular repair. The crew that had laid the original track was now working its way back down the line, repairing and cleaning up, making certain the roadbed was firm and the rails secure.

The muscular, generally diminutive men swinging the hammers and hauling the iron glanced up with interest as the towering mountain man rode into camp. So did the beefy supervisor charged with overseeing his imported workers. Though he came from a line of prejudiced folk, he would brook no insults toward his men. They might have funny eyes and talk even funnier, but by God they'd work all day long and not complain a whit, which was more than you could say for most men.

"All right. Show's over," he growled, aware that work was slowing all along the line as more men paused to gaze at the stranger. "Get your backs into it, you happy sons of heaven!"

The pounding of hammers resumed, echoing down the canyon, but alert dark eyes still glanced in the direction of the silent visitor.

They widened beneath the brows of one broad-shouldered worker when the stranger leaned close and whispered something to him in a melodic, sing-song tongue. The man was so startled, he nearly dropped his hammer on his foot. The stranger had to repeat his query more slowly before he got a reply.

"Most unusual. White Devil speaks fluently the tongue of my home. You have traveled that far, honored sir?"

"Once or twice. I'm never for sure how many. Canton's a nice little town, though the food's a bit thin for my taste. Now, how about my question?"

The man hesitated at that. Despite his size and strength, the worker seemed suddenly frightened. He looked past the visitor's horse as though someone might be watching him.

Mad Amos followed the other man's gaze and saw only tents. "Don't worry," he said reassuringly. "I won't let the one I'm after harm you or any of your friends or relatives back home. I will not allow him to disturb your ancestors. Will you trust me, friend?"

"I will," the worker said abruptly. "The one you seek is called Wu-Ling. You will find him in the third tent down." He leaned on his hammer and pointed. "Good fortune go with you, White Devil."

"Thanks." Mad Amos chucked his horse and resumed his course up the track. The men working on the line watched him intently, whispering among themselves.

Outside the indicated tent he dismounted, pausing a moment to give his horse an affectionate pat. This unique steed was part Indian pony, part Appaloosa, part Arabian, and part Shire. He was black with white patches on his rump and fetlocks and a white ring around his right eye. This eye was unable to open completely, which affected the animal with a sour squint that helped keep teasing children and casual horse thieves well away.

"Now you wait here, Worthless, and I'll be right back. I hope." He turned and called into the tent.

"Enter, useless supplicant of a thousand excuses," replied an imperious voice.

Seated on a mat inside the tent was a youthful Chinese clad in embroidered silk robes and cap. He wore soft slippers and several jade rings. There were flowers in the tent, and they combined with burning incense to keep out the disagreeable odors of the camp. The man's back was to the entrance, and he gestured with boredom toward a lacquered bowl three-quarters filled with coins.

"Place thy pitiful offering in the usual place and

then get out. I am meditating with the forces of darkness. Woe to any who disturb my thoughts."

"Woe to those who meddle with forces they don't understand, progenitor of a hundred bluffs."

The genuflector whirled at the sound of English, only to find himself gaping up at a hairy, ugly, giant White Devil. It took him a moment to compose himself. Then he folded his hands (which Mad Amos thought might be shaking just a little) back into his sleeves and bowed.

Mad Amos returned the bow and said in perfect Mandarin, "Thy ministrations seem to have exceeded thy knowledge, unomnipotent one."

A hand emerged from silk to thrust demandingly at the tent entrance. "Get out of my tent, Devil. Get out! Or I will assuredly turn thee into a lowly toad, as thy face suggests!"

Mad Amos smiled and took a step forward. "Now let's just settle down, inventor of falsehoods, or you'll be the one gets done to. I can't turn you into a toad, but when I finish with you, you'll look like a buffalo carcass a bunch o' Comanches just finished stripping."

The man hesitated but did not back down. He raised both hands and muttered an important-sounding invocation to the skies.

Mad Amos listened a while, then muttered right back at him.

The would-be sorcerer's eyes went wide. "How comes a White Devil to know the secret words of the Shao?"

"That's a long, nasty story. 'Course, I don't know *all* of 'em, but I know enough to know you don't know what the hell you're invoking about. I suspect that's what got you into trouble the last time. I know enough to know this is all a show to impress your hardworking kinfolk out there. You ain't no Mandarin, Wu-Ling, just as you ain't no Shao sorcerer. You're nothing but a clever amateur, a dabbler in darkness, and I think you got yourself in over your head with this dragon business."

"So that is what inflicts you upon me. That damnable beast!" He threw his cap to the floor. "May its toenails ingrow a thousand times! I knew it would bring me problems from the moment the incantation expanded beyond my ability to control the signs." He sat heavily on a cushion, no longer bold and commanding, now just a distraught young would-be lawyer whose pact with the forces of darkness had been overturned by a higher court.

Watching him thus, Mad Amos was able to conjure up a little sympathy for him, no small feat of magic in itself. "How'd you come to have to call him up, anyways?"

"I needed something with which to cow my ignorant kinsmen. There had been mutterings . . . a few had begun to question my right to claim their support, saying that I was not a true sorcerer and could not threaten them as I claimed or work magic back in the homeland for their relatives and friends. I required something impressive to forestall such uncertainties once and for all."

"I see. How'd the railroad feel about your brothers supporting you in luxury while they worked their tails off?"

"The White Devil bosses care nothing for civilized behavior so long as the work is accomplished on time."

"So you finally had to produce, magically speaking, or risk going to work with your own delicate fake-Mandarin hands. That about right?"

"It is as you say." He turned and assumed a prideful air. "And I did produce. A dragon of whole cloth, of ancient mien and fierce disposition did I cause to materialize within the camp one night. Since then there have been no further mutterings among my kinsmen, and my support has multiplied manyfold."

Mad Amos nodded and stroked his luxuriant beard. "Yup, you got a nice little racket going here. 'Course there might be some trouble if I were to stroll outside and announce that you've got no more control over this dragon than I do over a thunderbird's eye. I think your toiling kinsfolk would be a touch unhappy."

The young man's boast quickly turned to desperate pleading. "Please, you must not tell them that, White Devil! Please . . . they would linger over my killing for weeks if they once learned that I have no power over them." His gaze sank. "I confess all this to You Who Know the Words. I have no control over this dragon. I tried to make it vanish once its purpose had been accomplished. It laughed at me and flew off toward the high mountains. I have tried to call it back, to no avail. Now it does as it pleases, threatening your own people as well. I was an overanxious fool, determined to overawe my people. I should have settled for a less dramatic materialization."

Mad Amos nodded sagely. "Now you're learning, inheritor of troubles. It's always best to make sure you've put all the parts back into a disassembled gun before you go firin' it. I kinda feel sorry for you. The main thing is, the damage this dragon's already done wasn't by your direction."

"Oh, no, Honored Devil, no! As I confess before you, I have no control over it whatsoever. It does as it desires."

"Okay, then, I'll strike you a bargain. You quit dealing off the bottom of the deck with your brothers out there. Pick up a hammer and go to work alongside them. I promise it won't kill you, and you'll gain merit in their eyes by working alongside 'em when you supposedly don't have to. Tell 'em it's time for you to put aside wizardly things and exercise your body for a change. You do that and I'll keep my mouth shut."

The young man rose to his feet, hardly daring to hope. "You would do this for me? My ancestors will bless you a hundred times."

"They'd damn well better. I'll need all the help I can gather if I'm going to do anything about this dragon you cooked up, Wu-Ling."

"But you cannot! It will surely slay you!"

"Sorry. I'm bound to try. Can't just let it wander about, ravaging the countryside. Besides which, this country of mine is a young one. It ain't quite ready to cope with dragons yet. Havin' enough trouble recoverin' from the war and the devils *it* spawned. Now, this ain't one of those types that likes to carry off women, is it?"

"It would be in keeping with its lineage if it chose to abduct and consume a virgin or two, I am afraid."

Mad Amos grunted. "Well, even so, that ain't a worry. There ain't a virgin between here and Kansas City. That means it's just this gold affinity we got to worry about. That's a new one on me, Wu-Ling. What's it want with this gold it keeps stealin'?"

"I thought one so wise as thyself would surely know, Honored Devil. Gold is a necessary ingredient in the dragon's diet."

"It eats the stuff? Well, I'll be dogged. And all this time I thought it was doin' something normal with it, like buying up spare souls or accumulatin' a memorable horde of riches or some such nonsense. Gulps it right down, you say?"

"Truly," Wu-Ling admitted.

"Huh! World's full of wonders. Well, gives me something to think on, anyways." He gazed sternly down at Wu-Ling. The would-be sorcerer paid close attention. A baleful look from Mad Amos Malone was something not to be ignored. "Now, you mind what I told you and quit leeching off your kinsfolk out there. They're good people, and they deserve your help, not your imaginary afflictions. It's tough enough gettin' by in a foreign land. I know; I've had to try it myself. I've ways of knowin' when someone gives me his word and then backs off, and I don't like it. I don't like it one bit. You follow me, son of importunate parents?"

"I follow you, Honored Devil."

Wu-Ling allowed himself a sigh of relief when the giant finally departed. He wondered by what method the dragon would slay him.

Mad Amos worked his way up into the heights of the Medicine Bows despite the signs that winter was arriving early that year. It would be bad if he were caught out on the slopes by a blizzard, but he'd weathered bad storms before and could do so again if compelled to.

Near a fork of the Laramie River he paused and made camp, choosing an open meadow across which the river ran free and fast. To the west the crests of the mountains already slept beneath the first heavy blanket of snow.

"Well, Worthless, I guess this is as good a spot as any. Might as well get on with it. Oughta be an interesting business, unless I've figured it all wrong. In that case, you hie yourself off somewhere and have a good time. These mountains are full of herds. Find yourself some fine mares and settle down. Bet you wouldn't be all that sad to see me go, would you?"

The horse let out a noncommittal whinny,

squinted at him out of his bad eye, and wandered off in search of a nice mud wallow to roll in.

Mad Amos hunted until he found a willow tree of just the right age. He cut off a green branch, shaped it, and trimmed off the leaves and sproutings. Then he sharpened the tip with his bowie, fired it in charcoal, and used the white-hot, smoking points to etch some strange symbols in the earth around his kit. Some of the symbols were Chinese ideographs, some were Tibetan, and a few were not drawn from the lexicon of man.

Next he rummaged around in his battered old saddlebags, which some folk whispered held things it were best not to talk about. Out came an owl's head, a bottle of blue goo, several preserved dead scorpions, three eagle feathers bound together with Zuni fetishes, and similar debris. He reached in a little farther and withdrew a shiny metal bar. It was five pounds of enriched tumbaga, a gold alloy made by the Quimbaya Indians of the southern continent, composed of roughly sixty-five percent gold, twenty percent copper, and the rest silver. This he set carefully down in the center of the inscribed symbols.

Lastly he pulled the rifle from its fringed and painted holster. The holster had been fashioned by one of Sacajawea's daughters. Good gal, that Sacajawea, he mused. Some day when they were both ruminating in the Happy Hunting Ground he hoped to meet her again.

The rifle had an eight-sided barrel, a black walnut stock, and a breech large enough for a frightened cottontail to hide inside. It was a Sharps buffalo rifle, fifty-caliber, with a sliding leaf sight adjustable to eleven hundred yards on the back. It fired a two-and-a-half-inch-long cartridge loaded with a hundred grains of black powder and could drop a full-grown bull buffalo in its tracks at six hundred yards. The bandoliers draped across Mad Amos's chest held oversized three-and-a-quarter-inch shells packed with 170 grains of black powder.

The Sharps was a single-shot. But then, if you could fire it proper without busting your shoulder, you only needed a single shot. To Mad Amos's way of thinking, such built-in caution just naturally led to a man bettering his marksmanship.

He loaded it with more care than usual this time, paying special attention to the cartridge itself, which he carefully chose from the assortment arrayed on his chest.

Then he settled down to wait.

The moon was waning and the sky had been temporarily swept clean of most clouds when he heard the wings coming toward him out of the west, out of the mountaintops. Soon he was able to see the source of the faint whistling, a streamlined shape dancing down fast out of the heavens, its long tail switching briskly from side to side as it sniffed out the location of the gold.

It landed between the river and the camp and stalked toward the lonely man on feet clad in scales of crimson. Its neck was bright blue, its body mostly yellow and gold, its wings and face striped like the contents of a big jar stuffed with assorted candies. Moonlight marched across scimitarlike teeth, and its heritage burned back of its great eyes.

"Whoa up, there!" Mad Amos called out sharply in the dragon tongue, which is like no other (and which is hard to speak because it hurts the back of the throat).

The dragon halted, eyes blazing down at the human, who had one foot resting possessively on the golden bar. Its tail twitched, flattening the meadow grass and foxgloves, and the tendrils bordering its skull and jaws twisted like snakes with a peculiar life of their own. Its belly ached for the cool touch of yellow metal; its blood burned for the precious golden substance that purified and helped keep it alive.

"Oh ho!" it replied in its rasping voice. "A human who talks the mother tongue. Admirable is your learning, man, but it will not save you your gold. Give it here to me." It leaned forward hungrily, the smell of brimstone seeping from its garishly hued lips and parted mouth.

"I think not, Brightbodyblackheart. It ain't that I resent you the gold. Everybody's got to eat. But you scared the wits out of some good people hereabouts and killed a couple of others. And I think you're liable to kill some more afore you're sated, if your appetite's as big as your belly and your desire as sharp as your teeth. I'm not fool enough to think you'll be satisfied just with this here chunk." He nudged the bar with his foot, causing the hungry dragon to salivate smoke.

"You are right, man. My hunger is as deep as the abyssal ocean where I may not go, as vast as the sky which I make my own, and as substantial as my anger when I am denied. Give me your gold! Give it over to me now and I will spare you for your learning, for though gluttonous, I am not wasteful. Refuse me and I will eat you, too, for a dragon cannot live by gold alone."

Casually, Mad Amos shifted the rifle lying across his knees. "Now, this here's a Sharps rifle, Deathwing. I'm sure you ain't too familiar with it. There ain't the like of it where you come from, and there never will be, so I'll explain it to you. There ain't no more powerful rifle in this world or the other. I'm going to give you one chance to get back to where you come from, hungry but intact." He smiled thinly, humorlessly. "See, I ain't wasteful, neither. You git your scaly hide out of this part of the real world right now or by Nebuchadnezzar's nightshade, I'm oath-bound to put a bullet in you."

The dragon roared with amusement. Its horrible laughter cascaded off the walls of the canyon through which the Laramie runs. It trickled down the slopes and echoed through caves where hibernating animals stirred uneasily in their long sleep.

"A last gesture, last words! I claim forfeit, man, for you are not amusing! Gold *and* life must you surrender to me now, for I have not the patience to play with you longer. My belly throbs in expectation, and in my heart there is no shred of sympathy or understanding for you. I will take your gold now, man, and your life in a moment." A great clawed foot reached out to scratch contemptuously at the symbols so patiently etched in the soil. "Think you that these will stop me? You do not come near knowing the right ways or words, or the words you would have uttered by now." It took another step forward. Fire began to flame around its jaws. "Your puny steel and powder cannot harm me, worm-that-walks-upright. Fire if you wish. The insect chirps loudest just before it is squashed!"

"Remember, now, you asked for this." Quickly, Mad Amos raised the long octagonal barrel and squeezed the trigger.

There was a crash, then a longer, reverberating roar, the thunderous double *boom* that only a Sharps can produce. It almost matched the dragon's laughter.

The shot struck Brightbodyblackheart square in the chest. The monster looked down at the already-healing wound, sneered, and took another step forward. Its jaws parted farther as it prepared to snap up gold and man in a single bite.

It stopped, confused. Something was happening inside it. Its eyes began to roll. Then it let out an earthshaking roar so violent that the wind of it knocked Mad Amos back off his feet. Fortunately, there was no fire in that massive exhalation.

The mountain man spit out dirt and bark and looked upward. The dragon was in the air, spinning, twisting, convulsing spasmodically, thoroughly out of control, screaming like a third-rate soprano attempting Wagner as it whirled toward the distant moon.

Mad Amos slowly picked himself off the ground, dusted off the hollow cougar skull that served him for a hat, and watched the sky until the last scream and final bellow faded from hearing, until the tiny dot fluttering against the stars had winked out of sight and out of existence.

From his wallow near the riverbank Worthless glanced up, squinted, and neighed.

Mad Amos squatted and gathered up the tumbaga bar. He paid no attention to the coterie of symbols he'd so laboriously scratched into the earth. They'd been put there to draw the dragon's attention, which they'd done most effectively. Oh, he'd seen Brightbodyblackheart checking them out before landing! The dragon might bellow intimidatingly, but like all its kind, it was cautious. It had taken the bait only when it was certain Mad Amos owned no magic effective against it. Mere mortal weapons like guns and bullets, of course, it had had no reason to fear.

He used his tongue to pop the second bullet, the one he hadn't had to use, out of his cheek and carefully took the huge cartridge apart. Out of the head drifted a pile of dust. He held it in his palm and then, careful not to inhale any of it, blew it away with one puff. The dust duplicated the contents of the bullet that had penetrated Brightbodyblackheart:

mescaline concentrate, peyote of a certain rare type, distillate of the tears of a peculiar mushroom, coca leaves from South America, yopo—a cornucopia of powerful hallucinogens that an old Navajo had once concocted before Mad Amos's attentive gaze during a youthful sojourn in Cañon de Chelly many years before.

It was not quite magic, but then, it was not quite real, either. The dragon had been right: Mad Amos had not had the words to kill it, had not had the symbols. And it wasn't dead. But it no longer lived in the real world of men, either. In a month, when the aftereffects of the potent mixture had finally worn off and Brightbodyblackheart could think clearly once more, it might wish it *were* dead. Of one thing Mad Amos was reasonably certain: the dragon might hunger for gold, but it was not likely to come a-hunting it anywhere in the vicinity of Colorado.

Carefully he repacked that seemingly modest pair of saddlebags and prepared to break camp, casting an experienced eye toward the sky. It was starting to cloud over again. Soon it would snow, and when it started it again, it wouldn't stop until April.

But not for two or three days yet, surely. He still had time to get out of the high mountains if he didn't waste it lollygaggin' and moonin' over narrow escapes.

He put his hands on his hips and shouted toward the river. "C'mon, Worthless, you lazy representative of an equine disaster! Git your tail out of that

mud! North of here's that crazy steamin' land ol'
Jim Bridger once told me about. I reckon it's time
we had a gander at it . . . and what's under it."

Reluctant but obedient, the piebald subject of
these unfounded imprecations struggled to its feet
and threw its master a nasty squint. Mad Amos eyed
his four-legged companion with affection.

"Have t' do somethin' about that patch on his
forehead," he mused. "That damn horn's startin' t'
grow through again . . ."

FERROHIPPUS

I never took Latin, but I kind of always wanted to. They didn't offer it in the Los Angeles public school system. Not at my school, anyway. Words fascinated me from the very beginning. The feel of them, the way a certain one would roll around in the air in front of you once it had been spit out, the flavors they conveyed to waiting minds. I used to have a game where I'd try to find words that sounded like the things they were describing (come to think of it, I still play that game).

Take gemstones, for example. Diamond doesn't have much of a resonance, nor does ruby. Emerald is better. But topaz: that rings on the ear. Or carnelian. Colors offer another example. Red is, well, red. But crimson and carmine, these conjure up real color.

Thersitical is one of my favorites. Sounds innocuous but packs a real bite (look it up). At the other extreme we have Kong, as in the King. A name chosen for its euphonious connotations. (How did you think Schoedsack and Cooper came up with that

*name? They wanted one that sounded the way their
protagonist looked.)*

*Sitting around doing nothing one day (which is to
say, writing), I started playing with a little Latin,
and out of it came, hey presto, this story.*

THE CLERK FROWNED AS THE INDIAN EN-
tered the hotel. Fortunately, it was late and the last
of the regular guests had already gone off to bed.
The nearby parlor was empty. He hurried around
from behind the front desk.

"We don't allow Indians in here. Get out."

The young man was simply dressed in pants and
open shirt of trade cotton. His black hair hung down
to his neck and was secured by a red headband. To
the clerk he appeared as one of the unclean. The
visitor ignored the order and stared with undis-
guised curiosity at the etched bowl of the imported
hurricane lamp that illuminated the entryway.

"I told you to get out," the clerk repeated, louder
but not loud enough to disturb the guests. He wondered if he should wake the owner, Mrs. Hedrick, or
maybe even send for the sheriff. "You understand
English? Savvy?"

"I'm looking for a man," came the soft reply.
"Big man."

"Listen, you, I don't care if you're looking
for . . ." He hesitated. "How big a man?"

"Very big. Bigger than man ought to be. Big
crazy man."

Reflexively, the clerk glanced up the stairs. By an

odd coincidence, someone fitting that terse description had checked in early this morning. "His name wouldn't happen to be Malone, would it?"

"That him."

"What do you want with Mr. Malone?"

"Got business with him."

"What kind of business?"

"What kind of business not your business."

"Look, heathen, I . . ." But again the clerk hesitated. Something about this young savage marked him as different from the tired members of the Gila River tribe the clerk saw in the village of Phoenix during the day, trading vegetables and hides and game for simple tools and muslin from back East. He decided that it would be better not to wake Mrs. Hedrick, better still not to fetch the sheriff.

He also noticed for the first time that his visitor was very tired, as though he'd come a long way through the January night in an awful hurry. Best not to cross a man in a great hurry even if he was only an Indian.

"Up the stairs . . . *quietly*. People are sleeping. Can you read?"

A single nod.

"Number six. Down the hall on your right."

"Thanks."

The clerk watched until the young man disappeared onto the upper landing. Then he quickly checked to make sure the pistol in the drawer behind the front desk was loaded, even though the Indian had entered unarmed.

As for the guest whose rest the visitor was about to disturb, that was none of the clerk's business, was it? Besides, he was more than a little certain that the occupant of room number six could take care of himself.

At the end of the hall the young man knocked on a door. A voice boomed back from within.

"Go away! Get lost! A pox on your privates, tarantulas in your boots, and ticks in your beard, and I promise you worse if you don't leave me in peace!"

The young man considered this thoughtfully, noted that he had no beard, and replied, "May I come in?"

Silence. Then, "Oh, hell, come on, then."

It was dimly lit inside. A single lamp glowed on a far wall by the window. His eyes adjusted to the weak illumination. Then he closed the door behind him. Quietly, as the nervous white man downstairs had requested.

Standing next to the lamp and blowing out a long match was a thickly bearded white man of indeterminate age. There was silver in his beard and hair, but in odd places. He reminded the young Indian more of a black bear than a man, and the profusion of visible hair did nothing to dispel the image.

In the middle of the room was a wide bed. The top sheets had been turned down, but the bottom linen was as yet undisturbed.

A quick examination of the visitor was enough to satisfy the guest that no harm was intended. So, in addition to putting down the extinguished match, he also put aside the big LeMat pistol he'd been holding in his other hand.

"Come on in, son."

"I am in."

"Well, then, come on in farther, dammit."

The visitor obeyed, staring at the stained long johns that were all that stood between the giant and nakedness of an unpredictable nature.

"What brings you to civilization, son, as the locals delude themselves into callin' it?"

"You crazy big man?"

"Haw! Guess I shouldn't laugh, though. Most folks'd agree with you. My name's Malone. Amos Malone. Or Mad Amos Malone, if you prefers the colloquial."

"I do not understand your words."

"You got company. Folks can be weird about namin' other folks. Unconventional I may be, but not the other. Leastwise, I think not."

"Amos Malone, I have trouble. My people have trouble."

"Well, now, I'm sorry to hear that. What did you say your name was?"

"Cheshey."

"Okay, Cheshey. Now if you'll just tell me . . . Cheshey? You got a grandpappy called Ma-Hok-Naweh?"

"That is my grandfather, yes." Cheshey began to feel more secure in this small dark room with the crazy big white man.

"Good ol' Ma-Hok-Naweh. Chief medicine man to the Papagos. Great man, your grandpappy. What brings his grandson so far north?"

"Do you know of the Big House that stands between here and the home of my people?"

"Casa Grande? Sure I do. A place full of long memories and much magic. Spirit home."

Now Cheshey was nodding eagerly. "Crazy white men want to run the trail for their Iron Horse right next to it. Grandfather says the shaking the Iron Horse makes will make Big House fall down. If this happens, times will be made very bad for Indian as well as white man."

Malone frowned and stroked his impenetrable beard. "Sure as hellfire would. I'd *heard* that the new Southern Pacific was goin' to cut north so they could make a station here in Phoenix. Goin' to lay track right alongside the Big House, huh? We'd better do somethin' about that right quick. Your grandpappy's right."

"He waits for us at Big House. He told me to find you here, said you would help. Would you really help us against your own people?"

"What makes you think the railroad men are my people, son? There's only two kinds of folk in this world: the good folk and the bad folk. Mine's the good folk. They come in all shapes and colors, just like the bad ones. Don't never let nobody tell you different."

"I will remember, Amos Malone," Cheshey said

solemnly. "You must come quick, while there is still time. You have a horse?"

"If you can call Worthless a horse. I'm comin' as fast as I can, son." As he spoke, he was dragging on his buckskins, then the goatskin boots. When at last he was ready, he paused for a last loving look at the still-unused bed. "Real sheets," he muttered darkly. "I almost made it. Them railroad people better listen to reason, 'cause I'm mad enough at 'em already."

Of course, they didn't.

"Let me make certain I understand you, sir. You want me to alter the route of the line several miles eastward to make sure that the vibrations from passing trains won't knock over a pile of Indian rocks?"

"That's about the sum of it," Malone agreed.

The foreman took his feet off the desk, rose, and stalked over to the wall where the map was hung. The only reason he didn't laugh at his outlandish visitor outright was because he had the distinct feeling that to have done so would have been unhealthy. He would have to be satisfied with being in the right.

He ran one finger along the map.

"Look here, sir. I didn't buy this godforsaken territory from the Mexicans, and I wouldn't give you a plate of fresh spit for the lot of it! There's nothing here but cactus, sagebrush, mesquite that sucks the water out of the earth, and Indians too poor to spit it back again. But buy it we did, and the Southern Pacific is chartered to span it from Texas to California. I aim to see that done exactly as laid out by the company's surveyors."

"But why do you have to pass so close to Casa Grande?"

"If you must know, I think some fool with a sextant and too much time on his hands decided the old relic would be worth a passing glance from passengers."

"Not if it falls down, it won't."

"That's not my problem; that's the Indians' problem." He walked back to his desk so he could be closer to the Colt that rested in the top compartment there. "Anyway, the decision's already been made. What's the big ruckus over an old stone tepee, anyway?"

"It's not a tepee. This ain't the Plains Country, friend. Big House is thousands of years old."

"Sure looks it, but how do you know that?"

"You can taste it. The air in them old rooms reeks o' antiquity. So do the red clay pots you dig up inside sometimes. It was built by a people the local Indians call the Ancient Ones. Still the tallest building in this territory, if you don't count a few mission steeples. You go shakin' it to bits, and there'll be hell to pay."

"Are the Indians making threats, Mr. Malone? I have the authority to request Army protection, if necessary."

"No, they ain't makin' threats. I'm just relayin' to you what ol' Ma-Hok-Naweh told me last night."

"Ma-Hok ... you mean that old savage who's

been living up there?" The foreman smiled. "I think we can handle any attack he might mount."

Malone leaned forward and put a big hand on the desk. The wood creaked under the rough, callused skin. There were some mighty peculiar scars in the skin between the thumb and big finger. "Listen, friend, I don't think you understand me. You're not just dealin' with one old shaman. You're dealin' with the Ancient Ones. Now, if I was you, I'd make it a point to shift the line a mile or so to the east."

Having had his say, he turned without a good-bye and strode out. The foreman was glad to see him leave. It would make a good story to tell the work gangs. Mountain men were kind of rare hereabouts, and it wasn't every day you got a visit from one crazier than a bedbug.

It was cold in the desert that night. In the Sonoran summer you prayed every day for the heat to dissipate, and then in the winter you prayed for it to return. Those who survived and prospered in that country realized early on that whatever deity was involved, it had made its decision about the land a long time ago, and constant pleading for change would get you nothing but a sore throat that no shift in the weather would make any better.

At Malone's back, Casa Grande—the Big House—the place of the Ancient Ones, rose four stories toward the new moon. Windows like square black eyes gaped at the clouds milling uncertainly overhead. A big rattler slithered into a crack in the

caliche, and Malone listened to the final surprised
squeak of a startled kangaroo rat.

For a while he concentrated on listening to the
sounds of the snake swallowing. Then he let his
gaze come to rest on the figure seated across the
small fire from him.

Ma-Hok-Naweh's age was unknown save to himself and a few intimate friends. A true shaman
keeps his real age private, which is understandable
since it's the age not of his body but of his soul.
Malone held Ma-Hok-Naweh in high regard. He
was a true medicine man, not an accomplished fake
like Broken Water of the Ute.

A few ribbed saguaros stood sentinel behind the
old man, guarding him from the night. At their
bases, lines ran through the sandstone, across his
face, to continue down into the stone on which they
sat.

"The Ancient Ones are restless. They are restless
because they are frightened for their house in this
world."

As Ma-Hok-Naweh spoke, his grandson Cheshey
sat cross-legged nearby, watching and listening
without comment. A wise boy. Like his grandfather
and like Malone, he wore only a breechcloth and
the ever-present headband.

"How will the Ancient Ones make their fear
known?" Malone asked.

"I cannot tell, my friend." The shaman studied
the sand pictures before them, watching as the wind
played with the granules stained that afternoon with

fresh vegetable dyes. As the sand shifted, the earth
shifted with it, for the sand is of the earth and
knows its ways. "All I know is that it will take the
form of the white man's own medicine, but seen
through the eyes of the Ancient Ones."

"Will many die?"

Again the old eyes examined the play of wind
and sand. "It may be. I am saddened. Though I argue with the white man's steel trail, I do not wish to
see him die. There are many who are as well-
meaning but ignorant braves who only follow the
orders of their chief, he who makes war upon the
land, and question not what he says."

Now the moon was hidden by dark clouds, and
the rumble of approaching thunder rolled over the
paloverde and the thornbushes.

"Can nothing be done?"

"Not by this old one. Perhaps by you, if you
would wish to try. You know the white man's ways
as well as our ways. The spirits might look kindly
on you as an intermediary. With help and will, you
might do something."

Carefully he reached down and collected a hand-
ful of green sand and put it in a small leather sack.
He did the same with a palm full of ocher grains.
Malone accepted both sacks and put them aside.

"Keep them apart, for they contain both life and
death," Ma-Hok-Naweh admonished him. "You
know the words. Use the sand and the words together and you may turn the unrest of the Ancient
Ones. Do not be startled by what you may see. Re-

member that it is only white man's medicine as seen through the eyes of my ancestors. And if you cannot work this thing, get out, get out quickly, my friend!"

Malone rose, his near-naked body massive against the ancient wall behind him. "Don't worry about that, old teacher. I don't aim to die for no damn-fool railroad man. But maybe I can save his braves in spite of themselves."

Ma-Hok-Naweh stared worriedly at the sands as his friend dressed, mounted, and rode off toward the south, toward the railhead. After a while his grandson spoke for the first time all evening, his voice a whisper as befitted the enormity of the occasion.

"Do you think he can do anything, Grandfather?"

"No, I do not think so. But he is a strange man, this Amos Malone, even for a white man. It may be that I am wrong and that he *can* do something. Also, you must always remember that he is crazy, and that is a great help in dealing with the spirits." Ma-Hok-Naweh looked to the ground. Dark spots began to appear on the dirt. "Now help me inside the Big House, Grandson. It is the best place now for me to be."

The boy looked around uneasily. "Because the wrath of the Ancient Ones is upon us?"

"No, you young fool. Because it is starting to rain."

Worthless was breathing hard when Malone rode into the railhead camp. But Worthless always breathed hard, whether he'd been ridden ten miles or ten feet. It was his form of protest at being subjected to the indignity of having a man on his back.

The foreman had a tent all to himself, set apart from those shared in common by the laborers. Malone strode inside, reached into the bed, and yanked the foreman to a sitting position. The man weighed well over two hundred pounds, but that didn't keep Malone from shaking him like a child.

"Wake up, Dungannon! Wake up, you son of a spastic leprechaun, or I'll leave you to die in your bed!"

"Huh? Whuzza . . . you! Let go of me, you bloody trespassing madman. I'll see you hung in Tucson if I can't have you lynched on the spot! Let go of me, or I'll . . ." He paused, and his voice changed. "What's that?"

"What's what?" So mad was Malone, so intent was he on shaking some sense into this fool, that he'd tuned everything else out. Now he let his senses roam.

Sure enough, there it was. Whatever it was.

He let go of the foreman's nightshirt. Dungannon pulled on his boots and in nightshirt and peaked cap followed the mountain man toward the doorway of the tent.

Dungannon sounded confused when he spoke. "Sounds like a train coming," he said. "Don't know why they'd be bringing in extra supplies at night. Funny they're not sounding a whistle. Guess they don't want to wake us . . . no, there's the whistle, all right."

Malone strained his senses at the night. There was more outside the tent than the smell and sounds of rain falling steadily, more than the suggestion of metal coming closer. He could sense it, and it wasn't good.

"That's no train a-comin', Dungannon, and that weren't no whistle you heard."

"Sure and it is, you great fool. There, hear it again?"

"Listen, man! That's no train whistle. That's a whinny, though like none I heard before."

He knew what he knew, and so did Worthless. He'd seen his docked unicorn fight off a wounded grizzly with his front hooves and dance neatly around a whole den of jittery rattlers without bucking or getting himself bit. But now Worthless was pulling frantically at the hitching rail where he'd been tied, eyes wild like with locoweed—even the squinty one with the white circle around it—bucking and yelling hoarsely.

The wind rose, bringing mournful thunder with it. Malone and Dungannon stepped out into the blowing rain and shielded their eyes. But finally Malone had to put a big hand on the foreman's shoulder and spin him around.

"You're lookin' the wrong way!" Malone shouted against the wind.

"But the line ends here" was the reply. Already Dungannon was soaked to the skin. "It *has* to be coming up from the south. There're no rails north of here!"

"What makes you think it's coming down the rails?" Malone yelled at him.

At the same time Dungannon saw it coming. His face turned pale as whitewash, and he turned and bolted. Malone let him go, stood his ground, and made sure the two leather pouches were close at hand while he fought to .keep the rain out of his eyes.

Worthless was loyal but no equine fool. With an astonishing heave on his bridle, he wrenched both posts out of the ground and went bounding off like blazes to the west, the hitching rail bouncing wildly along behind him.

"I'll be hornswoggled," Malone muttered as he stared northward. Ma-Hok-Naweh had been right: White man's medicine seen through Indian eyes.

Pounding down out of the scrub-covered hills came the Iron Horse. Lightning flashed on its metallic flanks. It breathed no smoke and whistled no greeting. Its eyes were the fiery orange of the wood box, and the spirits of the dead kept its engine well stoked. It rattled and banged as it ran, and there was a blind indifference about it that was more terrifying than an overt sense of purpose could have been. Looking at it, you'd think it had no more sense in its iron skull, no more care for what it was trampling underfoot, than did a train.

Big it was, bigger than any horse, iron or otherwise. It came crashing into the camp, kicking aside piles of big ties like they were toothpicks, orange eyes flaming, its massive iron hooves making pulp of wheelbarrows and buckets and storage sheds. While Malone stared, it took the most recently completed section of rail in its teeth and pulled, ripping up a hundred feet of new line as if it were toying with a worm. It turned and kicked out with both hind feet. The laying locomotive parked on the siding nearby went flying, too many tons of steel and wood, and landed loudly in a shallow pool of rainwater.

Then it came for Malone.

The wind and lightning and rain had drowned out its approach and kept the men in their warm beds, but when a locomotive flies a hundred yards through the air and lands hard on the ground, it makes a good bit of noise. A few sleepy-eyed, tough-skinned laborers began stumbling out of their tents.

Malone could smell steel breath and squinted against the iron filings that were spit his way. Taking a deep breath, he spoke in a voice as large as any the clouds overhead could produce:

"WHOA!"

That brought the iron monster up short for just an instant, more startled than intimidated. That was long enough for Malone to take aim and fling the two handsful of colored sand he held. Somehow that sand stayed compacted in spite of the wind and rain, long enough to strike the broad iron chest.

Without pausing to see if he'd thrown true, Malone began to recite in booming tones: *"Hey-ah-hey-hey, ah-wha-tey-ah, hey-hey-oh-ta-hoh-neh,"* and added for good, if unscholarly, measure: "Now *git!*"

A few shouts sounded dimly from those workers awake enough to see something towering over the camp there in the rain, but by the time they reached the place where Malone stood standing, hands on hips, staring off into the storm, the mountain man was all alone.

"What happened, mister?" one man yelled.

Another stuck his head into the foreman's tent. "Mr. Dungannon? Mr. Dungannon, sir!" He emerged a moment later. "He ain't here."

"Who're you?" Malone asked.

"Harold Sipes, sir. I'm tie and spike supervisor for this section of line. What the devil happened here, sir? I thought I saw something . . . something impossible."

"That you did, Harold."

"Where's Mr. Dungannon?"

Malone turned back southward. He thought he could still hear a distant clanking through the wind, but he couldn't be sure. His ears were full of rain-water and iron filings. "Mr. Dungannon told me he's tired of the railroad business and that he's gone south for his health. Before he left, he did tell me one thing to pass on to his immediate subordinate. I guess that'd be you, Harold. He said to be sure to tell you to move the track a couple of miles east of here before you start northwest up toward the Salt River. Said to be sure the company stays well clear of those old ruins the Indians call the Big House."

"He did?" The supervisor wiped water from his head. "He never said nothing like that to me before."

"Mr. Dungannon took a sudden interest in the culture of the local people. It was his last wish before he left."

"Well, sir, I don't know as how I have the authority to alter the survey."

"Harold, remember what you think you saw out here when you came stumblin' out o' your warm bed? Somethin' a mite impossible, you said?"

"Yes, I . . ." He paused and found himself staring into blue eyes so deep, they just went on through into that big hirsute head, never really stopping anywhere, just fading on and on into dark nothingness. "Actually, sir, maybe I didn't see much of anything. It was awful dark. Still is. Leastwise, I don't think I'd write my missus I saw it."

"Or your superiors, either. They wouldn't take well to such a tale, I think. Be a good idea to shift that line."

"Um, maybe it would at that, sir. Now that you put it clear like you have, I expect it would be the sensible thing to do, especially seeing as how it was Mr. Dungannon's last request."

"Before he left to go south," Malone added.

"Yes, sir. Before he left to go south. I'll see to it."

"Good man, Sipes." Malone turned from him. "Now, if you'll excuse me, I've got a date with a clean bed and new linen. But first I've got to run down my fool horse." He gestured toward two holes in the ground nearby, half-full of water. "Went and took off with the whole damn hitchin' rail."

Sipes glanced at the holes and smiled. "Not arguing with you, mister, but there ain't a horse alive strong enough to pull that hitching rail out of that rock. I saw them set in myself. There was talk of putting a small station here some day, and they were put in to last."

Malone was already wandering out of earshot, a sour expression on his face. "Then where do you expect that rail's got to, Harold? Worthless ain't no normal horse." As the rain began to close in around him, he raised his voice. "You hear that, you good-for-nothing, four-legged, useless hunk of coyote bait! Wait till I get my hands on you, you lily-livered, swaybacked equine coward!"

Supervisor Sipes listened until the falling rain swallowed up sight and sound of the mountain man. No, he thought, that wouldn't be no normal horse, mister. And you sure ain't no normal human bein'. Then he saw the torn-up section of track and wondered how the wind had done that, and then his eyes lit on the laying locomotive lying on its side like a dead mammoth a good hundred yards away, and he *knew* the wind hadn't done *that*.

Then he thought back to what he'd half maybe glimpsed through the storm and decided it would be a good time to get back into bed under the covers where it was safe. But by now there might be scorpions crawled in there to get out of the rain, and he hesitated.

Until something far way, but not far enough away, went *clank* and the supervisor decided that for the remainder of this night, anyways, it would be smarter to bed down with the scorpions . . .

WITCHEN WOES

You see them everywhere. The damn things are ubiquitous. Or as the Germans would say, allgegenvärtig *(please excuse me; that's the only really neat word I remember from two years of college German, college language courses being designed to do anything except teach you to speak a language and being more or less equivalent in enjoyment to, say, the fourth level of hell).*

You've seen them at so-called craft shows, which are usually ninety-seven percent show and three percent craft. Why "craftspeople" think everybody wants one of these things is beyond me. They don't do anything, they don't look particularly nice, and they're usually put together with about as much skill as a nine-year-old exhibits working on model airplanes. But they sell, they sell like crazy.

It's downright sinister, I tell you.

AMOS MALONE WAS SIPPING AT HIS FOURTH whiskey when the distraught woman wandered into the saloon. Her mere presence served to indicate the degree of her distress, for no female citizen of good repute would enter a hard-core drinking establishment unescorted unless her motivation arose from intentions indecent or insane.

Her arrival distracted several pairs of eyes from cards, drinks, and the unwholesome hostesses who were the only other nonmales present that afternoon in the Picadilly. Several hands groped for her, and her country prettiness provoked more than one lascivious proposal. She ran the gauntlet of hopeful debauchery as she searched the crowd for someone in particular, twisting out of one grasp after another, skirt and hair flying, yanking her shawl free of the grimy, rum-slick fingers that clutched at it.

One ex-miner was more persistent (or less drunk and therefore more accurate) than the rest, for he soon had her in a firm grip with both hands. "Now don't be so contrary, little lady." He leaned close and spoke with breath marked inflammable. "Howsabout a little kiss?"

Her back arched as she fought to dodge his mouth and the miasma that issued from the inebriated depths beyond. "I am a married woman, sir, and a decent one. I'll thank you to let go of me!"

Laughter rose from the surrounding tables at this pious declaration. "Shore you is, missy," her captor leered. "As to the fust, thet don' give me no trouble, and as to the second, it explains whut yer doin' in a fancy hotel like this!"

More laughter—which Malone found he could not ignore as he had the entire contretemps up to then. Generally he was of a mind to attend solely to his own business, but there was something in the woman's attitude and tone that led him to believe she might be as upstanding as she claimed. Anyhow, it was a slow afternoon in the sleepy town of Sacramento, and he didn't have anything better to do, so he downed the last of the amber liquid remaining in his shot glass, set the glass down slowly on the oak bar, wiped his lips, and turned. On his face was an expression that made the bartender make haste to sink out of sight. "Pardon me, friend," he said in a voice that sounded as if it were rising from the bottom of a mine shaft, "but it appears the lady has some trouble and doesn't need any additional of your makin'."

"And jest whut business be it of . . ." The ex-miner hesitated as he caught sight of his questioner. " . . . Mad Amos Malone?" he continued, his voice suddenly less than a whisper.

Mad Amos Malone stood a mite taller and spread a tad wider than most men . . . and not a few *bears*. He was—or had been—a member of that unique breed known as the mountain man: that peculiar subgenus of *Homo sapiens* closely related to both the angel and the Neanderthal. Sane folk left such individuals alone.

The young woman wrenched around, and her eyes grew wide as she caught sight of Malone. "Sir, if you are truly the Amos Malone they call mad, then you are he whom I have been seeking."

Danged if she didn't have green eyes, Malone

mused. He'd always been a sucker for green eyes. "Then that makes it personal." Malone took a step toward the ex-miner, who was no featherweight himself. "You kin understand my concern now, friend."

"Yeh. Shore I kin, mister." The other man kept his eyes focused on the mountain man as he let go of the woman and moved aside.

"Now then, ma'am," Malone said politely (such *limpid* green eyes!), "this is hardly the place to engage in genteel conversation. I suggest we step outside."

"Thank you, Mister Malone." Pulling her shawl protectively about her shoulders, she headed for the swinging doors, Malone following in her wake.

As they reached the doors, Malone sensed the nervous whisper of retreating air behind him. Air's funny that way. It can laugh, it can cry, and it knows when to get out of the way. Air ain't no fool.

Neither was Amos Malone, who whirled and brought his hand up as he jerked to one side. Several gasps were heard, and a few cards fluttered to the floor of the saloon as he plucked the knife out of the air not three inches from the place his head had been just seconds earlier.

The ex-miner let out a strangled cry and crashed through the back-alley door, pausing neither to recover his property nor to turn the lock.

Years later, a few who claimed they had been there swore that they saw the mountain man lean forward and whisper a few words to the knife before throwing it. One of those insisted that the knife answered back. At the time, though, none of them voiced their observations, not wishing to be thought of by their friends as unbalanced. On one account, however, all agreed. Malone threw that knife so hard, an echoing thunder trailed behind it like a dog worrying a wagon. It went straight through the hole the miner had made in the course of executing his precipitate exit, then turned sharply to the right, down the alley. A minute or so passed before a dim scream reached the attentive listeners.

The piano player circumspectly resumed his off-key rendition of "I'll Wake You When the Mail Boat Comes In," and the other inhabitants of the Picadilly Saloon returned to their poker and drinks.

"I hope you did not kill him, Mr. Malone," the young woman said as they exited into the street.

"No, ma'am. I don't cotton to killin' drunks. Most times they don't know what they're about. Just gave him a warnin' prick, so to speak, somewhere between his waist and his holster."

"I am glad to hear it. I would not want to be the cause of another man's death." She looked a little uncertain. "Am I mistaken, or did I clearly see that knife you threw make a sharp turn to the right upon leaving this establishment? Such a thing is contrary to nature . . . for a knife."

Malone shrugged, his expression noncommittal. "There's not much that's contrary to nature if you just know how to coax her along a little."

"Which is precisely why I have sought you out

among those ruffians, Mr. Malone. It is said among those in the know that you are familiar with many things the rest of us have no desire to be familiar with. I have desperate need of someone with such knowledge, for I am at my wit's end what to do."

She started to sob. Malone knew they were real tears, not merely tears concocted for his benefit. Real tears smell different from falsified ones, and mountain men are known for their acuity of smell.

Malone thought the tears looked faintly green.

"Now, ma'am, it's true I've been exposed to certain things they don't teach in eastern colleges, but I can't presume to help you until I know the nature of your trouble. Clearly it's affected you deeply."

"Not only me," she replied, "but my entire family as well. It's a calumny for which I blame myself."

"Family? Oh," said Malone, crestfallen (ah, fare thee well, ocean eyes). He drew himself up and put aside his disappointment. "I'll help if I can, of course. I was never one to turn away from a lady in distress."

"You are gallant, sir."

"No, ma'am, just stupid. What be your problem . . . and your name?"

"Oh. Excuse me for not saying to start with. Mary Makepeace is my name, sir, and Hart Makepeace my husband." She dabbed at her face with a tatted handkerchief redolent of lilac. "I have a kitchen witch, Mr. Malone."

"Call me Amos. Or Mad," he chuckled, "if you prefer." Then, seriously, "A kitchen witch? You

mean one of those little good-luck figures made out
of paper and wood and paint and scraps of old
cloth?"

"No, sir . . . Amos. A real kitchen witch, and the
very manifestation of horror she is, too. She won't
leave me alone, and she won't bring back my poor
family, and I . . . and I . . ." The flow of tears started
again from those vitreous green orbs, and Malone
found himself holding and comforting her—a not
entirely unpleasant circumstance.

A derisive snort sounded nearby. Malone glanced
toward the hitching rail, where a mongrelized, oversized, squint-eyed hooved quadruped was giving
him the jaundiced eye. He made a face at the sarcas-
tic creature, but he did take the hint. Reluctantly, he
pushed the unhappy Mrs. Makepeace an arm's
length away.

"A real witch, eh? In the kitchen? I've heard of
'em before, but they're supposed to be pretty scarce
hereabouts. They're the source of those little doll figures you find in kitchens, but the real ones are twice
as ugly and a hundred times more dangerous."

She stared up at him (with emeralds, he thought
. . . olivine and malachite). "You . . . you mean that
you believe me, sir . . . *Amos*?"

"I can tell a liar as far off as a month-dead wa-
piti, ma'am, and 'tis plain for any fool to see that
you're tellin' the truth. I'm not sure if I can be of
any help, though. For its size, a witchen—for that's
what you're afflicted with as sure as a djinn dry-

cleans his clothes—packs a mighty powerful wallop. But I'll do what I can. Where's your place at?"

She turned and pointed eastward. "That way, a day's ride, Amos Malone."

"Then we'd best get started, ma'am." He turned and mounted his horse, extended down a hand, and pulled her up behind him as though she weighed nothing at all. "Let's go, Worthless," he told his mount.

The horse turned and started eastward.

"Your pardon, Amos," said Mrs. Makepeace from her delightfully warm position immediately at his back, "but I don't believe I saw you unhitch this animal."

"That's because he wasn't hitched, ma'am." He patted the horse's neck. "Worthless don't cotton to bein' tied up. He's pretty good about staying in one place, though, so I don't insist on it. I only have trouble with him when there's a mare in heat around."

"That's understandable, of course," she replied gravely, putting both arms around his waist and holding tight.

At which sight the piebald steed of uncertain parentage let out a most unequine laugh . . .

The Makepeace farm was located on a burbling little stream not far from the north fork of the American River. Less than twenty years before, the entire length of that river had been aswarm with thousands of immigrants in search of instant fortune, for the bed of the American River had been paved with gold. Now the gold and most of the immigrants were gone. Only the scoured-over river remained, draining farmland that was worth far more than the yellow metal that made men blind. A few, though, like Hart Makepeace, had seen the richness in the soil that had been stripped of its gold and had stayed on in the hope of making a smaller but surer fortune.

Now, however, it seemed that something small and vicious was determined to quash that dream. Malone could smell it as they trotted into the fenced yard. His suspicions were confirmed by the sound of a plate shattering somewhere inside the modest little farmhouse.

"She's still at it," Mary Makepeace said nervously, peering around the bulk of the mountain man. "I'd prayed that she'd be gone by now."

Malone shook his massive head, squinting toward the house. The evil that lay within was strong enough to make his nose wrinkle and start a pounding at the back of his neck. "Not likely, ma'am. Witchens are persistent stay-at-homes, especially if they choose to make your home theirs. They're not likely to leave voluntarily, nor put to rights the damage they're fond o' doin'."

"Then what am I to do?"

"What we can, ma'am. What we can." He dismounted and helped her down.

The kitchen had been turned into a wreck worse than that of the *Hesperus*. Only a few pieces of porcelain and crockery remained intact. Cracked china littered the wooden floor, mixed with the contents of dozens of baskets and jars. Pickles lay scattered among fruit turned rancid. Home-canned jams and preserves had made the oak planks slick as river rock. A butter churn lay forlorn and shattered across the room, below the sink pump that had been torn loose from its mounting bolts. Broom straw was everywhere, sticking to walls and floor alike.

Buzzing and soaring through the air above this culinary wreckage on a sliver of wood the size of a good cigar was the tiny figure of a wrinkled old woman. Her gray hair flowed from beneath a little scrap of a bandanna, and her skirt was stained with pepper sauce. She had a nose the size and color of a rotten grape, and her skin was the shade of old tobacco juice. On either side of that heroically ugly nose flashed tiny eyes sharp and dangerous as the business end of a black scorpion.

"Hee-hee-hee-hee!" she was cackling as she tore through the air of the ruined kitchen like a drunken dragonfly. "More's the food and more's the pity, hee-hee-hee!" *Crash!* A pot of beans went spinning to the floor.

Mary Makepeace huddled fearfully behind the imposing bulk of Amos Malone. "M-m-make her go away, Amos. Oh, please make her go away and put to rights the damage she's done!"

"Where's the rest of your family?" Malone asked her.

"Over . . . there." She fell to sobbing again as she pointed.

Standing in a far corner of the kitchen, a fistful of cigars clutched in one frozen hand, was a wooden figure of startling realism. It was not made in the image of a stolid plains Indian, though, but rather in that of a young man clad in woolen white shirt, suspenders, work boots, a pair of Mr. Levi's revolutionary new pants, and an expression that mixed bafflement with sheer terror.

"That's my husband, Hart," Mary Makepeace bawled, "and those large cookie jars at his feet are our sons, Frank and Christopher."

Malone nodded, his expression grim. "This is a mean'un, for sure." He readied himself.

They waited while the witchen continued to engage in her orgy of destruction. At last the tiny evilness clad in the guise of an old woman zoomed over to hover in the air a foot in front of Malone's beard.

"Oh-ho-hee-hee," she laughed gleefully. "So the missy of the house has come back, eh? Good! I was so busy, I missed you the first time! What would you like to be? A nice harp, perhaps? You'd make a good-looking harp, missy. Or maybe that's too fine for such as you, yes, too fine by half. A beer mug, maybe, for some filthy-minded man to drink from? Or how about a slop jar? Hee-hee-hee! Yes, that'd suit you, yes, yes, a green-eyed slop jar!" She whirled around in a tight circle, delighted at her own perverse inventiveness. Mary Makepeace cowered weakly behind Malone.

The witchen tried to dart around him. Each time he blocked her path with a big, calloused hand. Finally the enraged little nastiness floated up to stare into his eyes.

"Now what's this, what's this what interferes with my housework, eh? I think it's alive. I think it does live, I think. At first I thought it was a big sack of manure the missy had pushed ahead of her to hide behind, but now I see that it moves, it moves, hee-hee-hee. Could it be that it talks as well, could it?"

"You are without question," Malone said studiously, "the vilest, most loathsome-looking little smidgen of bile it's ever been my displeasure to set eyes upon."

"Flattery'll get you anywhere, sonny," she cackled. Then, in a dark tone rich with menace, she added, "Perhaps if I put them out for you, you wouldn't be troubled with setting them on me, eh?" When Malone didn't respond, she said, "What shall I do with you, with you? You're too big to make into a piece of furniture for this besotted kitchen. Maybe I'll turn *you* into a kitchen, yes, yes? Yes, with a nice little cook fire in your belly." Her tiny eyes blazed threateningly. "I'll bake my bread in your belly, man."

Ignoring her, Malone whispered to Mary Makepeace, "Have you and your husband been fighting lately, ma'am?"

"Of course not," she started to say. "We were

happily . . ." then she recalled what Mad Amos Malone had told her about being able to smell a liar some good distance away and thought better of her response. "Yes, yes, we have been." She was shaking as she stared at the floor. "But if only I could have him back, Amos! We fought over such little, insignificant things! And the children . . . I'll never yell at my dear boys like that again!"

"Most folks don't think clearly about the consequences o' strong words when they're spewin' 'em, ma'am. That's what likely brought this badness down on you. Fightin' can poison a home, and a kitchen's especially sensitive to it. If the other conditions are right—not to mention the *ether* conditions—well, you've seen what can happen."

"Please give my family back to me, Amos," she pleaded. "Please . . . I'll do anything for another chance. *Anything.*"

Green eyes rich with promise fluttered at him, but Malone turned resolutely away from that beckoning gaze with a resolve a Kiowa pony would have envied. "Just stay behind me, ma'am. Just stay behind me." He turned his attention back to the waiting witchen.

"I don't think you're goin' t' turn me into no fireplace, filth-fingers," he told it, "and I aim to see to it that you don't hurt this lady no more and that you undo the damage you've already done."

"Hee-hee-hee, you do, do you?" She took her little hands off the nape of the tiny broomstick and waved them at him. "Hibble-de-glum, mubble-me-mock, fire and iron, kettle and stock, make of this mountain a . . ."

Malone didn't give her a chance to finish without interrupting. He had the advantage of volume, if not timing. "Bellow and roar all you wish, balloon-beak, but you won't sunder me. I've been circled round by the five fingers of Rusal-Ratar, Queen of the kitchens of the Earth and personal chef to Quoomander, Ruler of all the Djinn, Spirits, and Unassigned Ghosts of the Nether Regions!"

". . . two-armed stove crock!" the witchen finished.

There was a flash of smoke and fire as she threw something at him. Mad Amos Malone disappeared in a cloud of green haze. From behind it Mary Make-peace let out a despairing scream, and the witchen's "hee-hee-hee!" of triumph soared above it.

Her triumph, however, dissipated as rapidly as the haze, for within it Mad Amos Malone still stood in the kitchen doorway, unchanged, unharmed, and certainly unstoved, though a faint fragrance of un-holy boiling did issue from the vicinity of his slightly scorched belt.

"Now then, wart-heart," he whispered huskily as he reached toward his waist, "how'd thee like to try riding a bowie knife for a change?"

"No, no, no, not possible! It's not possible . . . eeeee!" The witchen found herself dodging Malone's huge knife, twisting and spinning for her life as the mountain man sliced and cut at her agile little form.

But she was quick and experienced, and while Malone was so fast that the knife seemed but a shining in his hand, he was not used to dealing with so small a target. "Hold up there," he finally told his quarry, gasping for breath. He bent over and put his hands on his knees as he fought for wind. "I'm plumb tuckered out."

So was the witchen. Exhausted, she landed on a shelf and climbed off her broomstick, dangling withered little legs over the edge. "Fast . . . so fast he is," she wheezed. "Almost too fast for old Beeblepwist, almost, almost . . . but not quite, not quite." A sly grin snuck over her extraordinarily ugly face. "Should be a better way to settle this, settle this. A better way, yes."

"Don't listen to her, Amos!" Mary Makepeace shouted from her position just outside the kitchen. "She'll try to trick you and . . ."

"No harm in hearin' what she has to say, ma'am." Amos took a last, deep breath, straightened, and was eye to eye with the sitting witchen. "I've no stomach for this constant chasin'. What have you in mind, corpse-cleaner?"

"No stomach for chasing, for chasing, eh? Have you stomach for some food? A cooking contest, yes? Yes, me and thee, hee-hee-hee?"

Malone considered the proposal carefully. He was a man of many talents. There were those who regarded him as a middlin' to clever cook. "Cookin' contest with what as its aim?" he asked guardedly.

"You win, I'll put this hovel to right and lose myself in the Bottomless Jar. I win . . . hee-hee-hee . . . I win, and you become part of the decor, along with little miss priss, there." She threw a short finger of fire in the direction of Mary Makepeace, who barely kept herself from swooning. "And one other thing," she said, her voice becoming less scratchy than usual, "one thing other. I keep your soul, man, your soul."

"I thought you wanted me for a stove," he said nonchalantly.

"I do, I do, but a soul's no good to a stove, and I can always find a buyer for a spare one."

Malone scratched his beard. "If you think a good stove don't need no soul, you ain't half the cook you think you are. I agree. What kind of cookin' do you propose? We ought to work similar, or there'll be no basis for comparison."

"I'm partial to spicy foods," the witchen said softly. "Think you the same, the same?"

Malone nodded. "I can handle tol'able condiments in my food."

"Then something spicy it shall be," cackled the witchen, adding, unsurprisingly, a "hee-hee-*hee*!"

Soul or surcease at stake, it was determined that the spiciest dish would be declared the winner. A truce blanketed that abused kitchen then, for both mountain man and witchen needed time to gather the ingredients for their respective dishes. Mary Makepeace saw a few of her precious utensils and pots restored for the purposes of the contest.

Three days slipped by. The sky over the farm

grew as dark and angry as the odors that began to issue from it. People remarked on the peculiar scents in the air as far away as San Francisco to the west and Chinaman's Bar to the east. Rabbits dug their burrows a little deeper that autumn, the birds moved their nests higher in the treetops, and for the first time since its founding, the citizens of Sacramento were not plagued by hordes of mosquitoes from the swamps along the Feather River—all the insects having dropped dead of unknown cause.

The heat that began to rise from those two steaming kettles blistered the wood of the farmhouse on the north fork of the American River. Paint peeled off furniture hauled undamaged clear across the country from New England, and rusty iron was scoured miraculously clean. Mary Makepeace huddled on the floor just outside the kitchen, not daring to peer inside, yet she still acquired a tan so deep and permanent that from that day on people mistook her for a Mexican.

By the third night the two dishes were nearly finished. A deep yellow-orange glow illuminated the kitchen, and no bullfrogs called along the length of the American River.

From the kettle above which the witchen danced and flew rose a pink glow alive with tiny explosions of spice. It emanated from a soup the color of pahoehoe, the thick ropy lava that sometimes flows from the lips of angry volcanoes.

Mad Amos Malone stood like a russet cliff above his own pot, stirring the contents occasionally with an iron bar until the mixture was thick and sizzling and the bar had melted clean away. The glow from both kettles suffused the room with the hues of hell. So spice-ridden were the two concoctions that the wood fires burning beneath each pot had begun to cower away from the metal bottoms, so that witchen and mountain man alike had to chide the flames back into heating them.

And when the smell and heat were at their highest, when both courses were ready for the tasting, the witchen floated in the hot air rising from her own pot and said with great anticipation to Mad Amos Malone, "You . . . go first . . . hee-hee-hee."

Mad Amos somberly removed his wolf-skull cap and unbuttoned his buckskin shirt. Ceremoniously, he downed half a gallon of cold stream water from a still-intact jug. The soup ladle burnt his fingers slightly when he picked it up, but he held tight to it. Cupped in the scoop of the ladle was something that bubbled and burst into little sparks. He brought his lips to the edge of the spoon. Mary Makepeace peered fearfully around the corner of the open doorway, one hand shoved reflexively into her mouth.

Malone hesitated. "What is it?"

"Why?" the witchen challenged him. "You afraid of a little soup, hee-hee-hee?"

"Nope. Just like to know what I'm eatin'."

"It's soup," she cackled, her eyes burning evilly. "Just plain red pepper soup, seasoned with brimstone and jellied kerosene and a few other personal spices. A delicate consommé sure to please as rugged and discerning a palate as yours, man. My own recipe . . . hee-hee-hee."

Malone nodded once, his face aglow with the light rising not just from the boiling kettle but from the liquid frothing on the ladle, and downed the contents in a single gulp. He smacked his lips and put the ladle back in the pot.

Water started to stream from the corners of his black eyes, to cascade down his cheeks and into his beard. The tears were so hot that the hairs of his beard curled aside to give them free passage and the hair on his head began to writhe desperately as if trying to flee his skull. Smoke began to rise from the region of his belly, and the leather there darkened ominously. The veins in his eyes swelled until there wasn't any white for all the red. A fingernail fell intact and smoking from the fourth finger of his right hand, leaving a steaming scar in its wake.

Malone opened his mouth, and a gust of fire issued forth that put to shame the roaring of the falls of the Yosemite—a great, intemperate blast of flame that turned the iron pump on the edge of the sink into a tired lump of slag. A sharp explosion shook the house as the heat of that exhalation blew out every one of the house's twelve imported windows, and Mary Makepeace held her head and screamed and screamed. Outside the kitchen, where the blast had struck, twenty-five feet of grass and brush was vaporized in a swathe five feet wide.

The force of his reaction had sent Malone slamming into the far wall of the kitchen, cracking a support log and threatening to bring down the whole upper story along with the roof. The log creaked, but it held.

Slowly, Malone picked himself up from the floor, his eyes still watering, and rubbed at his throat as he nodded admiringly toward the aghast witchen. "Not bad. Not bad at all." The lining of his mouth had gone numb, and his tongue felt like what a match is like after it's been used. "Now," he said softly, "it's *your* turn."

"Hmph! Waste of time this now, waste of time." She flew over to float above the steaming kettle at which Malone had labored. Some of the bravado had fled from her cackle. Malone ought not to have been alive, much less offering comments on the quality of her finest dish. She stuck her bulbous nose downward and sniffed contemptuously, then dropped lower and studied the simmering surface. "Maybe you survived the tasting," she said dangerously, "but you won't survive the contesting, hee-hee-hee." Using the end of an unlit match for a spoon, she dipped out a sample of the concoction and popped it into her mouth.

For a moment she chewed reflectively. Then it hit her. Her eyes bulged enormously, and her mouth dropped open, for what Malone had wrought was as feral and fey as it was flamboyantly effective. "Ohhh myyyyy!" she exclaimed sharply. Her skin turned from brown to pink to cherry red, and her tiny body ballooned up like a pig bladder. Bigger and bigger she swelled, until at last she burst in a cloud of red heat that filled the whole kitchen.

When the cloud had gone, so had the witchen.

A corner of the mountain man's mouth turned up, and he gave a loud snort of satisfaction. "Hee-hee-*hee*," he snapped at nothing in particular.

"Mary?" a querulous, uncertain voice murmured. "Mary?"

Malone watched enviously as Mrs. Makepeace rushed to embrace her newly restored husband and children, vowing as long as she was granted life to live in understanding and harmony with him again, to love and honor and all those other words so many people take so casually the first time around. Her only problem was that she didn't have enough arms to hug him and the children as tightly as she wished.

When the tearful reunion had settled down somewhat and the thankful Hart Makepeace had learned what had transpired during his cellulose sojourn, Mary was able to inspect a gleaming, completely restored kitchen. Even the ruined jams and preserves had been returned to their respective jars. Only the melted sink pump remained to remind all of what had gone before.

Unexpected side benefits arose from the confrontation. For the remainder of his life Hart Makepeace would smoke neither cigar nor pipe. The two Hart children, who spent the rest of the afternoon vomiting up cookies, chocolate, oatmeal, raisins, nuts, and other baker's material, were able to resist permanently the most tempting blandishments Sacramento's millers could proffer.

That night, as Amos Malone was preparing to take his leave of the farm, Mary Makepeace asked him, "What was it you prepared that affected her so, Mr. Mal . . . Amos?"

"A little something I learned from Tullie Kanotay, ma'am." He cinched the saddle a little tighter, and a warning groan issued from Worthless's throat. "Tullie Kanotay's part Apache, part Irish, part somethin' not entirely human, and all Texan . . . which latter often amounts to the same thing as the former. Bit o' the witch in her own right. That dish can only be made up once a year by any one individual, and then only by one who knows the proper proportions, has the touch of a master French chef and the heart of a Hindoo raj, or else the emissions might unbalance the ice which caps the head and backside of our world. Why, I can hardly eat more than a bowl or two of it myself.

"It's chimera chili, ma'am, and its effects can't be countered by any spell or magic makin' known, because the taste changes every couple o' seconds. It had to be that dish and that one only, or your nasty visitor could've spelled her way around it. But the flavor kept shiftin' too fast for her taste buds, not t' mention her counterspells, and she was done for." He patted the Sharps buffalo rifle slung next to the saddlebags on Worthless's back.

"The recipe itself ain't too hard to work up.

Hardest part's findin' chimera meat." He gestured toward the distant, moonlit, serrated crest of the High Sierra off to the east. "Ain't too many chimeras hereabouts, but you can track one down if you know how they work their meanderings."

Mary Makepeace listened to this quietly, then glanced back toward the farmhouse, which once more smelled of cleanliness and home. Inside, her husband and sons were reveling in being once more themselves instead of sterile objects of china and wood. She looked back up at the mountain man through eyes made of lime-green glass. "Dear, kind Amos Malone, whom I shall never call Mad, I don't know how to thank you, but I . . . I would offer you one last favor in return for your aid."

Malone eyed her uncertainly. "Now, ma'am, I'm not sure that I ought . . ."

"Would you . . . would you . . . stay for dinner?"

Malone wasn't sure whether to be disappointed or relieved. He rubbed gingerly at his stomach. The heat lingered . . . though it hadn't really been a bad soup at all. No, not bad at all.

"I'd be pleased to, ma'am. I don't get the chance to eat much in the way o' home cookin'. I'll stay . . . so long as there's plenty of plain meat and unsalted potatoes."

"I'll lock up the pepper," she assured him, smiling delightedly, and led him back toward the house.

Worthless watched them go, then ambled off toward the nearby barn. The forehead horn that Malone kept constantly trimmed back was itching again. That meant for sure there had to be a mare nearby who, like himself, would care nothing for the antics of silly humans but only for the things that really mattered . . .

JACKALOPE

Now, this one isn't fantasy at all. Nope, it's for sure absolutely positively real, as any local old-timer can tell you. At least, the first part is. The jackalope is not common in the Old West but with diligence and knowledge can usually be tracked down, as evidenced by the numerous neatly stuffed and mounted heads and full bodies visible in dozens of stores and restaurants. It's a wily creature: fast, alert, and quick to anger. Just ask anyone who's ever had the misfortune of being gored by a particularly large and aggressive specimen.

I see them occasionally when we drive the back way to L.A., through Yarnell and Congress, Salome and Quartzite. They're solitary critters, keep to themselves mostly. Fortunately I've never hit one. Probably lose a tire. Oh, and there's a fine musical group headed by R. Carlos Nakai, the foremost practitioner of Native American flute music, which has taken the same name.

It's a well-known fact that coyotes won't bother jackalopes. The ornery little cusses are too danger-

ous to bother with. But something must be keeping the population down . . .

"I'M SORRY, GENTLEMEN, BUT THERE IS NOTH-ing left to tempt me. I've killed everything there is to be killed."

Lord Guy Ruxton extracted an imported Havana cigar from a jacket pocket, utilized an engraved Italian cutter to snip the end, and turned slightly to his left so Manners could light it for him. As he puffed it to life, there was a subtle but unmistakable shifting of bodies in the saloon as cardplayers and drinkers leaned in his direction in a vain but hopeful attempt to partake, however infinitesimally, of that expensive aromatic smoke that would forever lie beyond their modest means.

Though they shared the best table in the house with him, Ruxton's audience of Butte's leading citizens was equally appreciative, if not nearly so obvious. Being connoisseurs of silver, they admired the cigar cutter as much as the smoke. The town of Butte would not exist save for silver.

Ruxton was a rara avis in Montana Territory: a wide-ranging world traveler and hunter of big game. A fine orator, he held his after-dinner companions spellbound with his tales of tracking exotic animals to the far corners of the earth. Miners and bankers alike were enthralled by stories of stalking tiger in British India, oryx in Arabia, and all manner of dangerous game in Darkest Africa. Ruxton was only mildly condescending to the colonials, and they responded in kind. Still, it was clear he was bored. He took a sip of the best scotch Butte had to offer.

"I think the time has come for me to pack it all in, gentlemen, and retire to my estate in Hampshire. You see, there is nothing left for me to hunt. The walls of my trophy room will see no further additions because there is nothing further to add. I lament the end of excitement!"

Silas Hooten had founded the town's first bank and watched it grow along with the production of silver. Now he smiled and put down his drink.

"If it's excitement you crave, why not have a go at hunting buffalo in Sioux Territory?"

Ruxton regarded his cigar rather than the banker. "Because there is nothing to hunt in the eastern portion of your benighted territory *except* buffalo, and I have found that animal a singularly uninspiring quarry, though I have hunted it with bow and arrow in the fashion of the savages as well as with rifle. The presence of red hostiles in the vicinity does not alter the object of the hunt." He sighed tiredly.

"No, gentlemen. I have sampled the best of your cuisine, your scenery, and your women. Now I fear it is time I return permanently to England. I do not fault your bucolic hospitality. America was the only land remaining to be hunted. That I have done. Would that there were more truth and less wind to some of the tales I have heard of this country."

"Jackalope."

Ruxton frowned and peered past Hooten. "I beg

your pardon, sir." His drinking companions turned
to stare with him.

"Jackalope, I said. Got ears, ain'tcha?"

The mouth that had given birth to the word was
hidden by a massive buckskin-clad back. The individual seated at the bar looked like a chunk of dark
granite blasted from the depths of one of the town's
mines, hauled in by mine trolley, and set up on a
stool like some druidic monolith. A hat fashioned of
an unidentifiable golden fur crowned the huge head.
Black curly hair lightly flecked with white tumbled
in an undisciplined waterfall from beneath the headgear.

As miners and bankers and visiting nobility
looked on, the man turned like an Egyptian statue
come to life. Deep-sunk black eyes regarded them
from beneath Assyrian brows. The hair at the back
was matched in front by a dense beard that might
have been forged of wrought-iron wire. Two thick,
gnarled fingers supported a beer mug full of whiskey.

"I was sayin', sir, bein' unable to avoid
overhearin' part of your conversation, that it might
be you've never hunted for jackalope."

"Yes. Well." Ruxton noted that his companions
were now smiling and chuckling softly among
themselves. He lowered his voice. "Who is this ex-
tremely large chap, and what is he nattering on
about?"

"Malone." Orin Waxman ran the biggest general
store in town. "Amos Malone."

"*Mad* Amos Malone." Hooten pointed a finger at the side of his head. "The man's crazier than a bedbug, but it's a rare soul who'll say so to his face."

"Looking upon him, I can understand that. You say he's mad?" Several of the men nodded. "What's this 'jackalope' thing he's on about?"

Waxman shook his head, grinning. "There is no such animal. Somebody somewhere faked one up, and it's turned into a long-standing gag for foolin' easterners. No offense, your Lordship. Someone will shoot a jackrabbit and a small deer or antelope. They'll take both to a good taxidermist with a sense of humor, and he'll stick the deer antlers on the rabbit's head. And there's your jackalope."

"I see. It is quite imaginary? You're positive of that?"

The men eyed one another uncertainly and left it to Hooten to reply. "Of course it is, sir. The mountain man's just having a little joke at your expense."

"A good joke, is it? At my expense?" Ruxton's eyes glittered as he turned back to the bar. "Here now, my good fellow. I am intrigued by your comment. Do come and join us."

Mutters of disbelief and distress came from Ruxton's companions, but none dared object when Malone lurched over to assume the lone empty chair at the table. Such men were not famed for their hygiene. Waxman and the others were relieved to discover that Malone, at least, seemed to have bathed some time in the not too distant past.

Obviously enjoying himself hugely, Ruxton swept

a hand toward his hosts. "These gentlemen insist vehemently that there is no such creature as the one you speak of. I interpret that to mean they are calling you a liar, sir."

Waxman choked on his liquor, while Hooten's eyes widened in horror. Malone simply eyed them intently for a long moment, then sipped at his tenth of whiskey. The resultant sighs of relief were inaudible.

"None of 'em knows enough to call me a liar. I ain't insulted by the denials of the ignorant."

His response delighted Ruxton. "Sir, you are a man of surprises! For the moment I intend to leave aside the matter of your sanity. As you overheard, I am something of a sportsman."

"Your claim, not mine."

Ruxton bristled slightly at that but restrained himself. "True enough. You claim I have not hunted this creature you call a jackalope. These good citizens dispute the assertion that it exists. I would put you and them to the test, sir." He made sure he met Malone's gaze evenly. "If you are game."

"I ain't, but the jackalope is."

Ruxton hesitated a moment, then burst out laughing when he was sure. "Upon my word! A rustic with wit. I like you, sir. 'Pon my word I do!" He stubbed out his half-finished cigar and tossed it over his shoulder, ignoring the near riot that followed its descending trajectory as a dozen men scrambled for possession of the butt.

"I would engage you, Mr. Malone, to direct me to

the place where I might find such an animal and add it to my collection. I will pay you well, in gold, to serve as my guide in such a venture. Our bargain will be that should we find nothing except fast talk, all expenses will be borne by you."

Malone considered, seeing the doubt in the others' faces. Then he gently set down his mug. "Done. It'll be you and me alone, though. I don't like travelin' with a crowd." He glanced at Ruxton's valet. "Especially slaves."

The valet stiffened. Ruxton only smiled. "Manners is a valued member of my household staff, not a slave. However, it shall be as you wish. I will accompany you alone. Where are we going, sir, or is it to remain a mysterious secret?" He was clearly amused.

Malone turned and nodded westward. "Up thataway. Into the Bitterroots."

"The Bitterroots!" Hooten half rose out of his seat. "Lord Ruxton, I implore you to reconsider this foolishness. The veracity of this—gentleman—is to be doubted. His reputation is eccentric in the extreme. There's nothing up in those mountains except Nez Percé and Blackfeet. You'll find only trouble and danger in that range, not nonexistent game!"

"Come now, gentlemen. Are you again openly disputing the good Mr. Malone's word?" Waxman's lower lip trembled, but like the others, he said no more. "Then it is agreed. When do we depart, Mr. Malone?"

"Morning'd be fine with me. We'll be gone a few

weeks. Take what you need, but it's best to travel light."

"As you say, sir. I understand the weather is good this time of year. I am looking forward to our excursion."

They headed northwest out of town despite the last-minute pleas of Hooten and his friends. The death of so distinguished a visitor to their territory would not be the best of publicity for a growing community, and they feared it; yes, they did. Ruxton's valet tried to reassure them.

"Lord Ruxton, gentlemen, is used to the life of the camp and the trail. He has been in difficult circumstances many times and has always emerged unscathed. He is a crack shot and an athlete, a man who relishes danger and its challenges. Your concern does him an injustice. No harm will befall him. If you must worry about someone, concern yourselves with this crude Malone person."

"Mad Amos is no genius, but he ain't dumb, neither," said one of the men who'd gathered on the porch of the hotel to bid the hunters farewell. "Ain't nobody never been able to figure him out noways."

"I assure you," Manners continued, "Lord Ruxton is more than a match for any situation this lout can place him in."

"Oh, I wasn't worried about how your boss is going to get on with Malone," said the man who'd spoken. "I was wondering how he was going to cope with the Rockies."

* * *

Once they left town, they commenced a steady
climb into mountains as serene and lovely as any in
the world. They reminded Ruxton of the Alps without the spas and fine hotels and other amenities of
that ancient region. By way of compensation, there
was a freshness in the air, a newness not to be found
at the watering holes of the wealthy that dotted the
Continent. Ruxton's packhorse trailed behind
Malone's.

"That is an unusual animal you ride, sir." He nodded at Malone's mount.

The mountain man spoke without looking at his
guest. "Worthless has been called plenty of names,
Lord. Most of 'em less complimentary than that."

The animal Malone called Worthless was black
except for patches of white at the tail and fetlocks.
A single white ring encircled one eye, giving the
horse the aspect of a permanent squint. He was a
cross among half a dozen breeds. For reasons
Malone chose not to elaborate on, a heavy leather
patch was affixed permanently to the animal's forehead.

Have to attend to that again soon, he mused. He
didn't worry about it out in the backcountry, but it
was just the sort of thing to provoke consternation
among simple city folk.

The horse snorted, just to let the two riders know
he was listening.

"Magnificent country, your West. Do you think

we might encounter some red Indians, as Mr. Hooten seemed to fear?"

"Only if they're in the mood for company. Nobody sees the Blackfeet unless they want to be seen, and sometimes the Nez Percé don't even see each other. I don't anticipate any trouble, if that's what you mean. I've an understandin' with the folks hereabouts. If we do meet up with any, you keep your mouth shut and let me do the talkin'. I ain't sure how they'd take you."

"As you wish, Mr. Malone. How long before—" he bent to hide a smile "—we stand to encounter one of your jackalopes?"

"Hard to say. They're shy critters, and there seem to be fewer of 'em each year. Seems to be as folks start movin' into this part of the world, certain critters start movin' out."

"Indeed? How inconvenient. Well, I am in no hurry. I am enjoying our excursion immensely. I took the liberty of stocking up on the finest victuals your community could provide. I shall enjoy dining au camp at your expense, Mr. Malone."

"Ain't my expense unless we don't git you a jackalope, Lord."

"Of course. I am remiss."

"Don't know about that, but you're sure as hell premature."

Many days went by without them encountering evidence of any other humans of any color. Malone seemed content to lead them ever deeper into the mountains. Snow-clad peaks soared ten thousand feet overhead as they picked their way across a rocky slope above a wide, white-flecked river. Ruxton marveled at Malone's ability to find a path where none was visible. The man was a fine tracker, like many of the primitives Ruxton had engaged in other lands.

He was watching his guide carefully now. Perhaps robbery had been his motive all along in agreeing to this trek. Ruxton had considered the possibility back in the saloon, but instead of deterring him, it only added spice to an expedition such as this. He lived for such excitement. If thuggery was indeed in the mountain man's plans, he was in for a surprise. Ruxton had dealt with drunken cossacks and silent-footed dacoits. Despite Malone's size, Ruxton knew that in the event of a fight, it would be an Englishman who returned to tell the tale.

He was careful to sleep on the opposite side of their campfire, Colt pistol at his side, the intricately carved pepperbox snug in its special holster inside his boot. Malone would not surprise him in the middle of the night.

So he was more than mildly shocked when he found himself being shaken awake the following morning. His hand lunged for the Colt, then paused when he saw that Malone was looking not at him but past him.

"Whisper," Malone instructed him, "and then speak softer than that."

"What is it?" Ruxton was up quickly, pulling on his jacket. "Savages?"

Malone shook his head.

"What, then?" Chilled fingers buttoned the coat. Even in late spring, dawn was cold in these mountains.

"What you come fer, Lord."

Ruxton's hands stopped. "Pardon, Mr. Malone?"

"Jackalopes, you damn idjit! You want that trophy or not?"

Ruxton gaped at him, then hurriedly resumed his dressing.

Malone led him away from camp. They crossed two small ridges before surmounting one slightly higher. The roar of the river masked their climb.

Clutching his .30-30, Ruxton peered over the crest of the ridge. There was no need for Malone to remind him to keep his voice down because he had no words for what he was seeing.

Not one, not two, but a whole herd of the utterly impossible creatures were feeding and frolicking in a small grassy meadow. They were bigger than he would have imagined, bigger than the largest jackrabbits he'd shot in New Mexico. They nibbled contentedly at the grass or preened themselves or lay on their sides soaking up the early-morning sun. Several pairs of young males were play fighting. They would eye each other intently, then drop their heads and leap like rutting rams. Heads made contact six feet above the ground. Antlers locked and clacked loudly before the combatants separated, tumbled back to earth, and gathered themselves for another charge.

"I don't believe it," he mumbled under his breath.

Malone was impatient. "I don't care whether you believe it or not, Lord, but I never did cotton to havin' my word doubted. I reckon we won't be hearin' no more of such nonsense. You think you can shoot one, or you want me to do it fer you?"

"What? Oh, yes."

Ruxton checked his weapon. He'd come to Montana in search of trophies, had gone along with Malone for the excitement of the wager, and now found himself in the position of obtaining far more than he'd sought. This expedition would yield much more. There would be articles in *The Times*, scientific honors, perhaps a special room in the British Museum.

Oh, he would take care to acknowledge Malone as his guide to this wonder. That would be proper. But recognition as discoverer would mean nothing to such a simple soul. The honor would be wasted on him. Ruxton therefore would graciously relieve him of the burdens it would entail.

Though nervous, he knew he could not miss. Not at this range. His valet had not exaggerated his master's skill with a rifle. Ruxton settled on the biggest buck in the herd, a magnificent ten-pointer. It was squatting off to one side, grazing contentedly. *Sorry, old fellow,* he thought as he squeezed the trigger.

The gun's report echoed noisily up the canyon. The buck screamed once as it jumped convulsively.

By the time it hit the ground, it was dead, shot cleanly through the heart. Like fleas exploding from an old mattress, the rest of the herd vanished in seconds.

But the dead buck jackalope did not vanish like a character from *Through the Looking-Glass*. It was real. Malone followed behind as the excited Ruxton scrambled over the rocks toward it.

He lifted it triumphantly by the antlers. It was heavy, at least twenty pounds. This was not some clever fake conceived at great expense to deceive him.

"Mr. Malone," he told the mountain man when he finally arrived, "I am sorry for doubting your word. Oh, I confess to being as skeptical as your fellow citizens. I thought I would be the one to have the good laugh. I apologize profusely."

"No need to apologize, Lord. Leastwise you had the guts to back up your words. And there's worse things to go a-huntin' fer than a good laugh. Come on, now, and let's be gettin' away from here."

"Why the rush? I thought I might have a shot at another one."

"I promised you one trophy. You bagged it, and a big one at that." He was scanning the canyon walls as he spoke. "Now it's time you and I were makin' tracks."

Ruxton frowned and joined Malone in studying the river and the enclosing canyon. "Why? Surely we're in no danger here. Or do you fear Indians may have heard my shot?"

"Nope. Ain't worried about Indians. Ain't none in this place. They won't come down this canyon."

"Well, then, what troubles you? Pumas, perhaps, or a bear?"

"Not them, neither."

Ruxton sighed, not wishing to spoil this historic moment with an argument. "I warn you, sir, I have little patience for linguistic obfuscation."

"Tell me somethin', Lord. What kind of critter do you think would be fast enough and strong enough to catch somethin' like a jackalope?"

"Why, I don't know. I should imagine that the usual predators manage to—" But Malone had turned and was already taking long strides back toward camp. Ruxton followed, too elated by his kill to remain angry with his irritating guide.

Having put the incident completely out of his mind, he was furious when Malone woke him in the middle of the night. He could see the mountain man outlined by the glow of the dying campfire.

"Sir, I have no idea what your absurd intention may be in disturbing me thus, but I am accustomed to enjoying a full night's rest, and I—"

"Shut up."

"Now listen to me, my good fellow, if you—"

He went silent as the muzzle of an enormous rifle tilted toward him. "I told you to shut up, Lord. If you do, maybe I can keep you alive."

Ruxton had plenty more to say but forced himself to keep quiet so that Malone could explain. That was when he noticed that his guide was staring anxiously at the sky.

A diadem of stars flattered a half-moon that turned the granite slopes around them the color of used steel. Far below, the unnamed river ran nervously toward the distant Missouri. Ruxton was about to mention the possibility of marauding Indians once again, when something man-sized filled his field of vision. Its eyes were like saucers of molten lead. He let out a scream and fell backward even as the gun in Malone's hands thundered. Something like a Malay dirk cut his shoulder, slicing through his shirt. Then all was still.

He lay panting as Malone rushed to reload the buffalo gun. Putting a hand to his shoulder, Ruxton found not one but three parallel cuts through shirt and skin. They were shallow but bloody and were beginning to sting as his body reacted to the injury.

Wordlessly, he started to stand, only to drop to hands and knees on Malone's terse command. He crawled over to the thing the mountain man had shot out of the sky.

It was not intact. Malone's Sharps blasted a three-inch-long cartridge through an octagonal barrel. The nocturnal attacker had been blown apart. But enough remained to show Ruxton it was no creature known to modern science.

"What the blazes is it, Malone?"

The mountain man continued to survey the sky, his eyes seeming to flick from star to star as though he knew each intimately. The horses pawed nervously at the ground, rolling their eyes and tugging at their reins. Of the four, only Malone's mount, Worthless, stood calmly, occasionally shaking his head and turning it sideways to gaze sourly at the two men.

"Wolful," Malone replied curtly. He set the rifle aside and drew his peculiar LeMat pistol.

The body was certainly that of a very large wolf. What lifted Ruxton's hackles were not so much the powerful, now-broken wings that sprouted from just above and behind the enlarged shoulders or the grasping talons on all four feet, one of which had slashed his shoulder and just missed his throat. It was the face that was really disturbing. The familiar long wolf muzzle was curved slightly, like some furry beak. The ears were too wide and long for any member of the *Canis* genus. And the now-dark eyes that had shone like the lamps of hell were so swollen in size, they nearly met above the bridge of the muzzle. It was a creature worthy of the imagination of a Dante.

He crawled back to camp and began pulling on his boots. Malone grunted satisfaction.

"Good. Reckon I don't have to tell you everythin'. We got to get under some cover." He nodded upslope from their trail. "Thought I might've seen a cave on our way in. Don't much care for dark places, but it might be big enough to hide us and the horses both." He rose and holstered the rifle, then began assembling their equipment with one hand. Ruxton noted that he did not at any time let go of the LeMat.

They lost one of the horses despite their caution. Neither man rode, and the unflappable Worthless led, but Ruxton's pack mare still broke her tether and bolted for the nearest stand of tall trees. As she charged across the slope, she shed cooking pots and utensils and food and tools, the equipment making a terrible racket as it banged and bounced off the rocks. Malone and Ruxton watched her go.

"She'll be all right," Ruxton declared hopefully. "We'll track her down come morning."

Malone's expression was grim in the moonlight. "Why do you think *I* didn't head for the woods?"

As the mare approached the first trees, the entire forest canopy appeared to rise from the topmost branches. Ruxton's mouth went dry, and he shivered. But what more natural than for nocturnal flying creatures to roost in flocks? The fleeing mare had disturbed them.

There were at least thirty of the huge wolfuls. They swooped down on the terrified animal, circling low and snapping with wolf jaws at her withers and neck. She kicked out frantically and sent one of her tormentors spinning. It yelped unnaturally.

There were too many to prevent the inevitable. A pair landed on her back, using their talons to cling to flesh and pack straps. They tore at her face and flanks. Others cut her legs out from under her, striking at the tendons until they had her hamstrung. Unable to run or kick, the mare was buried beneath an avalanche of snarling, tearing bodies. She whinnied wildly to the last.

Malone and Ruxton didn't linger for the end. Even as the mare went down, a couple of the flock were making exploratory passes at the remaining horses and men. Ruxton felt heavy feathers brush his head as he ducked. He was not ashamed to admit that he screamed. Malone's LeMat boomed several times. Once there was a deeper, sharper explosion as he fired the .410 shotgun barrel that was mounted beneath the revolver barrel. Ruxton found himself surrounded by blood and feathers. He had a brief glimpse of feral yellow eyes. Then the sky disappeared as they stumbled into the cave.

It tunneled far back into the mountain. As Malone had hoped, there was more than enough room for all of them, including the horses. They tied them to boulders near the back wall of the cave.

Bored with the carcass of the already dismembered mare, the flock began to gather outside the entrance, padding back and forth and flapping their wings excitedly. The cave was actually larger than Malone would have liked. There was flying room inside. A lower ceiling would have been much more comforting.

Ruxton was breathing hard, his eyes nearly as wild as those of his mount. While it had stopped bleeding, his injured shoulder was throbbing mercilessly. But he could still hold a rifle.

"I regret the loss of my large-bore," he told Malone as he checked the .30-30. "It was packed with my other supplies on the mare."

The mountain man grunted. There followed an uncomfortable silence.

"Look here, Malone," Ruxton said finally, "I'm sorry I doubted you, old chap. I've been a bit of an ass all along, and I apologize." He stuck out his hand.

Malone eyed it, then enveloped it in his own huge paw and squeezed briefly. "I like a man who can own up to his own mistakes. I just hope you'll live to regret it." He turned back to the cave entrance. "There'll still be some meat left on your mare. When they've cracked all the marrow out of the bones, they'll work themselves up for a go at us. We have to stop 'em before they get inside or we're done."

Ruxton nodded, resting his rifle atop a boulder that had fallen from the ceiling. "I've never even heard rumors of such a creature."

"Any folks whut sees one never gets away to tell of it. The Nez Percé know about 'em. They call 'em Sha-hoo-ne-wha-teh. Spirit wolves of the air. But the Nez Percé are unusual folk. They see things the Blackfeet and even the Cheyenne miss. 'Course, white folks don't find their way into this particular part of the Bitterroots.

"Way I figger it, no ordinary predator's fast enough or strong enough to take down a jackalope, especially when they stand and fight together. So these here wolfuls evolved to prey on 'em. Unfortunately, they ain't real particular about their supper. You and me, we're a damn sight slower than a sick jackalope. As for the horses, well, they're regular walkin' general stores far as these critters are concerned."

"Listen, Malone. Most of my shells were packed on that poor mare along with my big guns. If things start to look bad, I'd appreciate it if you'd save a round in that LeMat for me. I don't mean for my rifle."

"I know what you mean. We ain't somebody's supper yet, Lord. They got to get in here first. Meanwhile, why not have a go at askin' your namesake for help?"

"My namesake?" Malone's eyes rose as he jerked a finger upward. "Oh," Ruxton nodded somberly.

The wolfuls continued to gather outside, their massed wing beats a vast rushing that soon drowned out the livelier, healthier babble of the river below.

"First they'll sing for courage," Malone explained. "Then they'll start circlin' as they decide which one of 'em will get the honor of goin' for our throats first. After that they'll come for us. Try and pick your shots. One way or the other, it'll all be over quick."

Ruxton nodded, his teeth tightly clenched as he stared at the moonlit oval that marked the entrance of their sanctuary.

When the flock began its howling, it was as if all the graves at Battersea had opened to release the long dead. The sounds were higher in pitch than normal wolf calls, a sort of moan mixed with the kind of screech an enormous vulture might make.

The horses panicked at it, kicking up dust and gravel, pawing at the unyielding stone. Foam spilled from their lips. Only Worthless stood placidly, one eye half-open, swaying on his legs as if asleep. It made Ruxton wonder. Perhaps the animal was partly deaf and blind.

The flock leader was silver across his muzzle. He came in low and then rose abruptly toward the ceiling, awful talons spread wide to grasp and rend, vast yellow eyes staring hypnotically. They froze the startled Ruxton for an instant, but not Malone. The Sharps blew the wolful in half, the huge shell tearing through flesh and bone. Ruxton had no time to appreciate the difficult shot, because the rest of the flock followed close on the heels of their dead leader.

The terrified whinnying of the horses, the howls and roars of the wolfuls, and the rapid firing of both men's guns were deafening in the enclosed space. Ruxton saw Malone put down the empty LeMat and race to reload, his thick fingers moving as precisely as those of a concert pianist. He'd drawn his big bowie knife and was using it to fend off his attackers as he worked.

Then Ruxton saw him go down, the golden-furred hat flying as a diving wolful struck him across the forehead. The claws missed his eyes, but the impact was severe.

"Malone!" Ignoring the pain shooting through his shoulder, Ruxton rushed to the other man's side. His rifle cracked, and another wolful dropped, snapping mindlessly at its damaged wing.

The mountain man blinked dazedly up at him, bleeding from the gash in his head. It was a shallow wound. He was only stunned.

That was when the flapping and howling and gnashing of teeth ceased. So concerned was he with the guide that Ruxton didn't notice it at first. Only when he helped the much larger man to his feet did he see that the last of the wolfuls had turned tail and was fleeing the cave.

"They're leaving. We beat them, old man! Gave them a sound hiding!"

"I think not, Lord." Malone fought to penetrate the oil that seemed to be floating on his retinas. "The Sharps—gotta get the Sharps." He stumbled, blinking dizzily.

"Hang on. I'll get it. But we don't need it anymore. They've gone, you see, and—"

He stopped in midsentence, holding his breath even as he left Malone to pick up the heavy buffalo rifle. The last howling of the wolfuls had faded into the distance, but it was not silent outside. A dull booming, as of some heavy tread, was clearly audible and growing steadily louder as he listened. He forced himself to keep his hands steady as he loaded the Sharps.

The massive breathing was right outside the cave. Evidently they were not the first creatures to make use of its shelter. The horses were too terrified to whinny. They huddled together against the back wall, trembling.

The moon went out as something immense blocked the entrance. Ruxton raised the Sharps and tried to hold it steady. Though he was a strong man, it sent shivers along the muscles of his arms.

Whatever stood there had to bend to fit beneath the twenty-foot-high ceiling. Its eyes were red instead of yellow like those of the wolful. An overpowering musk assailed Ruxton's nostrils as the hairy leviathan paused to sniff loudly.

It growled, and Ruxton felt his knees go weak. Imagine a whale, growling. The growl became a snarl that revealed teeth the size of railroad ties in the blunt, dark muzzle. It was coming for them.

Ruxton pulled the trigger, and the Sharps erupted. He thought he'd prepared himself for the recoil, but he was wrong. It knocked him on his back. The echo of the gun's report was drowned by an incredible bellow of pain and anger as the monster stumbled backward.

The rifle was pulled from his numb fingers. Malone reloaded as Ruxton staggered erect. The owner of the cave was already recovering from the shock and preparing to charge again. This time it would not hesitate curiously. A second slug from the Sharps wouldn't stop it. Not this time. As well to try shooting a runaway locomotive.

Something went flying past him like black lightning: Ruxton had a glimpse of white fetlocks and flying mane. Worthless slammed headfirst into the belly of the monster like a Derby winner pounding for the finish line. The Gargantua went backward, falling head over heels down the slope.

"Dumb, stupid son of a spasmed mare!" Malone growled as he gripped Ruxton by the shoulder. "Let's git out of this damn possum trap!"

They stumbled outside. There was no need to lead the remaining horses. Freed from their tethers, they sprinted madly past the two men. Malone and Ruxton ran downslope toward the forest, which was now devoid of roosting wolfuls.

Ruxton risked a look backward. A less brave man might have fainted dead away right then and there or swallowed his tongue at the sight.

Worthless had become a darting, spinning black dervish on four legs, nipping at the ankles of the immensity that now stood on its hind feet. It swiped at the much smaller but nimbler horse with paws the size of carriages. Each time a blow capable of demolishing a house descended, Worthless would skip just out of its reach.

Only when the two men were safely in among trees too old and thick even for the leviathan to tear down did Worthless abandon his efforts. With a roar, the monster chased the horse a few yards. Then it bellowed a final defiance before dropping to all fours. Like a piece of the mountain come to life, it turned and lumbered back to reclaim its cave.

Running easily, Worthless galloped past both winded men. He turned the fleeing horses, circling them until they slowed, nuzzling Malone's pack mare until she stood quietly, spittle dribbling from her jaws. Then he snorted once, shook his head, and bent to crop the tops of some wild onions that were growing nearby.

"Mr. Malone, that is quite a remarkable animal you have there." Ruxton fought for breath as he rested his hands on his knees. "How did you ever train him to do something like that? 'Pon my word, but that was the most gallant action I have seen a horse take on behalf of its master."

"Train 'im? Gallant? The idjit bastard like to got hisself killed! I had a clean shot. Coulda stopped it."

"Stopped that behemoth?" Ruxton nodded in the direction of the cave that had initially been their refuge and had nearly ended as their grave. "Not even with that cannon you call a rifle, old chap. Your animal saved us for sure."

"Well—mebbee. But it was still a damn-fool thing to do."

Malone repeated the assertion to his mount's face, shoving his beard against that squinty-eyed visage while holding it by the neck.

"You hear me, you moronic offspring of a mule? Don't you never try nothin' like that again!"

Worthless bit him on the nose.

"What was it, anyway?" Now that they were well away from the nameless river and the canyon it had carved, Ruxton found he was able to relax a little. The sun was rising over his unsatisfied curiosity.

Malone had spent much of the morning muttering

curses at his mount while occasionally feeling gingerly at the bandage Ruxton had applied to his nose. It was an incongruous slash of white above the black beard. Personally, Ruxton had felt the animal justified in its response.

"Somethin' big enough to snatch a wolful right out of the sky. Nez Percé, they call it—wal, never mind what the Nez Percé call it. You wouldn't be able to pronounce it, anyway. Me, I call it a grizzephant. Only the second one I've ever seen. If the good Lord wills it, I'll never see another. Reckon you could call it *Ursus loxodonta.*"

"Why, Mr. Malone, sir. Latin? I do believe you are at pains to conceal a real education."

"Nope. Just don't use it much 'cause nobody around here cares one way or t' other. They don't believe half of what I try to tell 'em anyways, so I just keep my mouth shut." He leaned over to give his mount a reluctant pat on the neck. "Old Worthless here, I reckon he deserves a genus of his own. I just ain't come up with the right one yet, though I kinda lean toward *Equus idioticus.* With the emphasis on the 'cuss.' "

Ruxton leaned forward for a better look. As he did so, he noticed that the leather patch that normally covered the animal's forehead was hanging loose, having been dislodged in the fight.

"Mr. Malone, would I be remiss if I were to suggest that your horse has a horn growing from the center of his forehead?"

Malone leaned out for a look, straightened. "Drat.

Got to fix that before we git to Randle's Farm. Folks in these parts don't rightly understand such things as unicorns."

Ruxton couldn't keep from staring. The horn was six inches long and looked sharp. Undoubtedly it had helped keep the grizzephant's attention last night. He could just make out the marks where Malone had kept it filed down.

"I know an elderly Chinese gentleman who will give you a million pounds sterling and six of the most attentive and beautiful women you ever set eyes upon for that horn, sir."

"No, thanks, Lord. Be happy you got your jack-alope."

"Yes, my jacka—" Ruxton's eyes got very wide. "The jackalope! It was tied to the packhorse the wolfuls killed!"

Malone eyed him evenly. "Want to go back and try again?"

Ruxton turned around in his saddle. His shoulder still throbbed, but the injury was almost completely healed thanks to some strange-smelling herb powder Malone had rubbed on it while mumbling some nonsense about Tibet and Samarkand. He straightened resolutely, bringing his gaze back to the trail ahead.

"I will mount the memory in my mind," he said firmly, "and make do with that."

For the first time since they'd met, Amos Malone smiled. "I reckon mebbe you ain't as dumb as you look, then, Lord. Even if you do ride funny. Ain't that right, sweetie-dumplin'?" He caressed his mount's neck.

Worthless looked back out of his half-closed squint eye. A kind of thunder rolled across the Bitterroots one more time as the unicorn farted.

THE CHROME COMANCHE

I don't get it. I mean, I'm as relentless an enemy of the out-of-control political correctness in this country as anyone. For one thing, I never met a dedicated PC'er with a sense of humor.

But nobody except Native Americans seems to mind much that they're the only ethnic group in this country that's treated like a commodity. Do you see a football team called the Atlanta Negroes? How about a semipro baseball team yclept the New Jersey Jews?

Although sports make the most blatant use of this peculiarity, it can be found everywhere. In restaurants, on television, in thousands of brand-name products. It's weird, and I'm glad it doesn't affect me intimately. How can a country take so much pride in a people it tried so hard to exterminate? Talk about your love-hate relationships.

Product brands, yes.

ESAU WAS CHECKING THE WAGON'S REAR axle when the dog started barking. It was the middle of the day, and it made no sense. The dog ought to be asleep somewhere back of the barn, not out front barking in the sun. In any event, it stopped soon enough. The dog was as exhausted as the rest of them.

At first he didn't even bother to look up, so absorbed was he in his study of the wagon. It had to be loaded and ready to go by this evening so that they wouldn't have to spend another night in the cabin. It wasn't much of a house, but it was a home, a beginning. Rock and sod mostly, braced with rough-cut cedar and mesquite. What milled lumber he'd been able to afford had gone into the barn. It wasn't finished, and the chicken house wasn't finished.

The only thing that was finished here on the south bank of the Red River was them, he thought.

He didn't raise his gaze until the dog came over and begin licking him.

"What the blazes ails you, hound?"

"He's scared, I think," said a deep voice. "I hope not of me."

Esau hesitated, then realized that the wagon offered little protection. Might as well crawl out and confront the speaker, whoever he might be. Were they now to have as little peace during the day as they'd found here at night?

No spirit gazed back at him, though the animal the speaker rode was unusual enough. Esau knew horses, but this particular mount appeared more jumbled than mixed. The rider was nearly as unclassifiable, though from what could be seen behind the flowing black beard, Esau was pretty sure he was white. Esau had to squint to make out individual features. The more he squinted, the more indefinable the details of that face seemed to become. Though it was as full of lines as a sloping field after a storm, it didn't hint of great age.

The man himself was immense. The pupils of his eyes were of a blackness extreme enough to spill over and stain the whites. He wore fringed boots and buckskin, his attire not so much dirty as eroded. Like the face, Esau thought. Had man put those lines there or nature? Bandoliers of huge cartridges crisscrossed his chest, fuel for the Sharps buffalo rifle slung next to the saddle. The octagonal barrel was only slightly smaller than a telegraph pole.

"You're a long ways from the mountains, friend." Esau shielded his eyes as he spoke, while the dog began to sniff around the horse's hooves. The confused-breed piebald ignored the attention. "No beaver to trap around here. Not in north Texas."

"You'd be surprised what there is to trap in Texas." The mountain man considered the little cabin. "But you're right enough. I'm jest passin' through, out o' New Orleans on my way to Colorado." He nodded in the direction of the chimney. "Saw your smoke."

A vast growl arose from the vicinity of the giant's stomach, belly-thunder heralding the approach of an expansive hunger. Esau smiled slightly, relaxing.

"You're welcome here, stranger. Come in and set a spell. Be right to have company for our last meal here."

Though the giant slipped off his mount, he seemed to lose nothing in stature as he stood on his own two feet. "I thank you for your hospitality. Your last meal, you say?"

Esau nodded gravely, indicating the wagon. "Just checking out the frame and the springs before loading her up. Never thought I'd have to do that again. We'd planned to live out our days here. This is a good place, mister. River's always running, and the grass is high. Best cattle country I ever saw." He shrugged fatalistically.

The mountain man addressed the uncomfortable silence. "Name's Malone. Amos Malone."

"Esau Weaver." The rancher's hand vanished inside the giant's gnarled grasp. "Sarah's inside fixin' dinner. You're welcome to stay for supper, too, if it suits you. We'll be out soon after. Have to be."

"It ain't in me to linger long in any one place, but I appreciate your offer, Weaver."

Esau led the visitor toward the home he was preparing to flee, unable to keep from glancing at his companion. "Didn't think there were any of you boys left. Thought the beaver had all been trapped out, and the market for 'em faded anyways."

"There's still places in the backcountry where a feller can make a livin' if he works hard and has half a mind for figures. Only real trouble's that the country's gettin' too citified. Even Colorado's fillin' up with folks tired of city life." He chuckled, an extraordinary sound. "So naturally, soon as they arrive, they all light out for Denver. Folks sure are a puzzlement sometimes."

"Wish all I had to deal with were country neighbors." Esau opened the door and called to alert his wife. Malone had to duck double to clear the low doorway.

Behind them the dog concluded its inspection and disdainfully peed on the horse's rear right leg, whereupon the mountain man's mount did a most unequine thing. It raised its leg and liked to drown that poor unsuspecting hound, sending it shaking and yapping around the back of the cabin. The horse, whose name was Worthless, let out a soft snort of satisfaction and went hunting for fodder. Malone had not tied him. Would've been useless to try.

Sarah Weaver showed the lack of sleep the family had endured recently. She wore her hair pulled straight back and secured in a small bun, a simple long-sleeved dress, and an apron decorated with fine tatting. She hardly glanced at her husband and his guest. Her son, Jeremiah, was far less inhibited. He stared unabashedly at Malone, firing questions that the mountain man answered readily until the boy's mother warned him to mind his manners.

"Heck, ma'am, he don't bother me none," Malone said with a smile so ready and wide that the tense woman relaxed. "It's good to be around young'uns. Reminds a man what the future's for."

"I then take it that you're not married, sir." She dipped stew from the black cast-iron kettle that hung in the fireplace. Once things got settled, Esau had promised her a real stove, but now . . .

"Name's Malone, ma'am. As for lockin' up, I've had the urge once or twice, but as I ain't the type to settle down, it wouldn't be fair to the woman."

"I hope you like this stew." She set the bowl in front of the visitor. "It's all we have. What's left of all I could salvage from my garden before *they* destroyed it."

Malone inhaled pointedly. "Ambrosia and nectar, ma'am. Though if you cleaned out your barn an' boiled the results, it'd be bound to be better than my own cookin'."

She smiled thinly and sat down opposite her husband. Jeremiah took the high seat opposite Malone.

An unnatural silence settled over the table. Any slight creak or groan caused both rancher and wife to look tensely at walls or windows before resuming their meal. There eventually came a time when Malone could stand it no longer.

"Now, you folks tell me to shut my food hole if you want to, but I'm afflicted with a confusion I got to vent. Friend Esau, you told me what a fine place you had here, and havin' seen some of it, I don't find any reason to dispute. So maybe you'll sympathize with an ignorant bumpkin who sits here delightin' in your wife's fine cooking while wonderin' why you're in such an all-fired rush to leave."

Esau Weaver glanced at his wife, who said nothing. He started to resume eating, then paused as though considering whether to speak. Clearly it burned within him to share this matter with someone else.

"Spirits, Mr. Malone." The rancher broke a chunk of bread from the round loaf in the middle of the table. "Ghosts. Devils. Indian devils."

"They come upon us in the middle of the night, Mr. Malone." Sarah Weaver had her hands on the table, the fingers twisting and twining. "Horrible sounds they make. They terrify Jeremiah. They terrify me."

"Got no heads." Weaver was chewing his bread unenthusiastically, but he needed something to do with his mouth and hands. "Thought it was just raiders at first, till I got a look at 'em during a full moon. No heads at all. That don't keep 'em from howling and yelling and tearing up the place. They want us off this land, and by God, they're going to have their way. I can't take any more of this, and neither can the woman." Love filled his eyes as he gazed across the table at his wife, love and despair. "White men or Indians I'd fight, but not things without heads."

"Esau went into town and spoke with one of the pacified Comanche medicine men," Sarah Weaver murmured. "He told Esau that this part of the country along the river was sacred to the tribe. But he couldn't say how much. He did say there could be spirits here."

"There are spirits all over this country," Malone said. "Some places don't matter so much to 'em. Others do." He sat back in his chair, and it creaked alarmingly. "But you were told straight, I think. This lands reeks of medicine, old medicine. But not," he added, his face twisting in puzzlement, "this place right here."

"You know about such things, do you, Mr. Malone?" Esau's tone was sardonic.

"A mite. I sensed the medicine when I was ridin' in. But not where we're sittin'. If there's spirits about, I wouldn't see them choosin' this place for a frolic. Upstream or down, maybe, but not right here. Besides which, it ain't like spirits to drive off cattle and tear up vegetables. If they're real and they wanted you off, they'd be a sight more direct in their intentions."

"They're real enough, Mr. Malone," Sarah Weaver said. "If you don't believe us, stay and see for yourself, if you dare."

"Well, now, ma'am, I jest might do that. Been a while since I seen a gen-u-wine spirit. Oh, and that Comanche medicine man you talked to? He might've been right or he might've been wrong, but one thing's sure: he weren't pacified. You don't pacify the Comanche. They jest got plumb tuckered out." He glanced at his host.

"Now, you say these here no-heads keep y'all awake a-yellin' and a-hollerin'. Do they sound somethin' like this?" Somewhere behind that wolf thicket of a beard, lips parted as Malone began to chant.

Jeremiah's jaw dropped as he stared in awe, while his parents sat stock-still, listening. Night, not due for hours, seemed to encroach on the little cabin, and a breeze probed curiously where moments earlier the air had been as still as a bad man's eulogy.

"That about right?" Malone inquired.

Esau shook himself back to alertness. "Something like that but deeper, long syllables."

Malone tried again. "Closer?"

Sarah Weaver found herself nodding unwillingly. "That's it, Mr. Malone. That's it exactly."

"Interestin'. First chant was Comanche. Second was Shoshone. Now, the Comanche and the Shoshones are related, but there ain't no love lost between the tribes and there ain't no Shoshone in these parts. Too far east, too far south. Makes no sense."

"Neither do headless devils, Mr. Malone."

The mountain man nodded somberly at the rancher's wife. "That's a truth fine as frog hair, ma'am. The devils I know always keep their heads about them, if not their wits. A head's something man or spirit tends to get used to and downright lonely without.

"You said they're about to run you off this land, but all they've done is make your lives more miserable than north Texas weather?"

"Maybe you're not afraid of devils, Mr. Malone,

but I have a family to protect. I'll take no chances with something I do not understand."

"I comprehend your position, Esau. You're a good man in a bad spot. Now, a fool like myself loves to take chances with what he don't understand. Mrs. Weaver, I will take you up on your offer to stay and see for myself. But I don't fancy doin' so all by my lonesome. You've stuck it out this long. Could you see your way clear to stickin' around one more night? If my suspicions are wrong, I'll be the first to up an' confess my sins."

"Another night?" Sarah Weaver's exhaustion showed in her tone and expression. "I don't know. What would be the good in it?"

"Might not be any good in it, ma'am." Malone didn't mince words with her. "Might be only understanding, and that ain't always to the good. But I've got a hunch it ain't your place the spirits hereabouts are concerned with."

Esau Weaver leaned forward. "Then you believe there are spirits here?"

"Didn't I say that? This is old Comanche land. Lot of coups counted here, lot of warriors' bones interred along this river. What I said was I don't see why they'd bear you folks any malice. You ain't even turnin' the soil."

"Why should you want to help us? You said you were just passing through."

"That's my life, Esau. Passin' through. The time to stop's when good people like yourselves are havin' trouble. It's what we do in the passin' that's remembered." He beamed at Sarah Weaver, and despite her exhaustion, she surprised herself by blushing. "Notwithstandin' that I owe you for the best meal I've had since leavin' New Orleans."

Weaver was wrestling with himself. His mind had been made up for days. He would not go so far as to allow himself to hope, but this towering stranger was so damned sure of things.

He glanced one last time at his wife, who acquiesced with her eyes. Then he turned back to Malone. "You mind sleepin' in the barn with the horses?"

"Not if the horses don't object. Uh, you got any mares in heat?"

Weaver made a face. "No. Why would you ask that?"

"Don't want to cause a ruckus." He jerked a thumb in the direction of the door. "Worthless may not look like much, but he's able to do more than trot when his back's up."

"I'll find you some blankets, Mr. Malone." Sarah Weaver started to rise from the table.

"Now, never you mind me, missus. I've got my own blanket. Buffalo robe's good enough for me. Warmer than homespun and strong enough to keep the mosquitoes away."

"Thick pile, is it?" Weaver inquired.

"Not especial. But it ain't been washed in a bit, and the smell's strong enough to mask my own."

Jeremiah gazed wide-eyed at the mountain man. "What if the headless spirits come for you, Mr.

Malone? What if they come for you in the barn when you're asleep and all alone?"

That huge wrinkled face bent close. The boy could smell the plains and the mountains, the sea and suggestions of far-off places. For just an instant those black eyes seemed to shine with a light of their own, and Jeremiah Weaver was sure he could see unnameable things reflected within them.

"Why, then, son, we'll have ourselves a set-to and gamble for souls or answers."

Malone guessed it was around two in the morning when Worthless's cold, wet tongue slapped against his face. Grunting, the mountain man swatted at the persistent protuberance as he sat up in the darkness, hunting for his boots.

"Godforsaken miserable son of a spavined mule can't let a man get a decent sleep." Worthless snorted and turned toward his waiting saddle and blanket.

"No, you stay here." Malone hop-danced into one boot, then its mate. "Bright night like this, you'd stick out like Tom Sawyer's fence. I won't be too long. Meanwhile, you leave those two mares alone. They ain't interested in you, nohow."

As Malone traipsed out of the barn in the direction of the faint sounds, his mount stuck out his tongue at him. Then Worthless turned to begin chewing at the rope that secured the paddock gate.

There was ample moon, though Malone didn't need it. He could track them by their movements. They were chanting already, but softly, as if practic-

ing. Peculiar and peculiar. Spirits didn't need re-
hearsals, and it was hard to imagine any Indian, real
or ghostly, crashing through the brush like a runaway mine cart.

But there were spirits here. That he knew. So he
continued to tread silently.

Then he could see them. There were about a
dozen, advancing slowly on the cabin, crouching
as they walked. They wore painted vests and leggings and, just as the Weavers had insisted, had no
heads.

Maybe that explained why they were so clumsy,
Malone thought. Spirits floated. Comanche floated,
almost. These critters, whatever they were, bulled
their way through the brush.

Only one of them was chanting louder than a
whisper. Malone focused on him. There was something about the way he moved that was real. His
feet caressed the earth instead of bludgeoning it,
and he wore moccasins. His companion spirits wore
boots. A few were equipped with spurs. Odd choice
of footgear for a ghost.

The crackling anger of a thousand crickets made
Malone look down and to his left. The snake was
already tightly coiled. So intent had he been on ob-
serving the advancing "spirits" that he'd neglected
to note the leathery one close by his feet.

The rattler's tongue flicked in Malone's direction.
Malone's tongue jabbed right back. If it had any
sense, the rattler would bluster a few seconds more

and then slither off in the grass. Snakes, however, were notoriously short on sense. This one struck, aiming for Malone's left leg.

The mountain man disliked killing anything without good reason, and the snake's unwarranted attack was evidence enough it was already deranged. So instead of drawing the bowie knife, Malone spit, faster and more accurately than was natural. His spit caught the snake in the eyes as its target leapt to one side.

Confused and queasy, the rattler lay silent a moment. Then it hurried off into the brush. It would not come back.

Unfortunately, it had been heard. Four headless figures surrounded Malone. All of them carried Colts, distinctly unethereal devices. The man in their midst regarded them thoughtfully.

"Didn't think you'd chance it forever on your singin' alone."

The one nearest Malone reached up and yanked at his chest. Painted fabric slid downward in his fingers, revealing a quite normal face. At the moment the expression on it was pained.

"You're a big one. Where'd you spring from?"

"The seed of an eagle and the loins of a cat—not that it's any of your business." Malone studied his captors thoughtfully as the speaker carefully removed bowie knife and LeMat pistol from the mountain man's person. Malone made no move to retain them. "What're you boys doin' out here in the middle o' the night in those getups? I didn't know the circus had made it this far west."

The speaker's expression turned sour. He was about to reply, when two other figures arrived. Those holding the Colts quickly made room for the newcomers. One of them was the real chanter. Malone studied his features intently. Shoshone, all right. Teetering the horizontal side of half-drunk and, by the look of him, not caring much about his condition.

His companion was bigger and older, made up to look like what he wasn't. He was neither ghost nor spirit, though the scent of the Devil was surely about him. He had about him the air of one with no time to waste, clearly a man poisoned by impatience.

"Who the hell are you?" he inquired belligerently of the mountain man.

"Malone's the name. Amos Malone. Mad Amos to some."

"That I can believe. Well, Mr. Malone, I don't know what you're doing out here, but I am told that the country on the north side of the river is more hospitable to strangers. I would suggest that you betake yourself there as soon as possible. Perhaps sooner."

"Your solicitude is touching, but I like it here, Mister . . . ?"

"Cleator. This is my associate, Mr. Little-Bear-Blind-in-One-Eye." He clasped the Shoshone possessively on the shoulder. It was enough to shake his none-too-stable equilibrium.

Malone murmured something in Shoshone to the chanter, who promptly and unexpectedly straightened. He blinked hard, as if fighting with his own eyes, trying to focus on the man who'd spoken to him. Meanwhile, the mountain man gestured at those surrounding him.

"Kind of an obscure locale for a theatrical performance, ain't it?"

"This is not theater, sir. This is seriously real."

"Might I inquire as to its purpose?"

Cleator gazed at him. "Why should I trouble myself to explain to a passing nonentity? Why should I not simply have you shot?"

"Because you don't want any shooting." Malone indicated the still-sleeping cabin. "If that's what you wanted, you'd have killed all three Weavers long ago instead of constructin' this elaborate masque."

"You are surprisingly perceptive. I am intrigued. You are, of course, quite right. I dislike killing because dead people cannot sign legal documents. It is much better for them to sign willingly, while they are still alive."

"This is all because you have a hankerin' for the Weavers' land."

"Certainly. It lies between two of my holdings. But that is not the most important reason." He paused, studying Malone, and then shrugged. "I will show you. Understanding will make you dangerous to me. Then I will have no compunctions about having you shot if you refuse to depart."

They led him to the edge of the Red. Little Bear followed but stayed as far away from Malone as possible. He was still fighting to focus his eyes.

Cleator pointed upstream, then down, and lastly at the far side of the river. "My land, Mr. Malone." He kicked dirt with his boots. "Weaver's land. Notice anything unique about it?"

Malone studied the river, the far bank and the near. "This is a narrows."

Cleator smiled, pleased. "Very good, sir. Very good, indeed. I may tell you that in fact this is the narrowest part of the Red River for many miles in either direction. Can you suspect why it is of such interest to me?"

"You need a bridge."

"Running cattle across a bridge saves the need of fording them to reach the railhead north of here. Every extra mile a steer runs costs weight and therefore money. I need this land to build my bridge."

"Why not simply lease the portion you need? I'm sure Weaver would be amenable to a fair offer. A bridge could be of benefit to his stock as well."

"Of course it would, but I don't want to benefit his stock, Mr. Malone. Nor do I wish the uncertainty of a lease. I want to own it all."

"You're goin' to all this trouble for that?"

"No trouble, Mr. Malone. I invent some mischievous spirits to frighten away the Weavers, and then I buy their land at auction."

"If you jest asked him, he might be glad to sell out direct."

"But in this fashion I obtain a much better price."

Malone considered. "Mr. Cleator, you are an evil man."

Cleator shrugged. "I am ambitious. They are not the same."

"I find it hard to separate the two much of the time. Joke's on you, though."

The rancher frowned. "What joke, sir?"

"You didn't have to invent no spirits to haunt this place. The spirits are here already. Have been for a thousand years or more." He turned sharply on Little Bear. "Ain't that right?" And he added something in Shoshone.

As wide as the chanter's eyes got, this time they had no difficulty focusing. Little Bear began to gaze nervously around him. Ordinary rocks and bushes suddenly caused him to retreat, to stumble.

"What did you say to him?" Cleator asked curiously.

"Nothin' he don't know. The whiskey you give him kept his eyes from workin', if not his mouth. He's seein' now, takin' a good look around, and he don't much like what he sees. Always been bad blood between Shoshones and Comanche. He's

feelin' dead Comanche around him now, and he
don't care for it. I wouldn't, neither, were I you, Mr.
Cleator."

A couple of the hired gunmen were starting to
glance around uneasily. Malone had started them
thinking. North Texas is a bad place for a man to be
thinking with the moon glaring down at him accusingly.

"Really? And why not? Am I supposed to fear a
few dead Indians?"

"I'm jest sayin' that if I were you, I wouldn't try
to put no bridge over these narrows."

Cleator was grinning now, enjoying himself. "Mr.
Malone, you are a caution, sir. I defy the Weavers,
I defy the Comanche, and I defy their dead or anything else that attempts to slow progress on this
land. Do not try to frighten me with my own invention."

"Sometimes it's healthy to be a mite afeared o'
progress, Mr. Cleator. It can jump up when you ain't
lookin' an' bite you severe." He looked up suddenly
at the opposite bank, his heavy brows drawing together like a small black version of the bridge
Cleator proposed to build.

The gunmen jumped when Little Bear let out a
cry and bolted. One of them raised his weapon, but
Cleator stopped him from shooting.

"Let him go. We'll track him down later. He'll be
in town, drunk."

"I wouldn't figure too near on that," Malone informed him. "I think our friend's seen the light. I

reckon by tomorrow he'll be headed northwest if he can find himself a horse. You see, he saw what was waitin' for him here and did the sensible thing by lightin' out."

One of Cleator's men stepped forward. "We're losin' the night, boss." A very large knife gleamed in his right hand. "Let me stick him, and we'll dump him in the river and get on with this."

"Very well. Now that he knows, by his own wish, he is a threat, and as previously stated, I can have no compunction about terminating a threat. Therefore, you may . . ."

He broke off, gazing across the river at the spot Malone was watching. One by one the men wielding the colts joined him in staring.

"Hell's bunghole," one of them stuttered, "what is *that*?"

It was larger than a bull buffalo, with teeth the size of an opium dream and burning yellow eyes. Even at that distance they could hear it growl as it raced toward them.

"Mr. Cleator, I wouldn't linger in this vicinity if I were you."

The rancher was shaken but otherwise unmoved. "I am not afraid of night beasts, Mr. Malone. That is no spirit. I don't know what it is, but if it is alive, it can be slain." He wrenched a rifle from the man next to him. "This will be my land, and I will build my bridge *here*. I will deal with any intruders." He glanced back and smiled. "You set this up, didn't you? You and the Weavers. Some kind of trick. It will not work. I am no gullible plainsman, sir. And you are dogmeat." He looked sharply at the man with the knife.

"Stick him or shoot him, as you please."

But the gunman was staring across the river, staring at the unbelievable thing that was coming toward them faster than a train could travel. As he stared, he kept backing up, until he prudently decided to turn and run. He was accompanied.

Cleator roared at them. "Come back! You cowards, idiots! Can't you see it's a trick! That damn farmer will be laughing at you tomorrow!"

A couple of the men slowed to turn, but what they saw made them tremble with fear and run faster still. The monster reached the far bank of the river. It did not stop but kept coming, soaring through the night air as easily as the fabled roc of legend, as cleanly as a bad dream. They were not particularly brave, those men, and they were not being paid well enough to stay and tussle with hell.

The scream made Cleator turn. So fast had it traversed the river gorge that it was already almost upon him. It screamed again, a cross between a bleat and a howl. Malone whirled to flee, yelling at Cleator to do the same.

Perhaps he didn't have enough time or chose to react instinctively. He raised his rifle and tried to aim.

The burning yellow eyes blinded him. He flung his gun aside and tried finally to dodge.

That was when Malone saw the Indian. He was riding the monster's muzzle.

It was solid and yet spirit, a brave clad in untraditional armor. Small but perfect, he thought as it turned toward the stumbling, half-paralyzed rancher and loosed a single shining arrow. It struck James Cleator squarely in the right eye, penetrating to the brain and killing him instantly.

Then the monster was upon him. Cleator was struck once and sent flying, his already dead broken body landing ten yards away in a crumpled heap. Malone slowed. It had not come after him but had vanished eastward, howling into the night.

Breathing hard, he waited until he was sure before returning to study the rancher's corpse. Nearby he found the monster's tracks. They were unlike any he'd ever seen. He knelt to examine them more closely.

A voice came anxiously from behind: "Mr. Malone! Are you all right, sir?"

The mountain man did not look up as Esau Weaver slowed to a halt beside him. The rancher was carrying a rifle, old and battered. There was nothing worn about his courage, however. He blanched when he espied Cleator's body.

"I know that man."

"Your antagonist, though you did not know it. Not spirits. Gold will buy a man much, but not truth and not the spirits of the dead. Too easy by half to defile yesterday as well as tomorrow. I believe he were done in by both." He put a comforting hand on the rancher's shoulder. "Nothin' more to be done here. Cleator was dead of heart before the rest of his body caught up with him. Let's go get some shut-eye. I'll have a go at explainin' it all to you and the missus tomorrow, while I'm helpin' y'all to un-pack."

Weaver nodded wordlessly. Together they re-turned to the cabin, which would be disturbed no more. Around them the land and all it contained were once again at rest. Yesterday and tomorrow slept peacefully, flanking the present.

"Hell of a restoration job." The attendant looked on approvingly.

"Thanks." The owner was standing before the ob-ject of the other man's admiration, examining it mi-nutely.

"Something happened; I can see that."

"Hit something coming over the bridge last night, just this side of Childress. Might've been a coyote. Might've been a small deer."

"Lot of damage?" The attendant was sympathetic. Out here you never knew what you might run into at night.

"Not as bad as it felt. Plenty of blood, though. That'll wash off okay. Then there's this." He fin-gered the Packard's nose. "Bent halfway around. And there's a little arrow that went right here, see? Must've lost it in the collision." He straightened, shaking his head sadly.

"These cars from the thirties and forties, they built 'em tough, but it seems like something's always happening to the damn hood ornaments."

AGRARIAN DEFORM

Okay, so they're cheap. So they're the proverbial lowest form of humor. So what? If it works, it works. The radiant Diana Rigg once starred in a one-season U.S. situation comedy. All that matters is whether it works.

Easy enough to get a cheap one-liner out of them. Damn difficult, not to mention frustrating, to build one into an entire story. Or build an entire story into one.

Aw, you know what I'm talking about.

"YOU TALK TO HIM, JESSE."

"Not me. Look at him. It can't be the right man."

"Have to be," said George Franklin. "Can't be another human being on God's green earth looks like that. It's him fer sure."

They argued vociferously among themselves. Since no one was willing to approach their quarry alone, they had no choice but to do so in a body.

"Shoot," Deaf Williams pointed out, "he's jest

135

sittin' there whittlin'. Ain't like he's gnawin' on baby bones."

"Yeah," said Slim Martin, "but you ever see anybody whittlin' with a bowie knife before?"

Having finally screwed up sufficient courage to approach the giant, they found they had nothing to say.

Amos Malone pushed back the wolf head that covered his scalp and regarded the sightseers. From somewhere behind that impenetrable black beard, luxuriant enough to offer succor and shelter to any number of small unidentifiable creatures, a surprisingly balsamic voice arose to break the uncomfortable silence.

"You folks never seed a man whittlin' afore?"

As the wealthiest and largest of the six, it fell to George Franklin to reply. Also, his erstwhile friends and neighbors were doing a fine job of concealing themselves behind him.

"Are you Amos Malone?" He swallowed uneasily. "The one they call Mad Amos?"

The bowie knife sliced. Wood chips flew. Standing there on the covered porch outside the hotel, Franklin was acutely conscious of the proximity of his belly to that huge hunk of razor-sharp metal.

"Wal, 'tis Amos Malone I am, but at the moment I ain't particularly mad. Next week, now, I wouldn't vouch fer that." He paused, squinting up at Franklin. "Kin I do something fer you folks, or are y'all just wanderin' art lovers?"

Jesse Kinkaid stepped forward. "Mr. Malone, sir,

we got ourselves a bit of a goin' problem. Word around is that you might be the man to help us out."

"We can pay," Franklin added hastily, grateful for the supportive voice of a neighbor.

"Ain't said I'd take the job yet." Malone sheathed the knife and scratched at the hem of his buckskin jacket with a huge, calloused hand. "What makes you think I'm the feller you need?"

The men exchanged glances. Though there were six of them, they were peaceable folk, and they felt badly outnumbered. "Now, don't be takin' this as no insult, Mr. Malone," Kinkaid said cautiously, "but the word in these parts is that you're some kind of magician."

"Black magic," said Deaf Jackson much too loudly before his friends could shush him.

Malone just smiled. At least, it looked like a smile to Kinkaid and Franklin. One couldn't be sure because only the center portion of the man's mouth was visible behind his black rat's nest of a beard. You couldn't tell what the corners of his mouth were up to.

"I'm no magician, gentlemens. Jest a poor seeker after knowledge. A wanderin' scholar, you might say."

"What kind of knowledge might you be seeking, sir?" Young Hotchkiss was too wet behind the ears to know that in California Territory it was impolite at best—and potentially lethal at worst—to inquire too deeply into another man's business.

Malone took no offense, however, and smiled at

the youth. Wiser men among the six heaved silent sighs of relief.

"Oh, this and that, that and this. Same thing as the poor feller Demosthenes. He has his lamp, and I've got that." He gestured out into the street, indicating a massive horse of unidentifiable parentage.

Young Hotchkiss would have asked who Demosthenes was ... sounded like a furriner ... but Franklin hastened to cut him off before he said too much.

"The point being, sir, that you are rumored to be in the possession of certain arcane skills." When Malone did not comment but instead waited patiently, Franklin continued. "We are farmers, sir. Simple farmers."

"I'd say that's right on both counts." Malone held his whittling up to the light, examining it carefully.

Franklin looked helplessly to his neighbors. Again it was Kinkaid who picked up the gauntlet. "Mr. Malone, sir, we got ourselves real troubles. Our land is, well, sir, it seems to be cursed."

The mountain man looked up at him. "Cursed, sir?"

Kinkaid nodded somberly. "Cursed."

"I wonder if you mightn't be a tad more specific, friend."

Emboldened, Slim Martin spoke up. "It's our crops, Mr. Malone. They get lots of water, plenty of sun. We work as hard as any folk in the Central Valley, but it don't make no difference. Corn tops out at less than a foot; apples just shrivel on the tree;

tomatoes never get ripe. It's a caution, sir. And it don't seem to matter none what we plant. Nothin' comes up proper."

Malone straightened in the chair, which groaned under his weight. "An' you think I kin help you?" It was not necessary for them to reply: their desperation was plain on their sunburned faces.

"Now, I ask you fair, gentlemens: do I look like a farmer to you?"

They eyed him up and down, noting the heavy goatskin boots, the wolf's-head chapeau, the bowie knife and LeMat pistol secured at his waist, and the twin bandoliers of enormous Sharps buffalo rifle cartridges that crisscrossed his massive chest, and the truth of what he said laid them low.

A couple turned to leave, but not Kinkaid. "Sir," he pleaded desperately, "if you can help us, we'd be more than just obliged. Most of us—" he gestured at his companions "—came to this country for the gold. Well, the placer gold's all run out, and big companies have taken over most of the claims up in the high country and on the American River.

"When the big money started moving in, a lot of folks picked up and left, but some of us stayed. My people are Illinois original, and I know fine farming country when I see it. A man ought to be able to make a good living out of this earth hereabouts. Plenty of folks are: those working the valley to the east of us.

"I don't mind bein' run off by bandits, or the weather, or grizzlies or Indians, but I'm damned if

I'll give up and just walk away from my spread without having a reason why."

Malone considered silently. Then he rose. Involuntarily, the little knot of farmers retreated a step. The mountain man had to bend to avoid bumping his head on the porch roof that shaded the sidewalk.

"Like I said, I ain't no farmer. But I don't like to see good folks driven off their places when mebbe there's a simple straight way their troubles kin be fixed. So I will have a look-see at your country, gentlemens. Don't promise that I kin do nothin' for you, but a look-see I'll have."

"As to the matter of payment," Franklin began.

"Let me see if I kin help you folks out first," Malone told him. "If I can fix your problems, then it'll cost you, oh, a hundred dollars U.S. In gold." Franklin inhaled sharply but said nothing. "Until then, bed and vittles will do me jest fine. A bucket or two of oats for Worthless wouldn't be turned down, neither."

Across the street the enormous multicolored nag looked back at the group and whinnied.

Franklin and Kinkaid exchanged a glance, then Franklin turned back to the mountain man and nodded. "Agreed."

Buoyed by their success but simultaneously wary of the man they'd engaged, the farmers headed for their own mounts or, in the case of Franklin and Kinkaid, a fine new buckboard.

"Think he's the man?" Kinkaid asked his neighbor.

"I don't know, Jesse." Franklin glanced back up the street to where the mountain man was mounting his ridiculous animal. "Might be he's telling us the truth when he says he doesn't know a thing about farming."

Kinkaid lowered his gaze. "Well, it weren't a farmer we come to find, was it?"

"I'm not very confident about the other, either," Franklin murmured. "I don't see anything remarkable about him except his size."

Deaf Jackson swung his right leg over his saddle. "What'd you expect to find, George? Somebody with horns growin' out of their head, breathin' fire and riding a cloud?"

"No, I expect not." Franklin heaved himself up into the buckboard while Kinkaid took the reins.

Young Hotchkiss mounted alongside Slim Martin. "Funny thing, back there."

"What's that?" Martin asked him as they turned up the street that led out of San Jose.

"That odd-looking horse of his turning back to us and whinnying when we were talking about him."

"What's funny about that?"

"Malone wasn't talking that loud, and there were wagons and horses going all the time we was there. How'd that animal hear him clear across that street?"

Malone had been studying the terrain ever since they'd ridden south out of San Jose. Rolling hills that gave way to flat, grassy plains. You could smell

the richness of the soil. Blessed as it was with ade-
quate water and California sunshine, there was no
reason why the soil they were traveling shouldn't
produce crops as fine and healthy as any in the
world.

But it was not. Something was wrong with this
land, something major unpleasant, Malone decided.

The men kept their distance from him, wary and
uncertain. All except young Hotchkiss, who was too
green to know better. He rode alongside, keeping
the stranger company and asking too many questions for his own good. But the mountain man
didn't appear to mind, and the others were delighted
to include among their number one fool whose chat-
tering ignorance served to free them of the accusa-
tion of inhospitality.

"That's quite a hat you've got, sir. Did you kill
the animal yourself?" The young farmer indicated
the wolf's head that protected Malone's scalp.

The mountain man kept his attention on the land
ahead, studying the soil, the increasingly twisted
trees, and the scraggly brush. Surely it was damaged
country they were entering. Sick country.

"I didn't kill it," he replied offhandedly. "It ain't
dead."

Young Hotchkiss hesitated as though he hadn't
heard correctly. "Begging your pardon, sir."

"It ain't dead." Reaching up, he adjusted the
wolf's head over his forehead.

Hotchkiss regarded the canine skull. "I wouldn't
be found calling you a liar to save my life, Mr.

Malone, but if it ain't dead, then where's the rest of it?"

"In a cave a thousand feet above the Snake River. Old wolf's denned up for the winter. Since he don't need his head while he's hibernatin', he didn't see the harm in lettin' me borry it till spring. I told him I'd look out for his family in return." Malone leaned close and whispered conspiratorially. "Don't talk too loud or you're likely to wake him up. I don't know what his head's likely to do without the rest of him, but it might not be real pleasant."

The wide-eyed young farmer nodded and spurred his mount to rejoin his companions up ahead. As soon as he'd gone, Worthless cocked his head back to peer up out of his good eye at the man on his back.

"What're you squintin' at, you useless offspring of a spavined mule? The boy was gettin' to be somethin' of an irritation."

The Percheron-*cum*-Appaloosa-*cum*-Arabian-*cum*-unicorn snorted with great deliberation, compelling his rider to wipe his left boot while visiting additional imprecations upon his mount, which plodded on, thoroughly unimpressed.

The town wasn't much: schoolhouse, church, smithy, barber, two general stores, a small hotel. It was the spittin' image of a thousand similar farming communities all across the country.

A woman with two kids was coming out of the general store. When she saw the riders approach,

she ran back inside. Several men emerged to greet
the tired arrivals.

"Well, we're back!" Deaf Jackson said loudly as
he dismounted.

"Yep. This is Malone," Kinkaid said. "The man
we heard about."

The two men standing on the store porch looked
uncomfortable. Franklin eased himself down from
the buckboard and mounted the steps to confront
them.

"Josiah, Andrew; what's going on here? This
isn't the greeting we expected. What is our friend
Mr. Malone going to think?"

The storekeeper picked at his apron. "You're late,
George."

Franklin frowned. "What's that got to do with
anything? It took considerable time to find our
man."

"Well, George," said the storekeeper's companion, "it's just that you all were gone so long, and
then this other gentleman rode into town ..."

Franklin's eyebrows rose. "Other gentleman?"

"Me."

All eyes went to the general store's entrance. The
man who stood there was as thin as Slim Martin but
taller. He had pale blue eyes and undisciplined
blond hair and rather more lines in his face than he
ought to have had. He wore a brightly checked,
long-sleeved flannel shirt over a new pair of Mr.
Levi's best pants and was masticating a chaw of the
store's best tobacco.

"And who might you be, sir?" Jesse Kinkaid inquired.

"Sam. Folks just call me Sam. You can call me Sam, too." His gaze rose to the silent, contemplative mountain man. "So can you, friend. That's me, just plain Sam. The farmer's best friend."

Malone touched the nose of his unusual headgear with the tip of one finger.

Franklin, Kinkaid, and the rest gathered around the two men from the store. Intense whispering ensued.

"Andrew, how could you go an' hire somebody when you knew we were lookin' for this Malone fella?"

"Well, George, he just wandered in, and we all got to talking, and he said he was sure he could help us. Before we go an' do something dumb, let's think this thing through. How much is that Malone gonna cost us?"

"Hundred dollars," Kinkaid murmured.

The storekeeper looked triumphant. "This Sam fella says he'll fix all our troubles for fifty."

"Fifty?" Slim Martin said eagerly.

"Now listen here," young Hotchkiss began, "we've as much as hired this gentleman Malone. He's rode all the way down from San Jose with us, expecting to be employed on our behalf, and—"

"Shut up, boy," Franklin snapped. "Pay attention to your betters. Fifty, hmmm?" The two men from the store nodded.

Franklin turned and put on his best smile, simultaneously checking to make certain that no one stood between him and the open doorway.

"Mr. Malone, sir, I don't quite know what to say. I'm afraid we've got ourselves a situation here."

The mountain man regarded him unblinkingly. "Situation?"

"Yes, sir." Franklin shaded his eyes against the March sun. "It seems that unbeknownst to the rest of us, our friends here have gone and hired this other gentleman to assist with our difficulties. I'm sure you understand that since he was engaged first, the conditions of his employment take precedence over yours."

Malone glanced at the tall, thin individual standing on the porch chewing tobacco, then looked back down at the big farmer.

"No problem, friend."

Franklin's heart, which had commenced to beating as if in expectation of the Final Judgment, resumed a more reasonable rhythm. "It's only business, sir. Perhaps we can make use of your services another time."

"Perhaps." Malone glanced down the narrow street. "I'll just find Worthless a stall for the night, and tomorrow I'll be on my way." Again a finger rose to touch the lip of the wolf's head.

He heard the footsteps approaching. It was pitch dark in the stable. In the stall across the way Worthless slept soundly, for a change not snoring. Two stalls farther up a mare shuffled against her straw.

Wil Hotchkiss quietly approached the recumbent bulk of the mountain man. No one had seen him enter the barn. He reached out to shake the man's shoulder.

Less than a second later Wil was lying on his back in the straw, a knife blade more than an inch wide so close to his Adam's apple, he could feel the chill from the steel. An immense shape loomed over him, and for an instant he thought the eyes glaring down at him were glowing with an internal light of their own, though whether they belonged to the man atop him or to the wolf-skull headpiece in the corner, he could not say.

"Hotchkiss." Malone sat back on his haunches, a mountainous shape in the dim light. The massive blade withdrew.

The young farmer sat up slowly, unconsciously caressing his throat. "You're mighty fast for a man your size, Mr. Malone, sir."

"And you're mighty stupid even for one so young." The mountain man sheathed his blade. "Don't you know better than to sneak up on a man in the middle of the night? Your head could've ended up a play-pretty for my wolf friend's cubs."

"Sorry, but I had to come get you without my neighbors knowing what I was about."

"Did you, now?"

"Mr. Malone, sir, it weren't right how my neighbors treated you today. It just weren't right. And I think they're wrong about that Sam fella. Something about him rubs me the wrong way.

"I'd like for you to come out to my place, sir, and see if you can't do something for my land. I'll pay you myself. I've got a little money put aside. I'd rather have you working for me than have that Sam fella."

"What, now? In the middle of the night?"

"If you would, sir. That way my neighbors won't be disturbed by my doing this behind their backs, as it were. It's them I've got to live with after both you and this Sam fella are gone."

Malone rose, grinning in the darkness. "And if I turn out to be the biggest fraud since Munchausen, I won't embarrass you in front of your peers, is that it?" He waved off Hotchkiss's incipient protest. "No, never you mind, son. This ain't a bad way to go about it. I don't like bein' embarrassed any more than you do. So if'n I can't extricate you from your troubles, why, this way there won't be none others to see me fail."

Hotchkiss waited nervously until the mountain man had saddled his complaining, grumbling mount. The animal's spirits picked up considerably once outside the stable, however. Hotchkiss had come into town on a wagon pulled by two mares, one of which was near coming into her time.

Nor had the young farmer come by himself. Seated on the wagon, holding the reins and bundled against the evening chill, was a vision of pure country grace.

"Mr. Malone, this is my wife, Emma."

"Mr. Malone." She eyed him about the way

Worthless was eyeing the nearest mare. Malone pursed his lips.

"Ma'am."

She kept up a steady stream of chatter all the way out of town, laughing and giggling and batting her eyes at him like an advertisement for a minstrel show, all physical innuendo and sly music. Hotchkiss guided his animals, his attention on the road ahead, oblivious to nocturnal flirting so blatant that it would have put a blush on a bachelor jack-rabbit.

Nor did it cease when they reached the neat wood and stone farmhouse. Sweet Emma Hotchkiss managed to bump up against Malone once outside and once on the way in, where she made a grand production of removing her cloak and bending tooth-somely to stir the sleeping fire. Malone eyed her speculatively. She was a bumptious, simmering three-ring circus barely restrained by tight gingham and lace, and no ringmaster in sight.

Nor was she the only surprise awaiting him.

As Hotchkiss led him into the sitting room, a lanky shape uncoiled from the couch to greet him with a smile. "Malone, ain't it?" A hand extended toward him. "Ought to be an interesting evening."

Malone did not take the proffered hand but turned instead to his host. "What is this?"

Hotchkiss looked uncomfortable. "I said that I felt my neighbors had treated you unfairly, Mr. Malone, and I hold to that. But they're thinking of the money in their pockets instead of their futures,

and I'm not. I don't care who helps us so long as
someone does, right quick. Otherwise, everyone in
this part of the country is going to go under before
the next harvest.

"So I thought the only fair thing would be for me
to hire the both of you for one night to see what
each of you can do."

Malone stroked his beard as he eyed his host.
"Reckon I was wrong about you, son. You're only
half-stupid."

Emma Hotchkiss turned gaily from the fire,
which wasn't smoldering half so much as she, and
eyed each of her visitors in turn.

"I think Wil was ever so clever for thinking of
this. He's such a clever boy. And if both of you gentlemen can help us, why, then we'll be twice as well
off, won't we? I'll be ever so happy to thank the
best man with a nice kiss on the cheek."

Sure she would, Malone thought, watching her.
The way Venus wanted to kiss Tannhäuser in that
German feller's opera.

Hotchkiss seemed oblivious to it all, his mind on
his crops when he ought to have been paying more
attention to his field. "How long after you've finished your work will it take to show results? A
month? two?"

"Shoot, no, neighbor," said Sam the farmer's
friend. "I can't speak for Mr. Malone, but as for
myself, I think we can prove something right here
tonight." He smiled up at the mountain man. "What
about it, friend?"

"I don't like contests," Malone rumbled.

The lanky stranger shrugged. "Don't matter one way or the other to me. The other good folks hereabouts seem pretty convinced of my skills already. I don't mind accepting a forfeit."

Malone was being truthful. He didn't like contests, and he didn't like the way he'd been rousted out of a sound sleep on false pretenses. But he also didn't like the way this blond stranger was eyeing his host's young wife. Not that she wasn't encouraging him, along with probably every other human male west of the Sierras, but it wasn't very tactful of him to respond so readily.

"I don't like forfeits, either. Might be harmful to my reputation."

"And do you have a reputation, friend?" Sam asked him tauntingly.

"Here and there. Not always good. How about you?"

"Me? Why I'm Sam, just plain Sam. The farmer's friend." He winked at Emma Hotchkiss. Her husband didn't see it, but Malone did. She responded by licking her upper lip. From what Malone could see, it didn't look chapped.

"What say we have a look at these fine folks' uncooperative land, Mr. Malone."

The mountain man nodded. "I think that'd be a right sound place to begin."

Hotchkiss provided lanterns to complement the light of the full moon. The four of them walked outside, the young farmer and his wife leading the way

toward the nearest field. The stranger toted a large
canvas satchel, his eyes eagerly following Emma
Hotchkiss as he envisioned the bonus he imagined
would be his before the night was over. Malone carried a small pouch he'd extracted from one of his
saddlebags and with unvoiced disapproval watched
the stranger watching Emma.

The sound of wood striking ground drew their attention. Everyone looked toward the corral as two
shapes bolted into the moonlight.

"I tried to tell you, Wil, that your mare was coming into heat," Emma Hotchkiss said accusingly.

"Don't worry none, son." Malone followed the
galloping, rollicking pair with his eyes as they disappeared over the nearest hill. "Worthless won't
hurt her. They'll have themselves their run, and
he'll bring her back."

Hotchkiss looked uncertain. "Can't you call him
in?"

Malone shook his head. "Worthless pretty much
does as he pleases. I reckon they'll have themselves
a tour of most of your property before he feels
winded enough to amble on back."

"Hard to believe that a man who can't control his
horse can do much with the earth," the stranger ob-
served insinuatingly.

The mountain man looked down at him. "Tryin'
to control Worthless would be about like tryin' to
control the earth. Myself, I'd rather have a friend
for a mount than a slave."

The neatly turned field stretched eastward, bathed

in pale moonlight. Rye grass whispered warningly
beneath their feet. A single silhouetted tree stood
leafless, lonely, and bruised amid a mound of broken yellow rock. There was no wind, no clouds: it
was a place where a man could smell silence.

A deep creek ran between the two sloping halves
of the field. Malone studied it thoughtfully, then
bent to examine the soil. Lifting a pinch of dirt to
his nose, he inhaled deeply, then tasted of the earth.
He straightened.

"Sour," he declared brusquely as he brushed his
hands together to clean them.

The stranger nodded, eyeing the mountain man
with new respect. "That was my thought as well.
You do know something about the earth, friend."

Malone eyed him evenly. "This and that."

The stranger hesitated a moment longer. "Well,
then, this looks like as good a place to begin as
any." Reaching into his satchel, he fumbled around
until he found a pinch of seed. He flicked it earth-
ward and waited, eyes glittering.

"Father Joseph!" Wil Hotchkiss whispered, staring at the ground.

Where the seed had landed, tiny pools of light appeared in the sterile furrow. They spread, trickling
together within the soil, a pale green glowing efful-
gence staining the dark loam.

As the four looked on, tiny stems broke the surface. Vines first, climbing toward the moon like
umber snakes. Three feet high they were when they
halted. Like soap bubbles emerging from a child's

toy pipe, bright red fruit began to appear beneath the green leaves, swollen and red-ripe as the lips of a succubus. The stranger turned proudly to the farming couple. His words were directed at both of them, but his eyes were intent on Emma Hotchkiss.

"Well, now, that wasn't so difficult, was it?"

"Tomatoes," Hotchkiss was muttering. "Finest damn tomatoes I ever seen. In March." He eyed the stranger warily. "This ain't farming, sir. It's witchcraft."

"Not at all, friend, not at all," the stranger replied, smooth as cream. "Merely the application of sound agrarian principles." He glanced at the mountain man. "Wouldn't you agree, sir?"

"Too soon to say." Malone grunted and reached into the bag he carried. Choosing another furrow, he scattered seeds of his own.

The earth did not glow where they landed. Instead, it rumbled softly like an old man's belly. Emma Hotchkiss put her palms to her face as she stared. Even the stranger backed away.

Not vines this time, but entire trees emerged from the ground. Fruit appeared on thickening branches, bright and bursting with tart juice. At Malone's urging, Wil Hotchkiss tentatively plucked one from a lower branch and rotated it with his fingers.

"Oranges." His gaze shifted between the modest tomato bushes and the full-blown orchard, and he did not have to give voice to how he felt.

Frowning, the stranger selected and spread another handful of seed. This time the vines that arose with unnatural rapidity from the earth were shorter but thicker than those that had preceded them. With a grandiose wave of his hand, he beckoned the young farmer close.

Wil Hotchkiss knelt to examine the thumb-sized dark fruit. "Grapes," he exclaimed. "And already ripe!"

"Sam, that's fabulously clever," said Emma Hotchkiss, throwing her arms around the stranger and bussing him not anywhere near his cheek. He responded without hesitation, the both of them ignoring Wil Hotchkiss, who was wholly intent on the miraculous grapes.

Malone surveyed the scene and shook his head. Then he sighed and carefully dusted a nearby mound with seed. This time it was as if the earth itself coughed rather than rumbled, as if uncertainly trying to digest the unexpected fodder. New vines emerged with astonishing speed. To everyone's surprise except Malone's, they looked no different from those the stranger had just called forth.

"Well." Wil Hotchkiss sounded slightly disappointed. "A tie."

"Things ain't always as they seem, son. Taste one," Malone suggested.

The young farmer did so, and as the grape squinched between his teeth, his eyes widened. He stared wonderingly up at the mountain man.

"Already turned to wine . . . on the vine!"

"Mr. Malone!" his wife exclaimed. "How wonderful!" But her attempt to explore her other guest was doomed to defeat, as Malone was too tall for her to reach, even on tiptoe, and he declined to bend. She settled for favoring him with a look that despite his resolve raised his body temperature half a degree.

"I don't know how you did that." The stranger's disposition had passed from mild upset to middlin' anger. "But fruit isn't all that this land will produce if coaxed by someone who knows truly the ways of the soil."

He whirled and flung a handful of seeds in a wide arc. Where they struck, a section of earth the size of Hotchkiss's corral began to burn with cold green fire. Clods and clumps of earth were tossed aside as trunks two feet thick erupted from the ground. No fruit hung bounteous and ready to pick from the gnarled, newly-formed branches. Hotchkiss searched a black extrusion until he found the first of the small oval clusters that were as wooden-dark as the branch itself.

"Walnuts," he exclaimed, picking one. "Ripe and full-meated."

"Oh, yes," his wife murmured huskily.

The stranger eyed Malone challengingly. "That's quite a feat," Malone said. He held up his pouch. "Don't carry near that much seed with me. So I reckon one'll have to do." Digging into his much smaller sack, he removed a single seed.

The stranger smirked. "That's all you got left, friend? My bag's still near full."

"I don't much like to travel heavy." Carefully,

Malone pushed the single seed into the soil, using one callused thumb to shove it deep. Then he stepped back and waited.

The tree that blossomed forth was no larger than any one of the dozen walnut trees that now blocked the stream from view. As soon as it reached its full growth, Hotchkiss approached to pick from a lower branch.

"Walnuts," he declared disappointedly as he cracked the shell with the butt of his knife. With the point of the blade, he pried out the contents, popped them into his mouth, and chewed reflectively. "No worse, but no better."

"Pick another," Malone suggested.

Hotchkiss looked at him funny but complied. It seemed that his eyes couldn't get any bigger than before, but they did. "Pecans." He stared wonderingly at Malone. "On the same tree?"

"Thought you'd be the kind who'd appreciate good nuts," Malone told him. "Why stop now?"

The young farmer picked some more. His delighted wife joined him. Together they sampled the tree's bounty.

"Peanuts . . . on a tree!"

"Chestnuts," his wife exclaimed. She displayed the rest of her pickings to the mountain man. "What are these, Mr. Malone?"

He examined the contents of her perfect hands. "The big curved ones are Brazil nuts. Little curved ones are cashews."

"What are cashews?" Hotchkiss asked.

"They don't come from around here, but they're good to eat," Malone told him. "Those big round ones are macadamias, from Australia." He peered up into the tree. "I reckon there's some up in there I don't rightly know myself."

The stranger walked right up to his taller opponent to search his face. "You're a very clever man, friend. Very clever indeed. But you're no farmer's friend. And whatever you be, I swear you can't match this."

He stepped back and took a seed the size of a peanut from his sack. It pulsed with a faint inner light of its own, as though a tiny heart were beating inside the hard outer covering. Instead of scattering it carelessly as he had the others, he planted this one very carefully. Malone thought the stranger whispered some words over it as he ground it into the soil with the heel of his boot. Then he stepped back.

From a red refulgent patch of earth another tree emerged, its branches sagging under the mass of multihued fruit they carried. The trunk of the tree seemed permeated with that pale red glow, which did not diminish when the tree ceased growing. There were apples and oranges, lemons and limes and soursop, jackfruit and star fruit and litchi and rambutan—fruits that never should have grown in that dirt, in that country. It was a cornucopia of fruit sprung from a single unsuspecting square of soil.

Even Malone was impressed and said so.

"Go on," the stranger said proudly, "taste some of it. Taste any of it."

The mountain man carefully scrutinized one of the groaning branches. He picked a couple of rambutan and began to peel them, the sugary white centers emerging from behind the spiny red outer husks. The stranger looked on intently as Malone put one fruit to his lips. Then he hesitated.

"You must be gettin' a mite hungry yourself after so much hard work." He held out the other rambutan.

The stranger waved him off. "No, thank you, but I enjoyed a fine supper and am quite content."

"Oh, go on," Malone urged him. "I dislike eatin' by meself."

Hotchkiss frowned at the stranger. "Is something wrong with the fruit?"

"No, of course not." The blond man hesitated, then took the proffered fruit. Eyes locked, the two men ate simultaneously.

"Can I have some, too?" Emma Hotchkiss asked coyly. "I'm not full at all. In fact, I'm just ever so positively empty inside."

Malone smiled at her. "Maybe later, ma'am. We need to make sure it's truly ripe."

"Oh, I think it is." She smiled up at him. "But if you're not sure, then I'll wait until you are."

"Pretty good," Malone said, tossing aside the nut that lay at the center of the fruit. He wiped his lips with the back of a huge, hairy hand. "You know your crops, Sam the farmer's friend, but I ain't so sure you know your soil. This hereabouts is soured fer sure, and not all the fruits and vegetables and grains that you or I could grow on it in a night will cure that."

The stranger did not hear. His face had acquired a faintly green glow itself. A hand went to his stomach as he turned to Hotchkiss.

"Are you all right, sir?" the young farmer inquired, alarmed.

"I am. Just a mite too much of my own bounty, I fear. Might your fine little community be home to a competent physician?"

Hotchkiss nodded. "Dr. Heinmann. Travels between towns hereabouts. He's at the hotel for another day, I think, but should be leaving tomorrow."

"Then I'd best hurry." Suddenly the stranger was running back toward the farmhouse, exhibiting more energy than at any time that night.

"What happened to him?" Hotchkiss asked.

Malone followed the stranger with his eyes as the man reached the house, mounted his steed, and urged it into a mad gallop toward town. Retching sounds drifted wistfully back over the fields toward them.

"I reckon he got too full of himself. He has a lot of knowledge but ain't quite sure how to control it. Your land hereabouts is soured. With his kind of help it'd grow you one fine crop this year and probably fail the next, mebbe forever. By which time the likes of Sam the farmer's friend would have harvested whatever he desired from this part of the world and moved on." He glanced in Emma Hotchkiss's direction, but rather than mark his point, she only gazed back at him invitingly, ignoring such inconveniences as admonitory implications.

Hotchkiss was crestfallen. "You're saying that the trouble's still in the ground and that it can't be fixed? That all our efforts here are doomed to failure?"

"Oh, no, I didn't say nothin' like that, Wil. The problem can be rectified by the application of an appropriate nitrogen-fixin' substance, not by seein' how many outrageous fruits and vegetables one man can grow in a night by trickery and deception."

"Nitro fix . . . ?" Hotchkiss frowned up at him. "What kind of talk is that?"

"Science, my young friend. The same science that makes the telegraph work and steam engines turn wheels. There's all kinds o' science stalking about the world, even among vegetables."

"Where do we get this kind of substance?"

"Wal, now, it might take some time to gather what you need from certain islands I know, like the Galápagos, or certain holes in the ground, like in New Mexico, but seein' as how you folks have already had such a bad time of it and are so far down the road o' discouragement, I thought it best to attend to the problem as quickly as possible. So while we've been out here playin' farmer, your difficulties have already been attended to."

"Already? You mean the ground is fixed?"

"Yep," said Malone. "Won't grow you no already wined grapes or many-nut trees, but you'll do right well hereabouts with regular walnuts and grapes, wheat if you need it, and a bunch of other stuff I don't reckon you know much about yet. Like artichokes." He stroked his beard. "I reckon I'd try the oranges a mite farther south, though."

"But the soil; how did you put it right?"

Malone put a fatherly hand on the young farmer's shoulder. "Now, don't you worry yourself none about the hows here, son. Sometimes it's jest better to accept things than to question everything."

They walked back to the house, which seemed already to have taken on a cheerier, happier air. As they did so, Malone glanced toward the corral. Worthless and the mare had returned. It was difficult to tell which was worse winded, but it was plain to see that the stallion had been attending to business. No doubt he'd sprayed most of young Hotchkiss's property in addition to his mare.

How could Malone tell his host that a little unicorn seed invigorated everything it touched?

Emma Hotchkiss could certainly cook, he had to admit. She had changed and wore a smile and a dress that revealed at least two rings of that three-ring circus whose presence he'd remarked on earlier. Several of the acts repeatedly bumped up against Malone as she leaned over the table to serve the men. As always, her husband did not notice. He was too delighted, too thrilled by the knowledge that his farm had been saved, to note that his field was in danger.

After she slipped off to bed, leaving in her wake a trail of perfume and promise, the two men shared conversation and tobacco in front of the crackling fire.

"I can't thank you enough, Mr. Malone. My neighbors won't believe it."

"They will when your crops come up, son. I promise you that."

Hotchkiss regarded him curiously. "For a man who's fulfilled every promise he made and vanquished the opposition to boot, you don't sound very content."

"I'm troubled, my young friend. 'Course, I'm always troubled, but I reckon that's my destiny. I'm not talkin' about those kinds of troubles, though. Jest the local ones.

"Fer example, if'n I were you, I wouldn't be entirely convinced that this was such a fine place to put down roots."

"But I thought you set the earth here to rights."

"Oh, she's unsoured, that's certain, but whatever cursed this ground in the first place I ain't sure is entirely cured. It might cause problems somewhere down the line. I'm not sayin' it will fer you, understand, but it might fer your children and your children's children. When you've put a few good years in, you might consider sellin' this property at a good profit and movin' farther down into the valley, mebbee somewheres along the San Joaquin. Better water there, anyways."

Hotchkiss was silent. "Well, sir, I cannot but take

your advice, having seen what you've done here this night. I will certainly keep your words in mind."

"That's not the only thing. There's more cursed hereabout than jest your land."

"More than the land? I'm afraid I don't follow you, Mr. Malone."

The mountain man nodded in the direction of the bedroom, the firelight deepening the shadows that were his face. "It's your Emma."

Hotchkiss gaped at him, then jerked around to follow his gaze. "Emma, cursed? Good God, Mr. Malone. By what? She seems well and healthy."

"She is that. But she's also tormented by the worst curse than can afflict any woman, Wil. That of boredom."

Hotchkiss frowned. "Boredom? But how could she be bored, Mr. Malone? There's so much to keep a woman busy on a farm: caring for the garden, washing, feeding the chickens and hogs, cooking, mending."

Malone coughed delicately into a closed fist the size and consistency of a small anvil. "I don't think you quite follow my reasoning, son. There's activity, and then there's boredom, and the two ain't necessarily mutually exclusive." He leaned forward, his eyes intent on those of the younger man, as if he were trying to communicate much more than mere words.

"She needs a change, Wil. She ain't the stay-on-the-farm-all-year type. You're a hardworkin' young feller, and I kin see that you're gonna do yourself proud with your farmin', make yourself some good money. Spend some of it on her. Don't just tell her you love her. Show her. Take her up to Frisco for a while. Tell her how beautiful she is. Give her little gifts and presents, and not jest for her birthday and holidays. The best time to give a woman something is when she ain't expectin' anything." He rose from the chair.

"Where are you going?" Hotchkiss asked numbly.

"Out to the stable. You'll be wanting the house to yourself."

"But I promised you . . ."

"Never you mind what you promised me, son. Most beds are too soft for me, anyhow. I'll sleep fine in the stable." He glanced toward the front door. "Need to keep an eye on Worthless, anyways. Come springtime he don't always know how to slow himself down." He grinned. "Thinks he's still a colt."

"Wait!" Hotchkiss said suddenly. "What kind of presents should I give Emma? What kinds of gifts?"

"Don't need to be big things. Lots of times little'uns mean more to a woman." He donned his wolf's head, and Hotchkiss thought he saw tiny lights flare briefly again, though more likely it was the glow from the fire. "You might start with this."

He reached into a pocket and removed something that he handed to the young farmer. It was a small wooden sculpture, exquisitely detailed, of a man and a woman holding each other close, staring into one another's eyes. Some of the detail looked too fine to have been fashioned by human hands.

With a start, Hotchkiss recognized the piece of whittling Malone had been working on outside the hotel in San Jose when he and his fellow farmers had confronted him.

"I can't take this, sir."

Malone stood in the doorway, bending low to clear the jamb. "Sure you can, son. I jest gave it to you. Go on. She'll like it." Before Hotchkiss could protest further, Malone closed the door behind him.

The young farmer stood there, unnerved by the gift. Then he shrugged and carefully put out the fire, retiring to the bedroom. In the dim light he failed to notice that the man and woman depicted in the sculpture were in the exact likeness of himself and his precious Emma.

The following morning Emma Hotchkiss made Malone the best breakfast he'd enjoyed in some months: grits, toast, biscuits and gravy, bacon and eggs, and homemade jam and sausage. She hovered close to her husband, the two of them exchanging little kisses and touches, and both wore expressions of great contentment and affection. The circus, Malone noted with satisfaction, had folded its tents, pulled up stakes, and left town.

Hotchkiss escorted him back into town, the two men chatting like old friends in the morning sunlight. Worthless all but trotted the entire distance. Malone gave him a couple of knowing kicks, which with great dignity he studiously ignored.

They walked into the general store, only to find a meeting already in progress. Faces turned in their direction as they entered, only to look quickly away.

Seated in the center of the group was the blond stranger. He was smiling. Evidently the good Dr. Heinmann's ministrations had mollified his internal confusions.

"What is this?" Wil no longer sounded young and insecure. "What's going on here?"

"Well, Wil," George Franklin said as he slowly turned in his chair, "we were just finalizing our agreement with Sam here."

"But you can't do that." Hotchkiss started forward, only to be restrained by his much larger companion. "I mean," he said more quietly, "Mr. Malone here fixed my problems by himself last night. Now he's ready to do the same for the rest of you."

"We're sorry, Wil." Kinkaid was apologetic. "But we did have a prior agreement with Sam here. Whatever your Mr. Malone did last night was between you and him. The rest of us have made another arrangement."

The blond stranger held up a paper. "This here is a signed contract, all legal and irrevocable. Fifty dollars for fixing these fine folks' land. Which I will do."

"Pretty underhanded, running back here to have that drawn up when you knew Mr. Malone was tied up with his work out at my place," the young farmer exclaimed heatedly.

"Easy there, Wil." Malone gazed silently at the nervous faces of the farmers. "This how you folks want it?" No one had the guts to speak. The mountain man nodded knowingly. "All right, then. But I'm warnin' you to keep an eye on this feller. Some things he knows how to fix; other things I ain't so sure. T'other night his own handiwork made him sick. If you ain't careful, it might make you sick, too. Might make your land even sicker than it already is. I just want you to know that anything happens after I leave, any problems you have, 'tain't my fault. It's his."

Kincaid and Franklin exchanged a look. "We are prepared to deal with any adverse consequences, Mr. Malone, though we are confident there will be none. We are mature men, and we know what we are doing."

"Saving yourselves fifty dollars. That's what you're doing," Wil Hotchkiss muttered angrily.

"It's all right, son," Malone told him back out on the street. "Jest remember what I told you about considerin' that move."

"What did you mean when you said in there that he might make the land sicker?"

Malone lifted his gaze to the sunburned hills and fields that surrounded the town like a grassy sea. "I don't rightly know myself, Wil. That Sam's a right clever feller, but I think mebbe too clever by half. A little knowledge is a good thing, but a lot ... well, you better know what you're doin' when you start playin' around with the earth." He clapped the young farmer on the shoulder, a friendly good-bye.

"You take care o' yourself, young feller, and your good woman, too. Come later this summer, I think you're gonna come into a foal that might act a mite peculiar, but it'll be a good animal for you if you can learn to tolerate its eccentricities."

"I will bear that in mind, Mr. Malone, sir. And thank you." Searching a pocket, he found the double eagle he'd been carrying with him since yesterday. "It's only a part of what you're properly owed, but . . ."

"Thank you, Wil." Malone accepted the twenty dollars. "Fair payment for services rendered." He mounted the four-legged massif that was his steed. "Give artichokes a try."

"I will, sir." Hotchkiss shouted after him as he rode south out of town, even as he wondered anew what the devil an artichoke was.

Inside the general store, the stranger was holding court, promising the small-minded, shortsighted men around him bounteous crops and enormous profits. He knew a lot, he did, but less than he thought.

"You heard what the mountain man said," Kinkaid told him.

The stranger smiled: relaxed, supremely self-assured. "Sure I heard, and it don't worry me none. Shouldn't worry none of you, neither. I know what I'm doin'. When I finish my work, your farms will be more prosperous than you've ever imagined.

'Course, there might be a slight recharge fee each planting season, but nothin' none of you won't be able to afford. A trifle compared to what you'll be making.

"As for any problems that come up, why, I'll gladly take the blame for them. You think, if I didn't have confidence in my skills, that I'd stick around? I know my responsibilities, gentlemen, and am prepared to discharge them to the fullest. So if anything untoward should occur hereabouts, let it be deemed my fault. My fault, gentlemen, or my name ain't Sam Andreas, Sam the farmer's friend."

HAVING WORDS

I've had my share. Of words, that is. After the first few million you start to go a little nuts, wondering how you're going to describe the next sunset, the next shoot-out, the next planet in a way that makes it seem fresh, new, different, or God-help-me-please at least not boring. When you've exhausted the dictionary and the Roget's, *what do you do? Where do you go for inspiration?*

You can invent your own language, juggle the vowels and consonants like Anthony Burgess in A Clockwork Orange *or George Miller's kids in* Mad Max: Beyond Thunderdome. *Insults are a particularly fertile area for invention. The tragically lost and influential underground illustrator Vaughn Bode always had his characters farking one another. It's a grand ground for twisting the meaning of words.*

And as we all know, words have power.

"WE WOULD LIKE TO GO UP INTO THAT COUNTRY. There are many animals there. Good hunting and fine places to camp." Bending toward the fire,

171

Grass-in-Hair cut a choice piece of dog with his knife and passed it to his guest, who accepted the morsel with a grunt of thanks.

Amos Malone hunched closer to the tepee's central heat and chewed thoughtfully. When he'd ridden into the encampment early that morning, his imposing bulk had frightened the children, but now Grass-in-Hair's youngest son slept peacefully on the mountain man's legs like a rabbit nestled in a bear's lap.

"Then why don't y'all just do it?"

Two-Feathers-Falling sniffed and repositioned the heavy robe that lay across his shoulders. It was late, and cold despite the fire. He would rather have been lying with First Woman, but Grass-in-Hair had insisted he be present. As far as Two-Feathers-Falling was concerned, the meeting was at best a polite waste of time. Half as big as a bull buffalo the white man might be, but in this matter he could do nothing.

"Do you not think we would if we could?" he snapped.

The mountain man took no umbrage at the medicine man's tone. "What's stoppin' you?"

Two-Feathers-Falling shifted uncomfortably. He was no coward, but neither was he a fool. Grass-in-Hair let the silence lie as long as was decent, then saw that he was going to have to do the explaining himself.

"Tongue Kills lives there. He has claimed all that

fine land for himself and will let no one else in. Not
to camp, not to hunt. He is a greedy, evil person."

Malone swallowed the last scrap of dog, extracted
his pipe from a pocket, and commenced to chew on
the rose-hued stem, which protruded incongruously
from the otherwise impenetrable black-wire mass of
his beard. "How big's his tribe?"

"He has no tribe, no family. He is alone."

Malone's gaze narrowed. "Mean to say one warrior's been starin' down the whole Cheyenne na-
tion?"

Two-Feathers-Falling spoke bitterly. "Tongue
Kills is not a warrior. He is a medicine man. Like
myself. But his medicine is too strong for me. And
not just for us. No one dares to challenge him.
Those who go into his country do not come out
again."

"Except for One-Who-Carries-Stone-Behind-His-
Head," said Grass-in-Hair. "He was a war chief of
the Crow who announced to his people that he
would kill the medicine man so they could move
into his land. He did come out. But he lived only a
few minutes after returning to his village." The old
chief was solemn. "We heard the story when we
were trading with the Crow up on the big river last
autumn. Those who told it to us are known to be
truthful men."

Malone tamped some brown dried substance into
the bowl of his pipe. "What happened to him?"

"The warriors said that he was burned all over."
The chief's tone was hushed. "As if he had been in

a great fire. His pony had been burned, too. It lived two days longer. Since then the Crow, like us, have stopped trying to go into that country." Grass-in-Hair looked wistful. "But we would still like to. I should like very much to hunt there. It is more land than any one man needs. Even one as strong in medicine as Tongue Kills." He went silent, expectant.

The fire crackled. Along with silence, the tepee was permeated by the pungent rankness of cooked meat and unwashed men. Finally Malone said, "What makes you think I can help you?"

Grass-in-Hair looked up at his visitor. "I have met a few of the other white men who have passed through this country. Some spoke of you. They said you could do strange things."

Malone laughed as he lit his pipe with a blazing splinter from the fire. "They probably meant to say that I *was* strange."

"They also said you were crazy. Here." The disgruntled Two-Feathers-Falling meaningfully tapped the side of his head.

"Might be as they were right."

"Only a crazy man would challenge Tongue Kills."

Malone chose not to comment.

"If you will try to help us in this," said Grass-in-Hair, "I will give you my eldest daughter. She is a fine woman and will bear many children."

"Wal', now, that's a swell offer, sir, but I fear I

must decline. I ain't quite ready yet to start in on a family."

Grass-in-Hair nodded, disappointed but understanding. "What, then, could we give you?"

"Your friendship . . . and mebbee that knife. I've kind o' taken a fancy to that knife of yours."

Grass-in-Hair held up the blade he'd used to partition the dog. It was a good knife of the kind of shiny black stone that always held its edge. But it was not irreplaceable.

"I would give it to you gladly. But I must tell you that I do not think it is worth risking one's life for." He gestured toward the visitor's belt. "You already have a knife of metal, one that is better."

Malone shook his head. "Not necessarily better. Just different. Somethin' about your knife calls out to me, Grass-in-Hair. And when somethin' calls to me, I make it my business to listen."

"Then I make you a gift of it. Will you use it to slay Tongue Kills?" he asked curiously as he handed it over.

Malone took the knife, admiring the way the light from the fire shone through the carefully honed edges. "Hope not. After all, y'all don't necessarily want him made dead. Just agreeable." He slid the knife into his belt alongside its steel cousin and leaned forward.

"Now, then. What makes this Tongue Kills's medicine so strong? What songs does he use? What powders? What is his animal? Badger, bear, eagle?"

Two-Feathers-Falling replied tiredly, knowing it

would make no difference. "He uses no songs, no powders. He has no animal."

"Then how the devil does he make medicine?"

"With words," Two-Feathers-Falling explained. "Only with words."

Malone nodded as if this meant something, took a couple of puffs, then removed his pipe and passed it to the old chief, who inhaled experimentally.

"Good tobacco," he said as he handed the pipe back.

"Thanks," Malone told him. He grinned at Two-Feathers-Falling. "I kin tell you don't think I've much of a chance against this feller Tongue Kills, but don't count me out till you see me down. I know a few words of my own."

The sleepy Cheyenne medicine man started. For an instant the mountain man's eyes seemed to have disappeared, the whites and the dark blue to have vanished completely, leaving only dark pits beneath heavy black brows. Within those twin voids lay stars and music, tenderness and power, indifference and compassion. Wide awake, Two-Feathers-Falling blinked.

But there was only a very large white man sitting there opposite him with real eyes. A trick of the fire, he decided.

"What do you think?" Grass-in-Hair asked the next morning as they watched the white man ride westward out of camp. "Of course he must be as mad as the other white men say, else he would not try this for us. But that is not necessarily a bad thing."

Two-Feathers-Falling held his buffalo robe snug against his body. Though it was warming up as the sun rose, stars still lingered in the blueing sky, pieces of ice the morning was slow to melt. "I think you have lost a good knife," he muttered as he shuffled off in the direction of his tepee.

It truly was beautiful country, Malone mused as he nudged Worthless to his right. Green and heavily forested. While his mount usually could be left to his own devices to find the easiest path down a slope, sometimes his bad right eye played him false and Malone had to help out.

Plenty of forage, good water. Excellent country. Elk and deer in abundance and a host of lesser animals. Grizzlies, too, of course, but they didn't bother Malone. Those possessed of a cantankerous disposition usually sought alternative routes as soon as they set eyes on him.

He settled in by the side of a meandering stream lined with new spring growth. There were trees nearby from which he'd soon raised a fine lean-to against a smooth outcropping of granite. Upstream he found beaver and remarked the location for future visitation.

He was preparing to put a door on the lean-to one afternoon, when he heard footsteps approaching. He tensed as he turned, alert but in no way particularly concerned. His rifle lay close at hand, within convenient reach. In wild country a man always kept his rifle closer to him than anything else, including his woman.

His visitor's attire was simple and traditional, except perhaps for an unusual breastplate that was decorated with feathers from a bird Malone couldn't identify. They were orange tending to yellow at the tips. The man wore much red paint on his face and clothing. His braids were long and, despite his apparent age, black as soot. He carried no weapons. Worthless spared him a glance, snorted, and returned to cropping the fresh new grass behind the lean-to.

The visitor was shorter than Malone, but then, so was most of the human race. He stopped to study the mountain man. Malone waited for a while, then shrugged and returned to his work.

As the day wore on the visitor maintained his silent inspection, eventually taking a seat on a small rock that protruded from the bank of the stream. Malone finished the door, peeled two large poles, and used them to brace the roof by jamming them into holes he'd dug earlier. Then he fished three good-sized trout from the stream, gutted and filleted them, and set about building a cookfire. Not one word had passed between the two men.

When evening arrived, Malone put the spitted fish on the fire, crossed his legs, and sat down to wait for them to cook. "For someone who's supposed to be master of a lot o' words, you're downright stingy with 'em, friend."

"You know who I am." Tongue Kills did not have a voice. He was possessed of an instrument, nay, an entire orchestra. Strings and brass, woodwinds and percussion, all were present and active, vibrating and resonant within his throat. Each word that fell from his lips was of itself a self-contained speech, a declamation, an oration of conciseness and import admirable. It was a thing wondrous and beautiful to behold.

"Then you must know, white man, that you are a trespasser on my land."

Malone gestured expansively. "Plenty o' land here. Why are you so reluctant to share it?"

Tongue Kills sat a little straighter. "It is my wish. I have taken this place for my own."

"Your brothers think you greedy."

"They are not my brothers, and I do not care what they think. I do not care what you think. Like them, you must leave."

Malone arched his back, stretching. "Shucks, I was jest gettin' comfortable here. Reckon I might stay awhile."

Tongue Kills leaned forward. Light danced in his eyes like individual flames skating on sheets of mica. "I say that you will leave. If you try to stay, I will make it bad for you."

"With what? Some words? Mister, I've been around. I've seen a lot and heard a lot. Why, you're lookin' at the original lover o' words. I know all the words of my own people as well as those of the Crow and Shoshone. Not to mention the Assiniboin and Kwakiutl, the Zuni and Arapaho, the Choctaw and the Seminole and Sioux. I know words in languages you ain't never heard of: Chinee and Nippon, Tamil and Urdu, Basque and Romany and pidgin. I know words in languages that was, like Assyrian and Maya, and words in languages that ain't yet, like Swahili and Hip-Hop.

"Better to share the plenty you got with your fellows. That's the proper way for one to live."

Tongue Kills smiled unpleasantly. "You speak of many strange things, but I see no signs of power. It matters not the kind of words but how they are used. I, too, know of other languages and other words. I have made the knowing of them my hobby." His tone deepened ever so slightly. "You do not want to know of them, white man."

Malone plucked a sprig of grass between thumb and forefinger and stuck it between his teeth.

"Shoot, I'm always willin' to learn. And since I ain't goin' nowhere, why don't you take the time to enlighten me?"

Tongue Kills's expression darkened. He nodded once, cleared his throat with a rumble, then spoke afresh. That extraordinary booming, reverberant voice spoke out, rustling the grass, its tone and emphasis sending birds fleeing from their nests and insects rushing to burrow deeper into the ground as the ominous speaker dropped one turbid obloquy after another into the previously calm pool of reality.

"Man, your spirit cannot escape the cradle of dung in which it was originally nurtured, a place

shunned by the lowest living things, a birthplace so
vile that it is avoided even by the beetles that seek
to feed in such holes. The odor of the misbegotten
clings to you and can never be washed off, so that
the stink of your ever-putrefying soul turns others
from you no matter whither you may seek to flee."

As Tongue Kills spoke, Malone felt himself
growing distinctly hot under the collar and, somewhat surprisingly, not only there. Looking down, he
saw that the fringe of his deerskin leggings was beginning to curl slightly at the tips. Wisps of smoke
emerged from several as if they were not strips
of cured leather but rather thick, sweat-sodden
matches. He began to perspire and, despite the chill
of approaching evening, experienced an unexpected
desire to be rid of attire become suddenly suffocat-
ingly warm. It was clear that Tongue Kills played
for keeps.

Not that Malone was about to take those words
lying down or even standing up. He'd picked up a
turn of phrase or two in his travels, damned if he
hadn't: the rapierlike accusations of cotton auction-
eers in Savannah, the seasoned dressings-down of
unyielding Prussian drill instructors. The lamenta-
tions of Calcut merchants and the withering com-
plaints of the camel traders of old Araby. Lisboa's
fisherwomen had shared their best and most scato-
logical insults with him, and once, severely in need
of a trim, he'd had his scalp professionally singed
by the singsong calumnies of a famed Canton trader
in opium.

Why, subsequent to one pleasant evening's drinking and concomitant commentary on Washington
politics, none other than Dan'l Webster himself had
ventured admiringly that when properly inspired,
Amos Malone's palate was truly an anvil of imprecations on which the mountain man's tongue could
hammer out insult after admirable insult, a river of
inventive invective as grandiosely appalling as New
York City's sewer system after a major summer
storm.

"I might tolerate that," he replied carefully, "if it
didn't come from someone so ugly that mere sight
of 'im would shock the feathers off a constipated
buzzard, the taste of whom would induce in a flock
o' starvin' mosquitoes permanent indigestion soon
as they discovered that their quarry had urine for
blood. Why, your countenance'd drive a dozen o'
the world's homeliest women to sworn celibacy an'
turn the Medusa herself to stone."

As he listened to this, Tongue Kills's expression
did indeed begin to harden, if not actually to fossil-
ize. His skin began to redden noticeably until, in
the gathering darkness, he was actually glowing
slightly. Currents of agitated air streamed upward
from his head and shoulders like heat waves rising
from a paved road on a blistering July noon.

"Your mother," the medicine man retorted, his
voice crackling like a newly-set bonfire of Georgia
fatwood, "must have mated with a snail, for it is
clear that slime was the sole offspring of that union.
You reek of man's civilization, of noxious hypocrisy

and embalming greed, of the air you have infected and the water you have poisoned. The soil itself recoils from beneath your feet, and the air screams as it is tortured by your lungs. The fecal matter that emerges from your body is the only pure thing you give back to the suffering earth, on which you are the foulest of parasites, in which even other parasites refuse to dwell."

Malone was forced to remove his heavy jacket, from which dense smoke was beginning to billow. He threw it down and began jumping madly on it to stomp out the flames that were trying to spurt from the sleeves. His exposed forearms, big around as aspen trunks, began to blister, and the sweat pouring from his forehead threatened to blind him. Even his teeth felt hot.

But he who listens learns. It struck Malone as more than slightly significant that Tongue Kills had spoken not of white man's civilizations but of man's. As they continued to trade dysphemisms of greater and greater heat, it set him to wondering as to just exactly whom he might be contending with by the shore of the wandering stream.

Not only the palaverers but the atmosphere surrounding them grew hotter as their calefacting conversation sent the very molecules of the air into an agitated frenzy. They tried to flee, crashing into one another and raising the temperature near the campsite to nearly tropical levels. Malone's overheated pants and leggings joined his well-pounded jacket underfoot as he was forced to expand the range of his frantic dance. Even the mountain man's hair was beginning to sizzle.

Meanwhile, Tongue Kills's smile grew forced, and though he did not give off any smoke, he looked more than a mite disconcerted. Heat continued to pour off him in waves, and he glowed like the big lantern that hung outside the Three Whalers' Tavern in Boston's High Street.

When an uneasy Worthless whinnied, Malone realized he'd better do something quick. A mere glance from his mount was suggestive of something seriously askew, but when he whinnied, it was time for a man to give serious consideration to proximate possibilities. It meant ordinary folk had better clear out fast, and the commonly fearful seek cover.

From the beginning there had been a glow in Tongue Kills's eyes, a particular glow that made Malone suddenly squint with recognition. He realized that he'd seen that exact thing before in another place, far off in the southern seas. It wasn't a glow that belonged in a man's eyes, which led him to a corollary that was as revelatory as it was inescapable.

"You win," he gasped, his throat scalded, the skin on the back of his neck beginning to curl from the heat. "I can't match you fury for fury, hot word for hot word. You've beat me."

Tongue Kills's triumphant expression twisted into a sneer. "It is good that you realize this, but it will not save you. I warned you, and you did not heed but chose instead to challenge. You will die, as will all who try to come to this place."

Malone was down to his long johns now, and only the fact that they hadn't had any contact with soap or water for an inexcusable length of time kept him from being spontaneously combusted right then and there by Tongue Kills's unceasing cataract of execration.

"What'll happen to me, I don't know, but there's just one thing more I have to say about you," he rasped out. "It's a durn shame that your mastery of heated language happens to be inversely proportional to your humanity."

Tongue Kills gave a start, then a cry of outraged realization as the paradox wrapped him in its inescapable grip. His fury imploded, inescapably self-contained. Malone shielded his face with an arm as heat, the by-product of all that anger, rushed outward in waves from his antagonist. Frustration, volatile as black powder, erupted. Somewhere behind him Worthless was whinnying loudly while trying to simultaneously keep all four feet off ground grown suddenly intolerably warm.

"You vile apparition, you imposition that walks on two legs; your existence outrages the world!"

"Yeah, well," Malone bellowed in response as he continued to shield his face, "you ain't no rose o' creation yourself!"

Tongue Kills's skin began to ripple and run like taffy, his flesh to sag. Malone had been witness to that phenomenon before, too, in the same places where he had seen the unholy glow, both in the Sandwich Islands and in the still-farther-distant Land of the Long White Cloud.

Even as he continued to shower fulminations on the mountain man, Tongue Kills was melting, unable to deny the uncontrollable fury and anger that were reducing him to his natural state. The vibrant red and orange and yellow of him spread out upon the ground, racing to take possession of the fertile valley. Where his colors, like his words, ran hot, the ground split like stale pudding and belched forth fresh fury, the earth itself melting and bubbling, until the entire region seemed to be seething and echoing the maledictions of its master.

"Enough of words!" screamed the pillar of molten contumeliousness that had been Tongue Kills. It towered higher than the tops of the pines, bathing the lean-to in hellish yellow light, twisting like a tower of coiled sulfur. Malone prepared to defend himself against something stronger than heated language.

"That weapon will not protect you!" the quivering pillar snarled. "Nothing made of man can affect me!" A pseudopod of orange fire reached for the nearly-naked Malone, intent on securing him in its grasp and crushing him to a crisp.

The mountain man crouched and parried, flicking the flaming tendril aside. A moan of frustration emerged from the unstable column. Its cohesion spent, it promptly began to shrink and collapse in on itself.

Somehow Malone's voice carried above the dispersing hell that confronted him. He gripped the knife tightly. "This here blade's good traditional obsidian, and it ain't of man. It's of *you*."

"Excretion of carbon!" the disintegrating pillar shrieked. "Boil upon the earth's buttocks! You *cannot* take this place for your own. You cannot drive me from it. Here I have been, and here I will remain, to shout the words that will keep you from this place! Where I am now, no grass shall grow, no animals live! The land will be denied you, and the very water itself I will season so sharply that it kills! I will remain forever, deny burbleiss shussh . . . !"

Tongue Kills continued his epithetic diatribe without pause, but having been reduced by Malone's carefully applied paradox to his true self, he could speak now only in the language of the earth from which he'd sprung. Malone could comprehend that speech as few others could but protected himself from it not with magic but by the simple expedient of stuffing his ears with bits of duck down extracted from his bedroll. As Malone gathered up his scorched but still intact clothing, Tongue Kills continued to rage all around him. He had indeed managed to render much of the fertile region useless but had also been compelled to leave many places untouched. Malone had neither triumphed nor been defeated. He had half won and was lucky to have managed that.

Only when they were well clear of the valley and

beyond earshot of Tongue Kills's pursuing screams did man and mount pause gratefully at a clean, untrammeled pool to cool their blistered feet. Thus assuaged, a chastened but relatively pleased Malone sought additional absolution in the mountain man's ultimate sacrifice. He undertook to have a bath.

"Ah-weh," Grass-in-Hair muttered understandingly. "It is no wonder, then, none could outtalk him, for he was not a man but a spirit." The chief frowned slightly. "What happened to your face?"

Malone gingerly felt of his scorched pinnacle of a proboscis. "As it progressed, our exchange grew heated. In my face you see the result."

"You say he is still there?" Two-Feathers-Falling said uncertainly.

Malone nodded. "Still there, still a-screamin' and a-hollerin'. But the words he shouts now can't hurt y'all because you won't understand 'em proper unless you get too close to him. So stay clear o' the places where he's doin' his insultin' and complainin', and you'll be okay. There's still plenty o' game about and water he ain't poisoned with his anger."

Grass-in-Hair replied thankfully. "You have helped us much, and we are grateful. We will move camp in three days."

"Suit yourselves. Me, I think I'm gonna head on south. Friend o' mine name o' Bridger's supposed to be around. Seen all o' this Yellowstone country I want to for a spell." He leaned back against a heaping pile of buffalo robes.

"I mean it, though, when I say you need to keep your kinfolks away from the places Tongue Kills has kept for himself. His words may not be able to hurt you no more, but be damned if he can't still spit."

WHAT YOU SEE . . .

It's hard writing stories to order. Well, to request, anyway. I love writing short stories. I'd write a lot more if this was the 1930s or 1940s and the heyday of the pulps. But yo, you know, I don't make enough to pay Stephen King's tax bill (but then, neither does Mozambique). To stay alive as a writer you have to write novels, which fortunately I also enjoy doing.

Which brings us to Amos Malone's saddlebags. What's in them, nobody knows. Not even Malone, I think. They're big, and floppy, and full of compartments, and generally speaking not a real smart place to go rooting around in without permission.

It's dark in there.

". . . BUNIONS, LUMBAGO, BAD BACK, CONsumption, whooping cough, dysentery, yellow fever, heart problems, liver trouble, infertility! Afflictions of the eye, the ear, the nose, and the throat! Broken bones, sprains, strains, disfigurations of the skin, and suppuration of all kinds!"

Now, the blacksmith, he had a disposition not dissimilar to that of the mules he frequently shod, but so suave and convincing was the stranger's pitch that the square-brick man with the arms like railroad ties stepped to the front of the milling crowd and squinted up at the platform.

"Thet leetle bottle, it can cure all thet?"

From the back of the garishly decorated wagon Doctor Mohet Ramses gazed down benevolently at the first (and hopefully not the last) of the warm afternoon's supplicants.

"Sir, I would not claim it were it not true." He held up the compact, winsome black bottle, letting the sunlight fall flush on the florid label. "All that and more can the Elixir of the Pharaohs cure."

"Then you best take some yourself," shouted someone from the back of the crowd. "Maybe it'll keep you from runnin' off at the mouth!"

Doctor Ramses was undaunted by the scattered laughter this rude sally brought forth. He drew himself up to his full height, which though just over six feet seemed greater because of his parsimonious construction, and glared haughtily at the cloddish loquator.

"For twenty years I have endured the slurs of disbelievers, and yet fate finds me still plying my trade. Why is that? I ask you. It is because the Elixir of the Pharaohs works, my friends!"

The blacksmith scratched dubiously at his bewhiskered chin. "A dollar a bottle seems awful high, Doc."

Ramses leaned low, bringing his voice down with

him. "Only when compared to what it can buy, my friend. How much is your health worth? How much another year of life, or two, or ten? For you see," he said, straightening and raising aloft the inimitable, the peerless black bottle, "this venerable elixir not only cures, not only prevents, but actually *extends* the life of the user!

"Unlike the traveling charlatans you good people have doubtless encountered before, I do not claim that my wondrous tonic cures every ailment, every time. Only most ailments, most of the time. I have records of hundreds of exhaustively documented cases from across this great country and from the Continent itself in which the elixir has proved itself time and time again. I speak only the truth when I say that it can add to your life, actually make you live longer."

"How much longer?" wondered a woman in the front row on whose cheeks the blush of youth had grown stale.

"A year per bottle, madam. One year of life, of good and vigorous and healthy existence, for each bottle you ingest according to instructions. One dollar for 364 days of continued subsistence on this good green earth. Is that not worth a little sweat of thy brow?"

"A dollar a bottle's too high," said a farmer angrily. "At them rates we can't afford to try it."

Doctor Mohet Ramses smiled compassionately. "Ah, my good sir, all things are granted freely in heaven, but in this world, sad it is to say, nothing comes without cost. You should not think that you can't afford to purchase the Elixir of the Pharaohs but rather that you can't *not* afford to buy it."

Near the front a middle-aged lady looked at her husband. She hadn't been feeling well lately, had if the truth be known been in fact doing poorly. A dollar was a lot of money, but . . . if it did only a tenth of what the doctor claimed . . .

She struggled with her purse and dug out a handful of coins, holding them up toward the wagon. "I'll buy a bottle, Doctor. What have I got to lose?"

"A dollar," her husband muttered under his breath.

She glared at him. "See if I give you any, William."

Doctor Ramses's smile widened as he exchanged brimming black bottles for coins. When one well-dressed citizen eagerly pressed a quarter eagle into the erstwhile physician's perfumed palm, he positively beamed.

Bit by bit the crowd thinned, clutching the precious bottles tightly to shirt or bodice. Eventually there was but a single old woman left. She was so small and insignificant, Doctor Ramses hardly noticed her as he contentedly allied his take for the day. Time it was to move on. Other towns waited just over the horizon; other needful communities beckoned. All needed his services; all doted on his presentation as eagerly as they did on his marvelous solution.

The elixir really was a wondrous concoction, he

knew. Versatile as well, depending as it did for the bulk of its constituency on whatever creek he happened to cut across whenever his stock was running low.

He very rarely had trouble because, unlike that of so many traveling snake-oil salesmen, his pitch was different. Contrary to the rest of his silver-tongued brethren, he promised not merely cures but hope. For when his purchasers passed on, it was invariably with the conviction that the Elixir of the Pharaohs had truly extended their lives. He smiled to himself. A difficult assertion to disprove when the principal complainants against him were all dead.

Only then did he notice the woman. His initial reaction was to ignore her, but he hesitated. She had remained throughout his talk and remained still after all the others had departed. Her dress was simple patched homespun, and the bonnet she wore to shield herself from the sun was fraying. No fine Irish lace decorated the hem of her dress; no clever tatting softened the edge of her cuffs. Still, he owed it to her to repeat the offer one last time. Mohet Ramses was nothing if not magnanimous.

He knelt on the platform. "Can I be of assistance, madame?"

The woman hesitated. On her face could be seen the aftereffects of a long lonely life of hard work and toil. It was clear she was not used to speaking to anyone more educated than the town schoolmaster or the local parson. Her expression was a mournful mix of hope and despair. She managed a hesitant reply.

"It ain't fer me, Doctor, sir. It's Emmitt. My husband."

Doctor Ramses smiled tolerantly. "So I assumed, madame."

"He's in the wagon, Doctor." She pointed, and Ramses noted a gutted buckboard and team tied to a rail outside the nearby general store. "Emmitt, he's gettin' on to still be herdin', but he just tells me to shut up . . . he don't mean nothin' by it . . . and gits on with his work.

"It happened yesterday. Got the last of our twenty head in the corral; time to market 'em, don't you know, and that cursed old nag of his spooked. Still don't know what done it, but Emmitt, he went a-flyin'. Panicked the cattle, one kicked him, and, well, I'd be beholden if you'd come an' see for yourself, Doctor."

Ramses hesitated. It really was time to pack up the store and get a move on. There was invariably some local who would ignore the finely printed instructions and chug an entire bottle of the noxious brew in hopes of quickly curing some bumptious black eye, or constipation, or some other mundane ill, only to have his hopes dashed. Whereupon, fiery of eye and palpitating of heart, he would set out in search of the good doctor's whereabouts. As a purely prophylactic measure Ramses historically had found it prudent not to linger in the vicinity of prior sales.

As the streets were presently devoid of recent customers, however, this was an internal debate easily resolved.

"Tell me, madame; do you have a dollar?"

She nodded slowly. " 'Bout all I do have right now, sir. See, when the cattle git sold, that's the only time all year Emmitt and me have any foldin' money. I was goin' to pay the regular doctor with it, but he don't come to town but once a week, and this bein' Friday, I don't expect him for another four days." She sniffed, and the leathery skin twitched. "My man's a tough one, but he took that kick right hard." She rubbed the back of one hand under her nose. "I ain't sure he can last another four days."

Doctor Ramses reached down to take the woman's hand comfortingly in his own. "Fear not, good woman. Your husband is about to receive a dose of the most efficacious medication known to nineteenth-century man. Lead the way, and I shall accompany you."

"God bless you, Doctor!"

"There, now," he said as he hopped off the back of the floridly painted wagon, "control yourself, madame. It is only my Hippocritical duty I am doing."

He winced at the sight of the battered, lanky old man lying in the rear of the wagon. He lay on his back atop a dirty, bloodied quilt, a feather pillow jammed beneath his head. His eyes were closed, and his thin brown hair had long since passed retreating to the region above the temples. Several veins had ruptured in his nose, which reminded Ramses of a map he'd once sold that purported to depict in some detail the delta of the Mississippi.

A crude bandage had slipped from the left side of the old man's head. A glance revealed that the force of the blow he had received had caved in the bone. Dried blood had run and caked everywhere: on the pillow, on his weathered skull, on the floor of the buckboard. His mouth hung half-open, and his sallow chest heaved with pained reluctance. As they looked on, the aged unfortunate raised a trembling hand toward the woman. It fell back, and Ramses had to fight to maintain the smile on his face. Turning away from the disagreeable scene, he held out to the anxious woman a small black bottle.

"One dollar, madame. One dollar to extend your husband's life. A worthy trifle, I am sure you will agree."

She fumbled with her purse, and Ramses, eager to be away from this provincial municipality, waited impatiently while she counted out the money in pennies and nickels. Only when the count had reached one hundred U.S. cents did he pass to her the precious container. She accepted it with trembling fingers.

"You're sure this'll work, Doctor?"

"My good woman, it has never been known to fail. Ten years." He thrust high a declamatory finger. "Ten years did I live among the multitudes of heathen Aegypt, perusing the primordial scrolls, learning all there was to learn, acquiring great knowledge, until at last I understood the mystic formula of the great and wise pharaohs. Trust in me, and all will be well."

In point of fact, Doctor Mohet Ramses had never been to Aegypt. But he had been to Cairo. Cairo, Illinois, where he had practiced a number of trades, none of which were remotely related to medicine, until the furious father of an outraged daughter had gone searching for him with gun in hand. At which point Doctor Mohet Ramses, alias Dickie Beals of Baltimore, Maryland, had sought and found expediency in a life on the road. A most profitable life.

The sun was going down, the town's two saloons were lighting up, and the venerable doctor was anxious to be on his way.

"Good luck to you, good woman, and to your husband, who should begin soon to exhibit a salubrious response to the most noteworthy liquid. Give him a spoonful a day followed by a piece of bread and you will find yourself gazing in wonder upon the medical miracle of the age. And now if you will excuse me, there are others who have need of my services, access to which I am sure you would not wish to deny them."

"No, sir, no! And thank you, Doctor, thank you!" She clutched his hand and, much to his disgust, began to kiss it effusively. He drew it back with as much decorum as he could muster.

"A woman ought to consider carefully what she's kissin'."

The deep voice boomed out of the shadows, and a man rode into view from behind Ramses's wagon. He was enormous, as was the preposterous mongrel of a steed he bestrode. For an instant Ramses panicked. Then he saw that the man was an utter stranger to him and relaxed.

The rider wore thick buckskins and showed salty black hair that hung to his shoulders. An incipient conflagration in his beard would've died for lack of oxygen, so thick were the bristles. His eyes were the color of obsidian and darker than a moonless night.

He dismounted from the ridiculous stallion and lumbered over. A huge hand reached toward the woman, and she flinched instinctively.

"May I see that, ma'am?" His voice turned gentle as a cooing babe's.

"What . . . what for, sir?"

"I am by nature an inquisitive man, mother. I'd have a look to satisfy my curiosity." He squinted at Doctor Ramses. "Surely, sir, as a man of learning, you've no objection."

Ramses hesitated, then stiffened. "I, sir? Why should I have any objection? But you delay this poor soul's treatment." He indicated the wagon and its pitiful human cargo.

"Not for long, I reckon." He reached out and plucked the bottle from the woman's uncertain fingers.

Ramses had to repress a grin. If this stranger had been the aforementioned local physician, there might have been trouble, but there was nothing to fear from a gargantuan bumpkin like this. He watched amusedly as the giant opened the bottle and sniffed at the contents.

His smile vanished when the mountain man swallowed the oily contents in a single gulp.

The old woman let out a cry and, astonishingly, threw herself at the giant. She hardly came up to his waist, but that didn't stop her from flailing away at him with her tiny fists. She might as well have been trying to reduce Gibraltar to dust.

Gently the giant settled her. A thick finger wiped at her tears. "Easy, mother." He tossed the empty bottle to Ramses, who caught it reflexively. "There weren't nothin' in that bottle that could've helped your man."

"Now, sir," declared Ramses, a fount of mock outrage, "I really must protest! If you were a man of science, I might accept . . ."

The huge form turned to him. "Listen well, 'Doctor.' I am Mad Amos Malone, and I am a man of many things. But what is in any event called fer here ain't science." He jabbed a huge forefinger toward the buckboard. "That man there is dying, and he needs somethin' rather stronger than what you're offerin' him. He wants to live, and I aim to help him."

"You, sir?" It was growing dark rapidly. Night

fell quickly on the open plains. "How might you intend to do that?"

"By helpin' these folks to help themselves." He smiled reassuringly at the old woman, yellowed teeth gleaming from within the depths of the beard. "You just calm yourself, mother, and we'll see what we can do."

Ramses thought to depart. There was nothing for him here but a distraught old woman and a man crazy from too much time in the wilderness. But Ramses was curious, and he already had the woman's dollar. Maybe the mountain man was some sort of competitor. If he had something worthy to sell, they might, as any two men engaged in the same trade were occasionally wont to do, strike a bargain. The doctor was ever ready and willing to improve his stock.

To his disappointment, the mountain man returned from fumbling with his saddlebags with nothing but an old wooden cup. It was scratched and chipped and appeared to have been carved out of a single piece of some light-colored hardwood. It had a thick brim and was in appearance nothing remarkable.

He offered it to the old woman, whose tears were drying on her cheeks. "Here, mother. Use this to give your man a drink of water." He gestured toward the town pump, which sat in a small Spanish-style square in the center of the street.

"Water?" She blinked in bewilderment. "What good will water do my Emmitt? He needs doctorin'.

He needs this man's medicine." She indicated Ramses, who smiled condescendingly.

Malone spoke solemnly. "Let him drink from that old cup, mother, and if it don't help your husband, I'll buy you another bottle of this gentleman's brew myself." Whereupon he produced from a pocket a shiny gold piece. Not U.S. issue but a disk slick with age and worn by time. Ramses's eyes widened as he recognized the ornate cross and Spanish lettering on the visible side. In his whole life he'd seen only a single piece of eight. It had belonged to a New Orleans gambler. What the mountain man flashed was worth rather more than a dollar. Ramses was glad he'd trusted his instincts and stayed.

"Sir, you are as noble as you are curious."

The giant's eyes seemed to disappear beneath overhanging thick black brows that drew down like a miniature portcullis. "Don't be too sure o' that, friend." It was not a threat, but neither did the big man's tone inspire Ramses to move nearer the speaker.

Unsteady and bewildered, the woman shuffled to the well. The men heard the pump handle creak, heard the attendant splash of water. She made her slow way back to them and, after eyeing the giant blankly, climbed with surprising agility into the back of the wagon. There she dubiously but lovingly tipped the wooden lip of the cup to her husband's parted lips.

"Here now, darlin'. You got to drink, even if it is

just water. You got to, so's this man'll buy us another bottle of the doctor's medicine."

The dying old man wheezed and tried but failed to lift his head. Some kind of unvoiced communication passed between them, as it can only between two people who have been married so long that the two have become one. She spilled the water into his mouth, and he gagged, choking, the liquid running out over his parted, chapped lips and down his furrowed cheek. Ramses suppressed a smile. A pitiful exhibition but one that, given the circumstances, he was quite willing to endure. In the giant's fingers the piece of eight shimmered in the fading light.

The old rancher coughed again. A second time. Then he sat up. Not bolt upright, as if hit by lightning, or shakily, as if at any moment he might collapse again. Just steady and confident-like. His wife's eyes grew wide, while Ramses's arguably exceeded them in diameter.

With profound deliberation the old man turned to his wife and put his arms around her. The tears streaming down his face started to dissolve the coagulated blood. "Sorry, woman," he was mumbling. "Sorry to make you worry like thet."

"Oh, Emmitt, Emmitt!" She sat back from him, crying and smiling and half laughing all at once. "You gonna listen to me now and git yourself a hand to do the heavy work?"

"Reckon I ain't got much choice." The rancher climbed effortlessly to his feet and extended a hand toward the beaming giant and the flabbergasted Ramses. "Mighty grateful to you, mister."

The mountain man nodded as he shook the proffered hand. "Glad to be o' service, sir. I could sense you were a good man, and I could see how serious you wanted to live."

"It weren't fer myself. Heck, I done had a decent life. But the woman, it would've gone hard on her. This way I got a little time to make some better plans."

"It's good for a man to have plans, Emmitt," the giant said.

Leaping lithely from the buckboard, the rancher loosened the reins from the hitching rail, climbed back aboard, and lifted his startled wife into the seat alongside him. She almost forgot to hand the cup back to Malone, following which her husband chucked the reins. Jerking forward, the buckboard rattled up the dirt road that led out of town, kicking up dust as it passed the seeping pump.

Ramses had forgotten all about the piece of eight. His attention was now riveted on the old wooden cup. "Might I have a look at that vessel, sir?"

"Don't see why not." The giant handed it over.

Ramses scrutinized it as minutely as he'd ever inspected a suspect coin, turning it over and over in his fingers, feeling the scars in the old wood, lifting it to smell of the interior. It reeked of old rooms, and dampness, and something he couldn't quite place. Some fragrance of a faraway land and perhaps also a distant time.

With utmost reluctance he passed it back. "What potion did you have in that, sir, that brought that man back from the dead? For the country of the dead was surely where he was headed. I saw his skull. It was well stove in, and his brains were glistening in the sunlight."

" 'Tweren't no potion." The mountain man walked back to his lunatic steed and casually returned the cup to the unsecured saddlebag whence it had come. "That man wanted to live. Out o' love for another. That right there's a mighty powerful medicine. Mighty powerful. Didn't need but a little nudge to help it along."

"Yes, of course." Then it was no potion, Ramses thought furiously, but the cup itself, the cup! "Might I ask where you acquired that vessel?"

"What, the grail? Won it off the Shemad Bey, pasha of Tripoli, durin' a game o' chess we played anon my last sojourn along the Barbary Coast. After he'd turned it over, the old pasha confessed to me that it had been stolen many times afore comin' his way. So I didn't see the harm in relievin' him of its possession. I reckon it's better off in my care than his, anyways." He pulled the straps of the saddlebag through both buckles and notched them tight.

"Your pardon, sir," said Ramses, "but did you say 'grail'?"

"That's right. Belonged long time ago to a feller name of Emmanuel. Took his last swallow from it, I believe."

"You are jesting with me, sir."

"Nope." The giant walked down the street, his mount trailing alongside with a notable air of equine indifference. "When I jest, I laugh, and when I laugh, rivers bubble and mountains shake. You don't see no rivers bubblin' or mountains shakin' hereabouts now, do you?"

"Sir, we stand in the plains of the Missouri. There are no mountains hereabouts, and the nearest river is the Meramec some twenty miles to the south."

"Why, 'tis right you are. I reckon you'll just have to take my word for it, then."

"Sir, would you consider selling that gr . . . that drinking vessel? I will make you a fine offer for it, in gold."

" 'Tain't fer sale, friend. Fer one thing, I got plenty o' gold. Fer t'other, it wouldn't work for you nohows."

"And why not?"

"The grail, see, it don't do nothin' by itself. It's just a cup, an ordinary drinkin' cup. It's what's in the heart and the soul of whomever's drinkin' from it that makes a difference. Most times it don't make no difference. Sometimes it do. I was glad it did tonight, but you cain't never be sure." He halted, and Ramses saw they were standing outside the blacksmith shop and stable.

"Now, if you'll excuse me, friend, I've been three days and nights on the back of this lamentable alibi of a horse, and I've a might o' sleepin' to catch up on." With that he turned and entered the stable. Emerging a few minutes later, he strode off down the street toward the town's single hotel, from whose attached saloon could imprecisely be heard the brittle jollities of a banjo player in shifty voice.

Ramses was left standing solitaire in the starlight, thinking hard. The giant would be a bad man to cross, he ruminated. He'd seen the heavy Sharps rifle protruding from its scabbard on the side of the saddle. But the Promethean rustic had neglected even to lock the stable! And he'd taken careful notice of the fact that there were no locks on the saddlebags, not even a knot. Just a couple of straps on each one.

But Ramses was no simpleton. He returned to his wagon and mounted the seat, chucking the reins and making as much noise as possible on his ostentatious way out of town. The mountain man had refused to sell him the cup, and that was that, and like the honest soul that he was, he was moving placidly on.

A mile out of town he set up a hasty camp by the bank of a running stream, tethering one of his horses to a convenient cottonwood while hoping there were no acquisitive Indians or white men about. He made and drank some strong coffee, considered the night sounds and the stars, and round about three A.M. saddled up his other animal and rode quietly back into town.

The wooden buildings were shadowy now, the

two saloons as silent as the distant church that dominated the far end of the main street. Dismounting outside the stable, he kept a wary eye on the distant hotel. The door hardly creaked as he edged it aside just enough to slip through. His excitement rose as through the dim light he saw that the mountain man's animal stood where he'd left it in the farthest stall.

Ramses could move fast when he needed to, whether running from irate fathers or from official representatives of the law. He moved fast now, the straw hissing under his feet as he hurried to the far end of the building. The dozing horses and one mule ignored him.

Lifting the stall door as he opened it so the hinges wouldn't creak, he stepped inside. Facing him, the improbably large quadruped filled the smelly enclosure from wall to wall. At the back of the stall the saddlebags lay draped across a pile composed of saddle and tack.

Turning sideways, he attempted to slip between the animal's mass and the unyielding stall panels.

"C'mon there, boy. Give us a little room. Move on over just a bit, won't you."

Swinging its mottled face to cast a skewed eye at him, the ludicrous creature emitted a soft snort and promptly lowered its head to begin cropping at the straw underhoof.

"Come on, damn you!" Ramses put both hands on the animal's flank and shoved, bracing himself against the wall and putting all his weight into the effort. He might as well have been trying to convert a reluctant Jesuit.

Breathing hard, Ramses deposed on the four-legged barricade to his intent a few choice nonmedical terms. He bent and passed through the slats of the stall wall into the vacant stall next to it, then carefully slipped in again near the rear, taking care to keep an eye on the horse's oversized rear hooves. It continued to ignore him, wholly intent on the available fodder.

The saddlebag's straps yielded easily to his deft fingers. He'd filch the cup and be clean out of the county before morning.

Lifting the nap, he dug around inside until his hand closed over the unyielding wooden cylinder. Extracting his prize, he held it up to the available light. In the moonlight it was outstanding in its ordinariness, and for an instant he wondered if there were more than one of the vessels. That was absurd, he knew. There was only one of what he sought. Only one in all the world, and now it was his, his!

He turned it in his fingers, letting the moonlight play across the bowl and rim. So plain, he mused. So utterly unremarkable. It was slightly bigger than he remembered it, but then, his first and only previous view had been clouded by astonishment and the realization of inherent possibilities.

His gaze narrowed. There was a hint of movement within the vessel. Lingering water or possibly some more viscous liquid.

Something crept out of the bowl to wrap itself around his left wrist.

Startled, he inhaled sharply. At the sound of his soft gasp the horse looked back wearily. Then it delivered itself of a decidedly disinterested whinny and returned to its browsing.

A panicked Ramses tried to shake loose of the cup. He flung his hand about wildly and banged the vessel against the back of the stall. But the old wood was tough, and the sinuous band around his wrist was like a steel cable. It was gray in hue and ichorous and glacier-wet. As he fought to extricate himself, it began to snake farther up his arm. With his free hand he fumbled frantically for the derringer he kept always in his right shirt pocket. As he did so, he made rapid breathing sounds, like a dog after a long run, as he struggled to scream but failed.

Before his wide, disbelieving eyes a second serpentine coil emerged from the interior of the cup to wrap itself around his head, blocking one of his eyes. It was cold and slick, cold as ice. The tip forced itself past his clamped lips and down his throat. He started to gag.

Tilted toward him, the depths of the cup revealed a pair of eyes. They were about the size and shape of a sparrow's eggs, bright red with little black pupils centered on fiery crimson. Of any face they

might front there was no sign. As he goggled madly,
two more emerged below the first pair.

Then he saw that all four were all part of the
same countenance, which he finally got a good look
at. He did scream then, but the sound was muffled
by the tentacle swelling inside his throat, and no
one heard.

In the stalls across the way two dray animals, a
mare and a gelding, looked on motionlessly. Well,
they were not quite motionless. Both were trembling violently, and sweat was pouring down their
withers.

The mountain man's steed munched straw while
ignoring the flailing, thrashing man who occasionally bounced off his hindquarters and legs.

More tentacles erupted from the abyssal depths of
the cup, far more than it should have been able to
hold. They lashed and bound the softly screaming,
utterly desperate Mohet Ramses before they began
to retract, dragging the unfortunate doctor with
them. As he didn't fit inside the bowl of the vessel
nearly as efficiently, there ensued a great many
cracking and rending noises as he was pulled in, until only his spasmodically kicking legs were visible
protruding beyond the smooth rim. Finally they, too,
vanished, and lastly his fine handmade shoes, and
then he was all gone.

It was quiet again in the stable. Across from the
silent stall the dray pair gradually ceased their shivering.

As the other guests looked on in fascination, Amos Malone rose early and ate breakfast enough for any three men. Then he made his way outside. A few other pedestrians were about. They glanced occasionally in his direction, but not always. Unusual men frequented the frontier, and Malone was larger but not necessarily more unusual than some the townsfolk had seen previously.

At the smithy he chatted awhile with the owner, then paid him his fee and entered the stable next door.

"Well, Worthless," he informed his steed as he set blanket and saddle on the broad back, "I promise you some oats first decent-sized town we hit. You look like you had an uneventful night." The stallion snorted at Malone as he cinched the saddle tight, shaking its head and mane.

The mountain man hefted the bulky saddlebags and prepared to secure them behind the heavy saddle. As he did so, he noticed the cup lying on its side in the dirt. Plonking the awkward load astride Worthless's butt, he bent to pick up the stray vessel, considering it thoughtfully in the morning light. The old jet-black wood drew in the sunshine like a vampire sucking blood. With a sigh he moved to place it back in its container.

"Told him," he muttered. "That ain't the way it works. A smart man doesn't go foolin' around in another feller's kit." Reaching inside the near saddlebag, he pulled out a second cup and held it up to the light. The morning rays turned the burn-ished cedar the color of Solomon's gold, pure and radiant.

" 'Course, it didn't help him that he got ahold o' the wrong grail."

NEITHER A BORROWER BE . . .

Roy Rogers had Trigger. Still has him, in fact. The grand old stallion stands big as life in Rogers's museum in Apple Valley, California, stuffed like a Christmas turkey. The Lone Ranger had Silver. Hopalong Cassidy had . . . c'mon now, western trivia buffs. All the great western heroes had great western horses.

It made me sick.

I mean, come on, now. Who wants to watch a film or TV show where the horse is obviously smarter than the hero? Not to mention braver and better-looking. The giants of animation recognized this contradiction and jumped on it with all four pencils. In Robert Clampett's Red Hot Ryder *the horse can barely stand his idiot master. Tex Avery (as one would expect) frequently gave the horse as many lines as the other protagonists in his western-theme cartoons. Chuck Jones satirized the western horse in* Drip-Along Daffy, *even allowing two of them their own shoot-out on Main Street.*

And the inimitable Jay Ward gave us a heroine in

the Dudley Do-Right *cartoons who quite sensibly (and with just a hint of borderline bestiality) preferred horse to hero.*

No, sir, pardner. If I'm expected to survive in the real Old West, I don't want no gussified, slicked up, pommaded palomino between my legs. I want a horse that'll kick and spit and bite and go all day on a diet of sagebrush and tumbleweed. That's to match me. One to match Amos Malone would be something.

Might not even be a horse, strictly speakin'.

FOR THREE DAYS IT HAD SNOWED HARD enough to freeze a preacher's sermon to his pulpit. Now it had let up some, but while Mother Nature had become less profligate with her precipitation, sporadic flakes still spiraled to earth fat and flat, heavy with moisture, while a blindingly blue sky flirted with the fast-moving clouds as intermittently as a Swedish dancer.

The little brown box of a cabin was two-thirds blanketed and buried. Smoke curled fitfully from the stone chimney, winkling its laborious way skyward, cutting a sinuous path through the drifting snow. The rough-hewn unpeeled logs of which the modest structure was fashioned differed in appearance from the surrounding pines and firs only in their spatial orientation. The living trees towered above shelter and snowpack alike, their branches slack and burdened with hermetic whiteness. They dominated the surrounding mountain slopes, clawing toward the barren, rocky tree line.

A bit away from the building the crest of a split-rail fence barely showed above the snow. It enclosed a partially cleared oval of bare ground. Accepting of the deceptive moderation, the scraggly grass thus revealed thrust bravely toward a bright sun and a false spring.

The clearing fronted a crude lean-to beneath which clustered three horses. A chestnut mare stood nose to tail with a roan gelding. Slightly off to one side the third member of the equine contingent leaned against the rear of the shelter. It was a stallion of . . . well . . . of indeterminate lineage, being mostly black with white markings on rump and fetlocks and a distinctive white ring around its right eye. Thin straps secured a leather patch to its forehead. Part Shire, it loomed over its more svelte cousins. While they browsed on the newly-sprung grass, quick-frozen exhalations emerging from their nostrils like the signatures of miniature steam engines, it chose to doze contentedly in the shade.

A slight noise from the nearby forest caused the massive conglomeration to straighten. Lifting its muzzle, the stallion sampled the air and peered into the dense woods with its good eye, the one that was white-ringed being half-shut in a perpetual squint. It stood thus for a long moment. Then it snorted a small cloud and relaxed again.

When the heavy horse huffed, Fifth John froze. Only after it had turned away from where he stood crouched in the snow did he move, turning and hurrying back to where his companions waited anxiously by the little stream that flowed clear and free beneath sheets of reluctant ice.

Having mocked the warnings of wiser, more experienced men, they'd sure enough found themselves caught out unprepared by the early spring storm. With hopes and bravado dashed in equal measure, their thoughts had hitherto been only of making it safely back to the lowlands with nothing to show for their recklessness. Until now.

His wide-brimmed, floppy hat slumped down over his face, and Fifth John cursed improvidently as he angrily shoved it back. It was nearly as filthy as the rest of his outfit, but then, he'd never been one much for personal hygiene. It wasn't his mother's fault, either, though his name was. A poor, simple woman gifted with minimal powers of cogitation, she and her dour husband between them had possessed just enough skills to feed themselves and about as much imagination as a Denver omelet.

They'd had ("raised" being too genteel a term) five children, all of the male persuasion. The father's name being John, they'd named the first boy John. And the second, and the third, and so on unto Fifth John, whose handle anyone could rapidly discern related no more to that portion of the good book than he did.

He was the de facto leader of the importunate trio by virtue of determination and sheer meanness rather than any inherent talent, his skills consisting pretty much of humble expertise with a sharp knife and the ability to lie like a Tennessee lawyer.

"There's smoke comin' from the cabin, but no movement. Couldn't smell nothin' cooking. I reckon they must all be asleep."

"Any pickin's?" asked Great Knox, chewing on a finger. It was a wonder the huge mule skinner had any left. He always had a well-gnawed digit between his brown and yellow tobacco-stained teeth. John had seen him chew on his toes, too, at which times the bulky Yankee displayed unexpected physical dexterity. It was good that he was comfortable in his habits because he wasn't apt to be invited to a plethora of cotillions. He wore a hat too small for his head, a narrow brown beard that traced the lower curve of his face from ear to ear, and an old tobacco-juice-stained vest over his heavy winter clothes.

Halfweed crouched nearby and listened. Though he was quite capable of speech, he chose not to say much, which was fine with his companions. Wiry and ruddy-hued, with a thin, down-arcing mustachio, he was good with both animals and a gun on the rare occasions when his brain and eyes managed to act in concert. His name descended not from his scrambled ancestry but from an addiction to peyote, which he'd acquired during a nefarious enforced sojourn down in Santa Fe.

These three solid representatives of the republic squatted in the snow by the creek and contemplated larceny.

"Three horses." Despite their cover and the distance from the cabin, Fifth John was careful to keep his voice down. "All of 'em healthy and well rested, though one's kinda weird-lookin'."

"What d' you mean weird-lookin'?" Great Knox pursed badly chapped, swollen baby lips.

"I ain't sure." John scratched under his left arm. "Just weird. Big, though. Biggest damn animal I ever seen." Beneath the brim of the battered hat iniquitous eyes glittered. "Great for packin'. Bet he'll fetch twenty, maybe thirty dollar in town."

Knox nodded. "We're wastin' time sittin' here talking about it, then."

John agreed curtly. "You stay with the horses. Halfweed and I'll do it." The half-breed broke out into a wide, gap-toothed grin as he rose.

Knox watched them go, pleased that their ill-conceived journey into the mountains wouldn't turn out profitless, after all. He wondered idly whose animals they were stealing, hoping he hadn't at some time in the past made their acquaintance.

Leaving a man stuck in these mountains without a horse was not too different from shooting him in the back. Just slower.

Caiben was preparing to clean the previous night's dishes when he noticed the empty makeshift corral. As he straightened, his gaze instantly swept the surrounding forest, but there was no sign of movement. Setting the laden bucket aside, he dashed over to the fence line, ignoring the powdery

snow that clung to his faded long johns and slid
with icy slyness down into his boots.

He yelled even as he was checking the gate and
the double set of footprints nearby.

In response to his shouts, two men emerged from
the cabin. One had to bend low to clear the lintel.
His companion replied, his words sharp in the chilly
afternoon air as if they'd been chiseled from granite
and hung in the sky to read.

"What's happened, Caiben?"

The other man rejoined them, looking grim. "Bad
doin's, friends. Horses are gone. Two men. Whites,
not Indians." He shaded his eyes against the snow
glare as he looked back and nodded toward the
trees. "Reckon they got about a four-, five-hour
start."

"Damnation." The other man spit into the snow,
making a tiny stained crater. "What you think,
Amos?"

The giant who stood next to him gazed phlegmat-
ically at the forest, an incongruous sight in his
bright red, custom-sewn oversized long johns. As he
considered the situation, he slowly stroked the impenetrable tangle of black wire that was his beard.
There were some folks what thought strange small
critters lived within that ebon brier patch, but none
ever had courage enough (or the reach) to examine
the confusion for themselves. Beneath heavy brows
startlingly blue eyes the color of the deep ocean examined the distant line of tracks in the snow.

"Never catch 'em in this." He kicked absently at

the deep powder. "Not on foot." His expression was unreadable. "I don't know about you two, but first off I'm gonna fix me some breakfast. Then I think I'll go back to bed." He squinted skyward. "Not much point in checkin' the traplines while it's still snowin'."

His companions exchanged a glance. "Is that wise, Amos?" the man next to him wondered.

The giant peered down at him. "That depends now, Jim, on whether or not you think I am."

Caiben shook his head slowly as he eyed the forest. "I dunno. They get more'n a day ahead of us, we'll never find 'em even if this starts to melt."

"Don't reckon we'll need to." Malone had turned toward the doorway. "Cold out here. I'll put some wood on." He bent to clear the opening and glanced back at his companions. "Y'all comin'?"

They hesitated briefly. Then Bridger sighed. "Hell, I remember once he told me we could make it from New Orleans to St. Louis in half the regular time, and we did. Never did tell me how he'd knowed that the Mississip was gonna reverse her course that day. Danged if she didn't." He followed the giant into the cabin.

The third mountain man gazed longingly at the woods, then shrugged. The snow that had fallen into the bottom of his boots was starting to melt, a condition sufficiently incommodious to decide the immediate course of action for any man.

* * *

The three thieves allowed themselves to hoot and holler freely once they were certain. they were well clear of any immediate pursuit. Their plunder followed meekly behind Halfweed's mount, each animal tethered securely to the one trudging on before it, with the unclassifiable prodigy bringing up the rear.

"Hell's fire if'n I wouldn't give a dollar to see their faces when they wake up and find their animals gone!" Great Knox chortled and slapped his leg gleefully, his hand returning immediately thereafter to his mouth, regular as a homing pigeon.

Fifth John rose and turned in his saddle to peer back the way they'd come, their trail as definitive in the deep snow as if it had been bashed out by a six-team wagon. He could see almost to the top of the ridge they'd just traversed, and his little piggish eyes were sharp. He forced himself to relax. There was no sign of any pursuit.

Damned if they hadn't brought it off, he thought with satisfaction. Tough for those marooned in the valley behind them, but it was their own damn fault for leaving good horses unguarded. Served 'em right. Fifth John sure enough knew all about life's lessons. If only he hadn't failed so many of them.

"Me, I'm gonna get me some whiskey with my share." Knox salivated around the finger he was masticating. "Not that cheap shit. Real drinkin' whiskey. And a *woman*. I'm gonna have me a pretty woman. A *big* woman. With red hair. All night, on a real bed, with sheets."

Fifth John struggled to avoid mental contemplation of such an invidious collusion. Great Knox was a useful associate, a good man to have in front of you in a fight, but was afflicted with constipation of the brain. Whereas Halfweed's hypothesized higher functions were much diluted by his daily intake of peyote, below the neck Great Knox was simply ill endowed.

Which was just as well. Fifth John was suspicious of anyone smarter than himself, which meant that suspicion was the country in which he most habitually dwelt.

"Get drunk." Halfweed mumbled aloud as he swayed atop his mount. "Stay drunk a week. Maybe a month." He grinned like a tubercular cherub.

"They ain't followin' us, that's fer sure." Fifth John was mightily well pleased with himself. He'd take three good horses over a stack of beaver and otter pelts any day. "Thought we might have to ride on through the night, but looks like we can have a camp, somethin' to eat. You boys done good." Knox tried to smile but was reluctant to remove his finger from his mouth. Halfweed was always smiling.

They found a good spot near the base of a steep slope, largely clear of snow and not particularly muddy. After making certain all six animals were secured, Fifth John broke out the jerky while Knox and Halfweed worked to start a fire. They lucked into a stack of dead *dry* wood that had accumulated in the hollow of an old lightning-blasted fir and by the time night fell had a crackling good blaze going atop stones gathered from the hillside.

Halfweed was making a last check of the tethers. Two of the horses they'd absconded with snorted and shied uncertainly at his approach, but the big stallion just stood motionless, watching him out of its good eye. Halfweed studied it intently.

"Me, I know horseflesh pretty good, *seguridad*. But I never seen nothin' quite like you, *grande*. What's this for, huh?" Reaching up, the half-breed took hold of the patch over the animal's forehead and tugged sharply. On the third pull it came away in his hands. His gaze narrowed in confusion.

"Hey! I think maybe this big one got something wrong with him."

Fifth John looked up from the fire. "What, fer instance?"

"I dunno." Halfweed reached up to gingerly feel the two-inch-high bump that protruded from the animal's skull. "He got some kind of risin' or somethin' on his head. But it ain't soft like a risin'. It's hard. Like bone."

"So he's got a funny head. Nothin' wrong with his teeth or his back an' legs, an' that's all what matters. We'll cover it up agin afore we sell 'im. Meanwhile, leave that piece o' leather off. Maybe the air'll help the spot heal."

Halfweed nodded to himself, turned to rejoin his companions, and found himself glancing back over his shoulder. He could've sworn that, just for an instant, the big stallion had been grinning at him. That was crazy. Horses occasionally smiled. They didn't never, ever grin.

Especially not like that.

Fifth John lit the stuffing in his pipe and leaned back on his bedroll, much gratified with the way things had turned out. It was not a sensation he'd been able to experience often.

Unfortunately, it did not last long.

The howl made Knox sit up fast. Then he smiled a trifle warily and lay back down again. The fire continued to sputter, and he tossed another broken branch in the middle of it. Embers flew up like escaping moths.

"Wolf," he mumbled.

"Yeah." Fifth John turned in his bedroll. "Shet up and go back to sleep."

Knox nodded and closed his eyes. He ignored the howl when it was repeated. When it was picked up by a second animal, he ignored that, too, and tried to cover his ears when the nocturnal choir was joined by a third.

The fourth howl, however, made them all sit up quick.

"*Madre de Cristo.*" Eyes wide in the firelight, Halfweed sat erect in his dirty roll and stared into the night.

"What in hell . . . ?" Fifth John squinted hard.

Twitching skittishly, their mounts were pawing the ground where they'd been tethered. Two of the stolen horses were also moving, though less restively.

Sitting back on its haunches, its long head thrown back, lips parted and teeth white in the firelight, the outlandish heavy horse was baying at the moon. Its howl was perfectly indistinguishable from that of the unseen carnivores, melding with and simultaneously inspiring the chilling moonlight chorus.

Great Knox was shaking his head slowly. He was so stunned, both hands hung at his sides. "That ain't no horse. No horse never made a noise like that."

Fifth John hesitated, then deliberately lay back down in his roll. " 'Course it's a horse, you dang fool. Looks like a horse, walks like a horse, smells like a horse. A mighty big horse, true, but a horse nonetheless."

"Don' sound like no horse." Halfweed's voice had dropped to a whisper, and he was looking around uneasily, as if the night itself were watching him.

John glanced up irritably. "An' you don't sound like no normal man, neither, but I still ride with you. But that'll come to quittin' if you don't shut your food hole and go to sleep."

The horse continued to howl. John tried, but with the woods by now resounding to what seemed like the concerted wailing of a hundred wolves, it was impossible for any man to rest. Frustrated, he rose to realign his sleeping kit, when he heard something else. Something different.

"You hear that?" he asked no one in particular.

Knox blinked sleepily. Somehow the great oaf had managed to fall asleep. "Hear what?"

"I hear it." Halfweed rose and stood trembling in his long johns, looking around edgily. "I hear it, yes."

As the two men listened intently, the suggestion became a whisper, then a rumble. Then a thunder that woke even Great Knox.

"Hey, Fifth. What's makin' thet . . . ?"

John's eyes became as wide as Halfweed's. "Run! It's the Devil's own signature! Run for your lives!"

Still half-asleep but waking up fast, Great Knox struggled with his bedroll. It had become all twisted around him in his sleep and reluctant to release his legs. The horses whinnied and shied, rolling their eyes. All except for the big black, which continued to sit and howl.

Fifth John's chest heaved until he thought it would burst as he raced down the mountainside in the darkness. He could feel the snow catching up to him, teasing him, toying with his backside. He slid, fell, and came up scraped and bleeding but still running, leaping over fallen logs, sliding down talus crumbly as stale johnnycake. When he could run no more, he scrambled desperately behind the biggest tree he could find and closed his eyes tight.

It was like being swallowed by an express train. The tree shook, quivered, even bent a mite, but stayed put. As quickly as it had gathered strength the avalanche began to spend itself, spreading out like white butter across the land. Only when it was done did Fifth John allow himself to leave the shelter of the tree and begin the long, difficult slog back uphill.

Of their camp there was no trace. Kettle, pan, bedrolls, clothing . . . everything gone, swept downslope and entombed beneath tons of snow. Only the horses remained. Apparently the angle of the cliff beneath which they'd been tethered had caused the bulk of the avalanche to roar past over them. It infuriated Fifth John to realize that had he kept his wits about him instead of panicking, he could have survived and completely avoided the dangerous downhill flight.

Halfweed joined him a few moments later as John was dragging his insufficient but nonetheless welcome spare clothing from the saddlebags they had providentially left near the horses. The skinny half-breed was terrified but otherwise unhurt. He looked around, blinking in the moonlight.

"Where's Knox?"

John continued to dig at the saddlebags. His good buffalo coat was gone, and he'd have to put on every stitch of clothing he had left in the world if he expected to keep from freezing. "Dunno. He ain't with you?"

"No, man." Shivering, Halfweed crossed his arms over his sallow chest. "I thought he'd be here."

"Well, he ain't, so I guess it's done for him." Fifth John grunted. "More for us. Split the horses two ways."

"Yeah. Hey, yeah, that's right." Halfweed relaxed

a little, his smile returning. It didn't stay long. "Hey Fifth; you notice somethin'?"

"No, what?" the other man replied testily.

Halfweed was looking around again, jerkily scanning the woods. "It's quiet. Howlin's stopped."

Fifth John eyed the night sky and the treetops, then returned to his hunting. "Yeah? What of it? Avalanche scared 'em off."

"Yeah, that's right."

"Check the animals."

Halfweed nodded, glad to have something familiar to do to take his mind off the misfortune that had just struck their camp and taken the life of their beloved friend. Friend, anyway. Well, maybe casual companion.

The horses, at least, had survived unharmed. The way east out of the mountains was clear, and their four-footed booty was intact. He was about to rejoin John when he squinted in the moonlight. The stallion stood munching a green branch it had pulled from a nearby tree. Once again it stood placidly and allowed him to approach. Halfweed reached for the broad forehead, ignoring the bad right eye, which swiveled up to watch him.

"Uh, hey, Fifth?"

"What now?" Fifth John did not look up as he wrestled a ragged shirt over the upper half of his long johns.

"That bump I told you 'bout? On the front of the big one's head? Pork me for a nervous nun if she ain't got larger."

John shoved his head through the reluctant shirt, wondering what his companion was babbling about. "What's that?"

"Come look for yourself." The half-breed stepped back.

Fifth John slogged over and frowned. The broad-backed stallion regarded him expressionlessly. Fingering his goatee, John ran his fingers the length of the protrusion, then gripped hard and pulled. The animal's head didn't move, nor did it otherwise react.

"Cabrito diablo." Halfweed tried to cross himself, nearly stuck his finger up his nose, tried again. He was more or less successful the third time, but by then he entertained serious doubts that the Virgin Mother was still paying attention.

"Naw, it ain't the Devil's goat," John groused, "though I grant you it's passin' strange. You're right about t' other, though. It is bigger. 'Bout six inches, I reckon. Grows fast, whatever it is." He shrugged, secure in his ignorance. "Don't matter none so long's the rest of the animal is sound. We'll cut it off before we sell." He turned away, grumbling to himself. "Now, where the blazes did I put those old coveralls?"

By morning his good mood had returned. Too bad for Great Knox but better for him and Halfweed. 'Tis not an ill wind that gives the other man pneumonia, he mused. There was still no sign of any pursuit, and by evening even Halfweed had mellowed. The half-breed didn't have sense enough to stay upset or happy for very long. Truth be told, he didn't have sense enough to find his ass with both hands.

As the sun scurried for cover behind the mountains, it started to snow again, just hard enough to be indifferent. Fifth John was thinking lean-to when he spotted the opening in the hillside.

Halfweed took one look at the shadowy fissure and shook his head violently. "I ain't goin' in there, man."

"What's the matter, toad *cojones*? You frightened?" John dismounted. Rifle in one hand, he hunted up the precious box of matches and fashioned a torch of reasonably dry pine needles and twigs. Burning taper in hand, he was able to enter the spacious cave standing up.

Halfweed held on to his reins and waited nervously, his face turned skyward, on the lookout for the tentative moon. A deep moan from within the cave made him sit bolt upright in his saddle.

He'd half turned to flee when John reemerged, smiling maliciously. "Scared you, didn't I? Damnfool crazy half-breed." He gestured curtly at him with his rifle. "There ain't nothin' in there. Ain't been for some time. It's dry an' warm, plenty of room for both of us to stand and walk around, even."

Halfweed slid out of his saddle, as much relieved as angry. "Dumb sunbitch. You didn't have to do that."

"Yeah, I know. But it was fun. Shoulda seen the

look on your face. For a moment you was even
dumber-lookin' than usual." John started to remove
the saddlebags from his mount. "Let's get a fire
goin'. Rate we're travelin', I figger by tomorrow
this time we'll be well on our way to startin' out of
these damn mountains. Then it's over the trail back
to town and the high life."

"Right." Halfweed perked up at the thought.

They built the fire near the entrance so it
wouldn't smoke up the cave. In such snug quarters
even the tired old jerky tasted good.

"Got to take a piss." John rose and headed toward the outside. Halfweed didn't bother to look up,
concentrating on his jerky.

Something close by went *snuf*.

"Hey, man, no more jokes, okay?" The half-breed
flailed absently behind him. Much to his irritation,
the sound was repeated. Smiling to himself, he deliberately extracted his revolver from the gun belt
lying nearby.

"Okay. I ain't afraid o' no *duende*. Since you
won't answer, I guess you some kinda animal now
and I got to defend myself, *verdad*?"

"Defend yourself ag'inst what, you loco freak?"
Fifth John stood framed in the entrance to the cave,
fastening his pants.

"Fifth?" Halfweed fumbled for a flaming brand
from the fire as he cocked his pistol. He tossed the
burning stick toward the unexplored recesses at the
back of the cave.

Something monumental rose up in the light. Primeval fire glinted from black eyes and off teeth the length of a man's hand. The bear raised forepaws equipped with claws like bent railroad spikes. It was ten feet tall, no, fifteen, with silver hairs shimmering among the brown. The Great Bear of the Arapaho, the bear overwhelming: the ur-bear.

"Jesus!" An openmouthed Fifth John stumbled backward, fumbling with his belt. In the confines of the cave the bear's roar was Vesuvius and typhoon and the Port Royal earthquake all rolled into one. It shook the ground underfoot and shattered rock from the walls.

"Oh, Gawd, John, help me!" Adding to the frantic pandemonium as the bear lumbered forward, Halfweed fired his Colt repeatedly, six times in all. All this did was make the brute mad, a tactical decision not dissimilar to Napoleon's decision to invade Russia.

Between the earthshaking roars of the bear, Halfweed's Colt going off, and its owner's terrifying screams as the monster dismembered him one limb at a time, it was a choice cut of purgatory.

"John, John, it's eating me, it's killin' me, oh Gawd, help me!"

Fifth John had not survived an upbringing among four tormenting elder brothers each as mean and ornery as himself without becoming pretty good at sizing up his chances in a fight. It was deuced clear to him that poor Halfweed was already as good as finished and that even with rifle in hand he didn't stand much of a chance against a grizzly from hell, and what would be the point, anyways?

Too bad, Halfweed, he thought sorrowfully as he swung into his saddle. Unlike Great Knox, who'd been tolerated, he'd genuinely liked the greasy, addled dimwit. The bellowing from the cave followed him down the mountainside as he struggled to lead five horses behind him. They were all understandably skittish and edgy. All except for the big black-and-white, who brought up the rear docile as an old hound.

He thought of the money he was going to make selling the five and how Providence had decreed he was going to have to spend it all by himself, and it did help to drown out the memory of Halfweed's final piteous shrieks.

When he was confident he was safely beyond the attentions of the monster bear should it have felt any unsociable inclination toward his person, he stopped and tied his animals. Then he passed methodically among them, speaking to each in a reassuring voice, rubbing its muzzle and neck until it calmed down. Only when that was done did he think to give a care to himself.

"I saw that!" He whirled, simultaneously drawing his gun. "You wuz grinnin' at me, you gawddamned big-butted squint-eyed sumbitch!"

Easy, Fifth, he told himself. *Horses don't grin. They dang well* can't *grin. You're jest tired an' upset. And no wonder, what with the past couple days' goin's-on.*

Mighty peculiar goin's-on at that.

Funny thing how that avalanche come up on that howlin' horse. He'd about forgotten that, but it came back to him now, sharp an' clear. That big old animal a-howlin' like a wolf, and then the snow crashin' down on them and buryin' poor Great Knox and somehow jest missin' all the horses. Then that bear. Biggest gawddamn bear ever was. But he'd checked that cave himself and woulda swore it was cleaner than the inside of a crinoline skirt.

Down the mountain then, all the animals a-frothin' and a-rollin' their eyes until he could quiet 'em. All except this one, this oversized, over-fed, great ugly four-legged bad-eyed bastard of a horse with a lump growin' out of its head. He blinked in confusion. Damn thing was more'n a foot long now, and pointed at the end, an' all twisty-curly round like a stick of store-bought peppermint candy.

Impossible or no, he'd have bet a quarter eagle then and there that it had winked at him.

"What are you, anyways?" He approached with caution. It raised its head from where it had been cropping the grass that poked green threads through the snow and gazed back at him blankly, innocently. Just another dumb animal.

Fifth John wasn't afraid, but he kept the muzzle of his pistol aimed straight at the creature's fore-head, just below the ivory-colored spiral spear.

"You cursed? Thet what it is? You a bad-luck

beastie? I heard tell o' such down in New Orleans. Island people come up and put curses on chickens an' such. Or maybe you're jest bad luck. I kill you, I still got t' other four to sell. You worth the trouble? I wonder." He was within arm's length now. As before, the animal just stood patiently and gazed back at him out of bland equine eyes.

Reaching out, he stroked the spear that grew from the creature's forehead. It was smooth and warm to the touch. Fifth John lowered his pistol. "You're different, that's fer sure. Reckon you might be worth a passle to the right buyer. Maybe you *are* worth the trouble. But from here on I'm gonna be watchin' you as well as my step, hear?"

Carefully but with increasing confidence he began to circle the animal, patting it on its flanks, inspecting its withers. It was sure enough an odd-lookin' concoction: a blind Quaker could've told that. But all muscle underneath that peculiar back. No, he wouldn't kill it. Too much money to be made, and he'd already put up with enough trouble to make it worth keepin' him.

He smiled and nodded at nothing in particular. "Guess you're all right, big'un. Somebody pay plenty to have you hitched in their team." A hot, wet sensation made him glance down at his boots.

The horse was pissing on his feet.

"The hell with it, you damn four-legged play-actor! I *knewed* you wuz grinnin' at me!" Irate beyond common sense, he raised the pistol.

The big animal swung its head around to regard

him thoughtfully. As John leveled his gun at his impassive target, he noticed that something else was different about it. Something new.

Lit from beneath, from inside, the white circle around the bad eye was glowing intensely. And that eye weren't squinting now, weren't more'n half-shut. It was full open, open all the way wide. And staring straight . . . at . . . him.

Mesmerized, Fifth John looked deep into that eye and let out a meager, completely involuntary moan. His whole body started to shake. That wasn't surprising because in an instant his mind had become as unhinged as his body. At the end of his arm his gun was waving up and down like a semaphore flag in the grip of a high gale. The precarious moan rose up in his throat as if trying to escape.

The animal was growling at him. That was crazy. Horses didn't growl. The growl became a snarl. Crazier still. Horses didn't snarl. Tremendous unsuspected muscles rippled and tensed in its back legs, its hindquarters, its neck, as it prepared to spring. That was madness. Horses didn't spr . . .

"I'll be hornswoggled and hog-tied." Caiben turned and yelled back toward the cabin. "Amos, Jim! Git out here and have a look at this!" Clutching the water bucket and heedless of the cold, he splashed through the stream back toward the cabin.

Amos Malone and Jim Bridger emerged, Malone

with skillet in hand. It was his turn to do the cooking. Bridger specialized in rabbit, while Caiben wasn't good with anything more than beans. They didn't much understand what Malone was talking about when he served them medallions of elk béarnaise au poivre or trout almondine with new potatoes and asparagus hollandaise or even how he came by the fixin's. Smart men that they were, they didn't push the question too hard.

Ignoring the icy water dripping from his deerskin leggings, Caiben joined his trapping companions as they watched the six horses, with Malone's in the lead, wander solemnly back into the crude corral from which they'd been abducted. Once within, they dispersed amiably and began to nibble at the greening grass.

No small man himself, Caiben got a crick in his neck looking up at Malone. "Well, you were right, Amos. Danged if you weren't right. They come back."

"Wonder what happened to the thieves," Bridger murmured.

"Reckon they had enough." Malone started toward the corral. His companions followed.

"What's that thing on your animal's head?" Caiben asked. "Looks like he got somthin' stuck in it."

"Just a growth," Malone murmured. " 'Tain't hurtful. I'll take care of it."

They entered the corral. Each man saw to his own mount and then collectively to the three they'd apparently acquired. Malone patted the stallion on the neck. It snorted as if bored by the attention.

"Well, Worthless, they give you a hard time? Other way 'round, I reckon. Some folks are just dumber'n dirt, thinkin' they could horsenap a unicorn."

"A what?" Bridger had come up behind him and overheard. "I know what that is. A mythical creature. Somethin' out of stories, that don't exist." The two mountain men regarded one another silently for a long moment. Then Bridger broke out into a wide smile. "Kind o' like you, Malone."

Malone smiled, too. *Have to replace that restrainin' patch quick,* he mused. "I reckon so, Jim. Tell me: you ever had crawfish étouffée on saffron rice?"

"Huh uh. Sounds like Frenchie food."

"Sort of. With lemon chiffon cake for dessert."

Bridger eyed him sideways. "Now, where you gonna git lemons up here, Malone?"

"Leave that to me, Jim." He gestured with a nod. "Better get cleaned up. Looks to me like you might've had an accident."

Bridger glanced around and down at his stained backside, thoroughly baffled. "Now, when'd I do that? I don't recall . . ."

Malone put an arm around the other man's shoulders. "Let's eat, Jim. Caiben, you ready for dinner?"

"Ain't I always?" The third trapper joined his companions as they sloughed back toward the cabin.

Behind them Worthless shifted his phenomenally

flexible anatomy and turned to thoughtfully eye the nearest mare.

Espying his implication, she gave a startled snort and bolted twelve feet.

THE PURL OF THE PACIFIC

A lot of folks don't know it, but part of the Old West just skipped over the Great Basin region and the West Coast to land in the Sandwich Islands. Different natives (same treatment) and even cowboys. The cowboys, in fact, are still there, hanging around Makawao and Wailea discussing weather and cattle and posing for the tourists.

But a different group of Native Americans were there first, with a very different and equally rich culture. Not that it would make a difference to Amos Malone.

The man is, after all, all business. Just what kind of business is sometimes hard to figure.

"SHARK!"

Amos Malone glanced back over his left shoulder. The men on the whaler *Pernod*, out of Nantucket, were running along the rail, shouting and gesticulating wildly. One native harpooner was actually hanging off the bowsprit as he did his level best

241

to draw the mountain man's attention to something in the water midway between himself and the ship.

Malone dropped his gaze and squinted. Sure enough, there it was: a dark, sickle-shaped fin cutting the water directly toward him. A couple of the whaler's crewmen had rifles out and were frantically trying to load and aim. Malone hoped they'd take their time. They were as likely to hit him as the fish.

Tiger shark, by the look of it, Malone decided thoughtfully. Fourteen, maybe fifteen feet. It was still a ways off, uncertain what to make of this unprecedented intrusion into its home waters. In its piscine bafflement it had been preceded by company both common and illustrious, for Mad Amos Malone constituted something of an intrusion no matter where he went.

Leaning to his left, he peered into his mount's eye. It rolled upward to regard him, its owner's dyspeptic temperament much in evidence.

"Shark over there, Worthless." He casually jabbed a thumb in the direction of the oncoming fin. "Just thought you'd like to know."

Beneath him the enormous stocky steed of mightily confused parentage snorted once, whether by way of acknowledging the warning or indicating its contempt for their present mode of travel, one had no way of knowing. Transporting them both, the stallion was swimming easily for shore, Malone having decided not to wait for the first boat to be lowered. He was anxious to see this new cattle country, even if the place was as hot as the Brazos valley in July and twice as humid.

The water above the reef was refreshing, though, and the island lay close at hand. The bustling whaling town of Merciless Sun lay before him, cloud-swathed green mountains rising sharply behind it. A brilliant rainbow arched over the heavily eroded gullies that flayed the slopes, looking for all the world like a gigantic advertising sign raised by elves. Or in this instance, Malone reminded himself, *menehunes*. Dozens of vessels, mostly whalers like the *Pernod*, swayed at anchor in the Lahaina roads behind him, their masts representing entire forests transported to the open sea.

They looked hot, too, Malone reflected. Everything hereabouts looked hot.

The *Pernod*'s captain had sympathized with his passenger's desire to get ashore but was dead set against any attempt to do so without the use of a boat.

"Most of these ships stink of whale oil, Mr. Malone, sir, and the great-toothed fish that ply these waters are always ready for a handout in the most literal sense of the word. Furthermore, if you will not be insulted by my saying so, no matter how well your animal may have weathered the journey from San Francisco, it is no seal, sir, to easily swim this distance to shore. Especially with a rider so large as yourself seated astride its back."

Malone had smiled down through his great, unfurled nimbus of a beard. "Now, don't you go

worryin' about ol' Worthless, Captain. He's a right
fine swimmer and takes to the water like a fish."

In point of fact, Malone's unclassifiable steed had
once swum Lake Superior from the American side
to the Canadian at the height of a ferocious autumn
storm. The captain would not have believed that, either, unless he happened to be familiar with a unicorn's extraordinary powers of endurance, which he
was not. With his horn kept cut down and filed flat,
Worthless's true lineage remained a necessary mys-
tery to all who encountered the exceptional, if
ill-dispositioned, creature.

The shark was quite close now, not even bother-
ing to circle. The men on the boat were frantic.

Worthless turned his head, located the shark, and
kicked out all in one swift motion. A portion of the
lagoon foamed. His left hoof caught the fish beneath
its jaw and knocked it clean out of the water. It lay
there belly up, floating and dazed. The frenzy
aboard the ship was instantly transformed into
stunned silence. A dozen or so sharp, pointed teeth,
forcibly ejected from their intimidating loci, spiraled lazily down through the crystal-clear water
and came to rest on the sandy bottom, but not before being thoroughly investigated by half a dozen
spotted butterfly fish, a couple of Moorish idols,
and one *humuhumunukunukuapua'a* (one *humuhumunukunukuapua'a* being more than enough).

The silence was replaced by several startled but
enthusiastic cheers from the crew. Malone leaned
forward and whispered in his mount's ear.

"Don't get no swelled head, now, horse. It were only a dang fish." Beneath him Worthless blew bubbles in the salt water. Perhaps recognizing a kindred spirit if not species, several sea horses had attached themselves to his tail.

The town of Merciless Sun (or Lahaina, as it was called in the native tongue) certainly lived up to its name. Emerging from the water alongside the short stone jetty, Malone carefully unpacked his kit and removed his mount's tack, spreading it all out in the sun to dry. Handling it as gently as a baby, he unwrapped his Sharps rifle from its waterproof oilskin holder. Not much use for a buffalo gun on an island with no buffalo, he knew, but the Sharps was as much a part of him as his beard or underwear. Or for that matter the great, white-dappled, jet-black, misogynistic stallion that stood nearby, nibbling at the exquisite tropical flowers that grew wild where the jetty met the land.

Not everyone glanced in his direction when he passed, but most did. At six foot ten and a slice of homemade chocolate cake over three hundred pounds, Amos Malone tended to draw the eye no matter where he went. Nor was the attire of a mountain man common garb in a seaport town situated in the middle of the great Pacific.

He'd come to this island as a favor to John Cochran, Esq., of Fort Worth, Texas. Père Cochran had been advised of the excellent prospects to be realized by raising cattle in the islands for export by ship to California, where there was an exploding

market for fresh beef thanks to the recent discovery
in that territory of a certain favored yellow metal.
Never having visited this particular island and ow-
ing Cochran a favor, Malone had agreed to evaluate
the possibilities in return for passage and expenses.

Certainly the town of Lahaina was booming.
Among its statistics the 1846 census had listed
3,445 natives, 112 foreigners, 600 seamen, 155
adobe houses, 822 grass houses, 59 stone and
wooden houses, and 528 dogs, among other items.
But not much in the way of cattle, though Cochran
had assured Malone that other entrepreneurs had
started to run them elsewhere on the island, using
imported Latin cowboys or espaniolas known to the
locals as *paniolos*.

Well, he figured to see for himself. Repacking his
now-dry kit and securing it to Worthless's broad
back, he set out to find lodging for the evening.

As it turned out, lodging wasn't the problem. It
was finding a place where a man could sleep. Used
to spending the night out in the wilderness beneath
the open and silent bowl of the sky, Malone had
been forced to endure for weeks the unending rustle
of sailors and ship. Looking forward to a little ter-
restrial peace and quiet, he discovered he'd made
landfall in one of the noisiest towns in Creation.
Whaler and sailor alike started partying early and in
earnest, the magnitude of their merrymaking only
intensifying with the lateness of the hour.

Giggling, laughing native men and women as

well as hopefully hymning missionaries contributed to the boisterous ballyhoo, and it was about two A.M. when a restless Malone recovered Worthless from his stable and set off in search of a piece of ground where the stars would serve as his sole company for the remainder of the night.

The shore south of Lahaina was rocky and difficult, but the trail that led to the central part of the island was well maintained from much use. When at last he came down out of the hills onto the flat, semiarid peninsula that divided the two mountainous halves of the island, he turned to his right and soon came to a beach of fine white sand. Slipping easily out of the saddle, he started forward in search of a quiet place among the *kiawe* trees in which to spend the balance of the night.

Not expecting to see any buildings, he was therefore much surprised when he found himself confronted by a six-foot-high wall of finely worked rock. Atop the solid stone platform stood a long, simple structure of wood posts and poles roofed with thatch. A small fire was burning at the near end, silhouetting the figure of a native seated crosslegged before it.

Malone examined the sky. Among the millions of visible stars were a few clouds. Rain, he had been told, fell in biblical quantities on the eastern side of the island but far less frequently in the west. Still, he had experienced one aqueous immersion already this morning and had no desire to spend the night enveloped in another.

"Aloha, y'all," he said, addressing the native.

The man jumped to his feet as if shot. Malone immediately saw that he was clad in the simplest of raiment instead of the contemporary European fashion favored in comparatively sophisticated Lahaina by so many of the locals. The woven tapa around his waist was complemented by a simple yet well-made headdress. In his right hand he brandished a formidable club carved of koa wood studded on two sides with sharks' teeth.

He started yelling in the local tongue until he saw by the light of the stars and his fire that his nocturnal visitor was neither demon nor commoner but something in between.

"Parlez-vous français?"

"Nope. English. I'm an American. Malone's the name. Amos Malone."

The man, who was quite large and well muscled but small compared to Malone (as was, for that matter, the great majority of the human race), stepped to the edge of the platform to confront his caller. After appraising the impressively indifferent Worthless with a critical eye, he crouched low to study the animal's rider.

"Malone," he repeated. "I know English good. Learned in missionary school." He gestured sharply with the club. "You come from Lahaina?" Malone nodded. "You must go away from here. This *heiau* is *kapu*."

"Sorry." Malone was properly apologetic. "Didn't know. You reckon there's a place hereabouts where a man could get a night's sleep without bein' disturbed by more hollerin' and howlin' than a pack o' coyotes make fighting over a dead buffalo?"

The man frowned. He possessed the exceptionally fine complexion of his people, and his eyes flashed alertly in the flickering light.

"Coyote? Buffalo?"

"Never mind." Malone turned to leave. "I'll just find another place."

There was silence for a moment. Then the solitary supplicant called out to his visitor. "You do not like the sounds of Lahaina?"

Malone turned back. "Fine for partyin'. Not so good for sleeping." He tilted his head back. "I prefer the company of stars to men."

"Ah." The man had a penetrating, piercing stare Malone had encountered before, but not frequently. "Come closer, haole." Malone complied and met the other's stare evenly.

After several moments during which the only sound was the crackle of fire and the cry of seabirds, the man nodded to himself. "Yes, I can see it. You are a kahuna. A teacher, a sorcerer. But what kind?"

Malone scratched through his beard. "Depends on the moment. There's folks think I'm a fairly versatile fella. You a kahuna, too, Mister . . . ?"

The native straightened, his coppery body glowing in the firelight. "I am . . . you could not pronounce my name. Call me Hau. In your English that means 'Iron.'"

Malone extended a hand, which the other grasped firmly. "Pleased to make your acquaintance. Hau you doin'?"

"Hau . . . ?" It brought a slow smile to the other's face. "You are not afraid? Many haoles find the *heiaus* frightening." He gestured at the temple behind him.

Malone gazed past his host to study the wooden structure and its imposing platform. "Places of power and reverence only frighten the ignorant. Or those with something to hide."

Hau nodded solemnly and turned aside. "Please. Come and share the fire with me. If you are truly a kahuna, or perhaps even a *kupua*, you are more than welcome here. It is the help of just such a one that I seek."

With a hop and a jump Malone was soon standing, and then sitting, across the fire from Hau. The native glanced in Worthless's direction. "You do not tie your animal?"

"Tie Worthless? That'll be the day. Don't worry; he'll stick around. Ain't nobody else would tolerate him, anyways." The unicorn glanced up and with great deliberation and malice aforethought turned its head and sneezed directly onto Malone's saddlebags.

"What's a *kupua*?"

"The child of a god. You can recognize them by their great strength and beauty. Or by their great ugliness and the terror they inspire in others." Hau studied Malone's face. "Possibly one can be both strong and ugly."

Malone grinned. "Thanks for the compliment."

"I am an *ali'i*, a noble." Hau sat straighter. "I will always tell the truth."

"And what is the truth tonight, Hau?" Malone picked up an unburned stick and casually toyed with the fire.

Hau leaned closer. "What do you know of Lahaina?"

Malone considered. "It's hotter than the hinges of hell, the whalers have made it the hottest port in the Pacific, and they're always going at it with the missionaries. I understand there's a real school above the town, too."

"Lahainaluna, yes. A copy of your New England schools and almost twenty years old now. A very good school that teaches both haole and local children modern ways." His voice dropped. "That is why Kanaloaiki hates it."

"Somebody hates a school? That ain't right."

"Not only the school," Hau continued. "He hates everything about Lahaina and what it has done to the people. Since King Kamehameha III moved the kingdom's capital to Honolulu, Kanaloaiki's ire has only increased."

Malone nodded. "Tell your friend things'll settle down. There's fewer whales this year than last, and fewer whalers. There'll be fewer still next year and the year after that. But the school should stay. It's a good school, I hear, and a good school is a good thing."

"Not to Kanaloaiki. He has vowed to destroy it, and all of Lahaina, and all who share in its life. He makes no distinctions. All are to die: haoles, missionaries, and local people alike. The town will be razed to the ground. Not even a breadfruit tree is to be left standing."

"I see." Malone considered the stars. "This Kanaloaiki, he's a powerful chief with a lot of warriors who'll follow him?"

"Worse." Hau shook his head. "He is a *kahuna 'ana'ana*, a sorcerer who practices black magic. For more than a year now he has been gathering the materials for a great spell that he plans to cast on a certain mountain." The *ali'i* pointed into the darkness. "*That* mountain."

Turning, Malone could just make out the dark ridgeline of a nearly six-thousand-foot-high peak.

"That is Pu'u Kukui. It has been asleep for as long as we can remember. But the island is not. Less than seventy years ago there was a modest eruption far to the south of here, on the slopes of the House of the Sun." He smiled. "I know this because I have been to the school. I know it did not happen because Pele was angry. It was geology."

"Don't be so sure," Malone murmured. "This Kanaloaiki, he thinks he can reawaken the old volcano?"

Hau nodded solemnly. "Lahaina lies at its foot. The town will die, buried beneath fast-flowing superhot aa. Nothing will remain. The school, too, will be buried, and the ships offshore will go away and not come back. So Kanaloaiki intends. Thousands of people will die."

"You can't stop him?"

"Nothing can stop the spell. Not now." Hau brooded over the fire. "Kanaloaiki began last week. Once begun, it can only be countered after it has started."

"What about your local kahunas? Do they all support Kanaloaiki?"

Hau looked up. "No. Most are against what he is trying to do. But they are all afraid of him. His power is very great. But *you* are not afraid of him, haole kahuna."

Malone shrugged. "Haven't met the old boy. Don't see offhand what I can do, though. How do you counter a spell that can't be countered until after it's begun?"

"I have been told there is a way. There is a tool. A special tool. The wisest kahunas say it still exists, but none believe them."

"Except you."

Hau nodded. "I would use it if I could to stop what Kanaloaiki intends. But while I am *ali'i*, I am not a kahuna. I do not have the power to use such a thing. If it exists. But another, one not afraid of Kanaloaiki or under his sway, might do so." He looked searchingly at Malone.

"Whoa, now. I'm just here to look over the cattle-raisin' prospects for a friend o' mine. 'Course, I

don't much like the idea of standing by while a few
thousand innocent folk get burned and buried alive.
Never much did. I just ain't sure I can do anything
about it."

Hau considered. "If I show you the best land for
cattle, will you consider helping me?"

"It's sure enough a good cause. All right, I'll see
what I can do. Now, where's this here good grazing
land you're talking about?"

"It's very interesting, but the place you are talking about and the place I am talking about are in
fact the same place."

Malone grunted. "Don't say? And what place
might that be?"

Hau turned and nodded to his right. "You will see
tomorrow, Amos Malone. Tonight it sleeps beneath
the blanket of night. Tomorrow I will take you to
the House of the Sun."

The House of the Sun, or Haleakala, as the natives called it, rose to a height of more than ten
thousand feet, completely dominating the entire island. It wasn't its height that impressed Malone,
who had seen far taller mountains elsewhere. It
wasn't even its breadth, which allowed for a slope
so gradual as to be imperceptible.

No, it was the weight of the mountain, which
plunged another 27,000 feet to the ocean floor.
Composed almost entirely of cementlike solidified
aa, the mountain was massive enough to dimple the
earth's crust beneath it. Unlike many mountains,
which were simply magnificently decorative, this

one had a presence you could feel. Malone sensed it as the light broke over the distant summit and commented on it to Hau.

"It is the House of the Sun," the native replied simply. "No one may go there save *ali'i*, and none may live upon its upper reaches but kahuna. You can go there. I cannot."

Malone reined in Worthless. Hau had been walking alongside the entire way, refusing to ride behind Malone or even alternate in the saddle with him. He was, he assured Malone, quite comfortable walking.

As they ascended, villagers came to gawk at the huge haole and his companion *ali'i*. The two travelers were given food and deference in equal quantities, and the locals marveled at Malone's appetite. A few of the children, grinning and giggling, tried to play with Worthless. The great black steed generally ignored them, even when they swung from his tail or tugged on his mane. He munched fruit in quantity and reacted only once to the juvenile attention.

One of the older youngsters stood directly in front of the stallion and reached for the patch on his forehead, intending to pull it loose and see what it concealed. The next moment he was running and crying for his mother, who was unable to determine exactly how he had been struck in the eye by a flying mango pit.

As they climbed, the air grew steadily cooler. About three degrees for every thousand feet, Malone reckoned. More than adequately protected in his buckskins and boots, he marveled at the nearly-naked Hau's ability to withstand the increasing chill.

At four thousand feet Hau pointed out excellent high grassland suitable for grazing cattle. At six thousand they entered and passed through a solid layer of cloud. At ten thousand they encountered isolated patches of icy snow.

Then Malone found himself gazing down into a black-streaked, rust-brown crater big enough to hold all of Manhattan Island.

Hau pointed to a distant cinder cone within the crater. "Down there, my friend. There is said to be a cave. In the depths of the cave is a tool. Only the truest of kahuna can recover it. Others have tried; none have succeeded. Whether anyone can even make use of it I do not know. I know only what the kahunas here tell me: that it is the only tool with which Kanaloaiki's terrible plan can be foiled."

Malone nodded. "Maybe it's a big hammer that I can whack him on the head with." So saying, he flicked Worthless's reins, and together man and unicorn started down into the barren, nearly lifeless crater.

Silversword grew in isolated bunches, thrusting their highly specialized leaves into a pristine pale blue sky. Exotic carmine, yellow, and emerald-hued birds fluttered in and out of the crater on air currents that rose from the volcano's rain forested eastern slopes, each one more brilliantly colored than the next. They reminded Malone of a rainbow's tears. Occasionally a *pueo*, the native owl, would dart low as Worthless's hooves disturbed a mouse.

The browns and blacks and russets and rusts of the crater seemed endless, but eventually Malone found himself approaching the indicated cinder cone. Trotting around its base, he skirted the edge of an undistinguished depression in the crater floor. According to what Hau had been told, the cave was to be found on the far side of the cone.

A few cinders slid away beneath Worthless's hooves, tumbling toward the center of the depression. Each step sent a few more skittering downward. Before long the slide had become continuous. Just to be on the safe side, Malone urged his mount higher.

But instead of ascending, Worthless, too, began to slide.

As steed and rider fought for stability, Malone saw that the sliding cinders were flowing rapidly toward the center of the depression, and not just from beneath Worthless's feet but from all sides. It reminded him of something he'd seen before.

Despite the unicorn's heroic efforts, they continued to slip. Finally Malone saw something else, something that at last brought back to him the memory of what they had found. It was very much identical, only on a larger scale.

A much larger scale.

Two projecting, curving, sharp-edged, sicklelike hooks, each taller than a man, clashed and clacked together expectantly in the exact center of the depression. The owner of those jaws would have been instantly familiar to anyone who had ever encountered them in sandy, dry soils. They belonged to an ant lion.

An ant lion that, to judge by the size of the depression and its now-visible jaws, must be as big as an elephant.

What it subsisted on here in this barren place Malone couldn't imagine, but he understood now why courageous but foolhardy travelers who defied the old *kapu* to visit this sacred place never returned to their homes. Why, even kahunas avoided the crater floor.

His first thought was to unlimber the Sharps, but even its fifty-caliber bullets would not be likely to have much of an effect on the slow-paced nervous system of the gigantic insect. Instead, as Worthless continued to slip and slide toward those expectant, waiting jaws, Malone began undoing one of his saddlebags. Fingering various vials and containers within, he sought desperately for the right one.

Those jaws, large and powerful enough to crack the bones of a man's skeleton like twigs, were much too near when he finally found the vial he'd been searching for. Unscrewing the lid, he tossed the entire open container into the center of the depression, only to see it swallowed immediately.

For a few moments nothing happened, and they continued to slide lower and lower. Then the descent ceased. With Malone whispering in his ear,

Worthless kicked and scrambled frantically to gain height.

The ground behind them began to tremble. It was an eruption, but not of Haleakala. With a violent, concussive roar the cinders and air behind them vomited skyward, forming a temporary but spectacular fountain. Malone held on to his wolf's-head cap, his saddle, and his dignity as best he could as the wild rush sent man and mount flying out of the depression.

It had been, he reflected as he and Worthless picked themselves up and continued on their way, one hell of a sneeze. But then, the open vial that he had thrown into the pit and that had found its way into the ant lion's mouth had contained purest essence of cayenne, a substance useful in numerous spells and Tex-Mex cooking and apparently not so ineffective when employed strictly on its own.

In contrast to the encounter with the crater dweller, the cave itself was very much an anticlimax, starkly unimpressive. Within, Malone found a few handfuls of bone tools, some old pots and desiccated baskets, and a frayed sleeping mat. Nothing more. Certainly nothing that on the face of it was potent enough to use against a formidable sorcerer.

Nevertheless, he knew from long experience that even the simplest object could be charged with considerable power. Gathering up everything he saw, he secured it to one saddlebag and started back toward the crater's rim, this time employing an entirely different route. Being completely out of essence of cayenne, he had no wish to tempt the ant lion's energy and appetite a second time.

What was worse, he mused as he rode, was that now he was going to have to have his evening meal inadequately seasoned.

Hau could hardly believe it when Malone rejoined him just below and outside the crater rim.

"You have survived!" the *ali'i* exclaimed. "No one has been to that place in living memory and returned to tell of it."

"I reckon I know why." Slipping down out of the saddle, Malone unpacked the artifacts he had accumulated. "Now, this here basket, what's it for?" He passed a finely woven container to the *ali'i*.

Hau's demeanor was less than reverent as he turned the object over in his hands. "Gathering fruit, I would imagine. It is a simple basket. What did you think it was?"

Malone grunted. "Never mind. How about this?"

They went through every item in the mountain man's perilously acquired inventory, Hau discarding one after another with nary a word. Malone was growing not just discouraged but angry, wondering if he'd risked his life only to recover some long dead kahuna's household goods.

So it was that when Hau's eyes grew wide and his hands began to shake as he held up an ordinary-looking fishhook, Malone hardly knew what to make of it.

"You must have much mana, Amos Malone, to bring this out of the House of the Sun."

"So I've been told ... in other ways." Malone squinted dubiously at the hook, unable to discern anything remarkable about it. "What do we do now? Go fishin'?"

Hau held the object piously in both upturned palms. "Of course you cannot know what this is. But by its shape, which I recognize, and its design, which I well remember from the old tales, and by the picture writing on both sides, I know it for what it is."

Malone was hungry. Behind him, Worthless whinnied impatiently. "A means for catchin' our lunch?" he asked hopefully.

Hau handed the artifact to his haole friend. "This, Amos Malone, is the *Manai ikalani*, the sacred fishhook which one of the god Maui's ancestresses fashioned at his request from her own jawbone. Using it, Maui raised from the depths of the sea all the land that became the islands of my people and those of their ancestors. When Maui caught the sun here atop Haleakala, the fishhook fell from where it was tied at his waist. It has lain here ever since." Without waiting to see if Malone would follow, he turned and started down the mountain.

"Come, my friend. With this even we may be able to stop Kanaloaiki from destroying Lahaina."

Malone swung himself up into the saddle and followed. "How? By bribing him with fish?"

Hau looked up and smiled. "You do not fool me,

kahuna. I know that when the time comes you will know what to do. Now that we have a hook, we must find a line to attach to it. The strongest line imaginable. There is good rope in Lahaina, fashioned to sell to the whalers. We will find the toughest there is and buy, borrow, or steal what is needed."

Malone considered. "That may not be necessary. You say we'll need a sturdy line?"

"The strongest that can be woven."

"Will that little hook hold a big line?"

Hau looked back and said in all sincerity, "It once raised from the bottom of the sea all the islands of Polynesia."

"Okay, I take your meaning. But I think I know where I can find us an even stronger line than you have in mind."

"Excellent. But we must hurry, Amos Malone. See that light on the far slope of Pu'u Kukui?" In the distance, on the upper slopes of the west Maui mountains, Malone could just make out a fitful, flashing light. "Kanaloaiki has begun his evil work. We have little time."

Malone sighed heavily. "In the wizardry business it seems like a man hardly ever does."

"What on earth d' you plan t' do with this ashore, Malone?" George Wilfong indicated the length of material Malone had sought to buy.

"You needn't know, George. Better you don't." Seated next to the whaler, Malone pulled hard on his oar. Around them lights flickered from murderous ships riding innocently at anchor.

"That's all well and good, I suppose. All I knows is that you'd better give me payment enough to satisfy the captain, as you promised, or there'll be hell to pay."

"There'll be hell to pay this night anyway. Rest assured the captain will be satisfied with the trade I have in mind."

Wilfong frowned. "He had better be, or he'll have me keelhauled right here in the roads. Malone, I don't know what you're up to this night, but one thing I am sure of: you owe me as well as the captain for this."

"Fair enough, George." Malone considered the looming bulk of the island and the tiny but intense light that was now clearly visible just below the shaft of the highest crag. "I hear tell you're thinking of giving up whaling."

"How'd you know that?" Wilfong looked startled.

"Sometimes a man thinks loudly, and I reckon myself a good listener. This is a sweet favor you're doing me, so I expect it's only just and fair that I slip you a sweet notion in return. The far side of this island is wet as any in the world, and the soil rich. Right now there's a hunger for all kinds of seasonings in California and gold to pay for them. Myself, I'm here to see to the possibilities of raising more cattle in this country, beef cattle to feed hungry miners. Someone's needed to see to other matters. It's a known fact that prospectors are most all afflicted with the sweet tooth."

"What are you saying, Malone?" Wilfong pulled steadily on his oar.

"Sugarcane, George. I've a thought that it would do well here. Why not try some on the well-watered side of the island?"

"Sugarcane?" Wilfong's brows drew together in thought. "I've seen how it's done in the Caribbean. But what would I use here to boil the juice? There's no manufacturing in these islands, and I couldn't afford to bring heavy gear over from the mainland."

"Use some of the big blubber pots off any whaler," Malone suggested.

Wilfong brightened. "Blubber pots. Now, that's a fine idea, Mr. Malone, a fine idea. It just might work, and Lord knows I've experience enough boiling things down. Sugarcane; yes, by God. I'll give it a try, I think, and thankee."

"Welcome."

"But there's still the matter of the captain's payment."

They were very close to shore now. Easing off on his oar while Wilfong did the same, Malone dug deep in a pocket and handed his companion a triangular-shaped object that seemed to glow from within with a supernal whiteness. On both sides were etched in black finely wrought scenes of whales, whalers, and whaling men.

" 'Tis the biggest sperm whale tooth I've ever

seen," Wilfong admitted, "and the scrimshaw is excellent, but scrimshaw to a whaling man is like ice to an Esquimaw. I'm not sure the captain will account it a fair trade."

Malone's tone was somber. "Tell him that so long as this sleeps in his sea chest, he need never fear that any ship he commands will come to harm. This here was given to me by a fella name of Herman after I rescued him from the natives down in the Marquesas." The mountain man chuckled. "Been writin' about it ever since, he has.

"The scrimshaw on this tooth was done by a Maori fella called Quehquoag, who pried it from the hull of a capsized lugger out of the Fijis. Came from a white whale, he told my friend. Last I heard, Herman was still workin' on that particular book." Malone turned thoughtful. "Ought to be out in a year or two, I reckon."

Wilfong was still doubtful but willing to be convinced. "All seamen are superstitious, captains no less so than common sailors. The size of it—" He hefted the enormous white tooth in both hands. "It's warm to the touch, as if still connected to the lower jaw of its owner." He nodded to himself. "I think the captain will accept it. You must be badly in need of this—" he gestured at the cargo they towed behind them "—to part with so powerful a talisman."

Once more Malone's gaze turned to the mountain. "The world's full of talismans, George, but short on good people and shorter still on good schools."

* * *

Hau led the way up the western slope of Pu'u
Kukui, which was steeper and brushier than that of
Haleakala. They were guided by the baleful light of
Kanaloaiki's work, which pierced the darkness like
a malevolent eye.

"There!" The *ali'i* pointed, and Malone found he
could see clearly.

The old man was as wrinkled and bent as an old
ohia tree, but his voice was unbowed. The fire into
which he was casting ingredients and words blazed
higher with each successive addition. Kanaloaiki
took those from a pile off to his right, a pile that
was growing smaller by the minute.

"See here," Malone suggested. "Why don't I
just ride on over and have a word with the old
gent."

"He is protected." Hau was looking around worriedly.

"By what?" Malone searched the *kahuna
'ana'ana*'s immediate vicinity. "I don't see anything."

"If you do, you will die."

"Pretty good protection," the mountain man
agreed solemnly. "How do we deal with guardians
if we can't look for 'em?"

"They will declare themselves. Listen for their
presence. Listen for the chanting. The old chanting."

They continued to approach. Once Malone
thought he saw Kanaloaiki glance in their direction

and smile evilly before returning to his work, but he couldn't be certain.

What he could be sure of as they drew very near indeed was the rise of a distinctive moaning, the echo of a dirge signifying the proximity of doom incarnate, and the smell of death drifting like black floss on the wind.

Hau shut his eyes tight and turned his back to the sorcerer's position. "That is it; that is the sound of which I spoke! The Marchers of the Night! To look upon them is to die."

Unperturbed, Malone spit to his right. A small spot on the ground sizzled. "Marchers of the Night, eh? What sort o' outriders might they be?"

"The souls of dead *ali'i*. Only a *kahuna 'ana'ana* can control them, because his withered soul is given over to evil. Somehow we must get close enough to Kanaloaiki to break the spell the instant it has begun, but we must do so without looking directly upon him."

"Kind o' like workin' in Washington." Fumbling in a saddlebag, Malone removed a scratched, chipped, but still serviceable mirror. Pulling hard on the reins, he turned Worthless about. Using the mirror to scope their route, they resumed their ascent, Worthless following Malone's guiding tugs on his reins while methodically advancing hind end first.

"A clever trick." Hau kept pace by the simple expedient of walking backward alongside Worthless. "What made you think of it?"

"Old acquaintance of mine name of Perseus had to deal with a similar dilemma once. Involved a woman." He adjusted the mirror. "Works better with a bronze shield, but it's danged hard to fit one in a saddlebag."

"Ah," Hau murmured. The moaning rose louder around them. "It will still be difficult to get close to Kanaloaiki with so many Marchers about."

"Actually, I had kind of another notion for dealin' with them." So saying, he extracted not from the capacious saddlebags but from a pocket a small tubular instrument. Placing it in his mouth and using the fingers of one hand to manipulate the notes, he began to tootle a winsome tune.

Hau winced. "A strange music but somehow attractive." Malone could only nod a response, his mouth being full of instrument.

The moaning grew shrill and strident. Then, astonishingly, it began to mellow, harmonizing with and eventually chanting in counterpoint to the tune Malone was playing. Still backing Worthless up the mountainside, he played on until he had all the dead *ali'i* moaning in perfect time to his music. Gradually they drifted away, moaning softly and, Malone was convinced, contentedly. Only when the last of them had vanished into the all-absorbing night did he remove the instrument from his mouth.

"Reckon we can turn about now. I expect they're gone."

"How did you do that?" Hau asked. Ahead of them Kanaloaiki saw that his protective spirits had departed and worked furiously to finish his spell.

"Friend of mine named Louie Gottschalk composed that little tune. It's a cakewalk; they're pretty much irresistible. This variation incorporates a little voodoo. Louie's from New Orleans, and he doesn't publish everything he composes. I figured an enchanted cakewalk was bound to work on any bunch of spirits called the Marchers. Just weren't completely sure it'd sound good enough on a kazoo. But they seem to have cleared out right promptly."

"Powerful magic!" Hau exclaimed.

"But not powerful enough," declared old Kanaloaiki with a sneer, overhearing them. Stepping back and raising his arms, he pronounced the final words of the spell. As the earth began to tremble, the old *kahuna 'ana'ana* started to laugh. "Say farewell to all the evil that is Lahaina, for the earth is soon to take her back! Sprite of Pele, heed my call!"

For the first time since Malone could remember, Worthless lost his footing. The mountain man was thrown to the ground. Recovering quickly, he staggered to the unicorn's side as the earth heaved and buckled beneath them. Hau didn't even try to rise. Sprawled helplessly on his side, the *ali'i* looked on in horror.

In front of old Kanaloaiki the ground split asunder. An unholy refulgence bolted from the depths as a hellish yellow-red glow illuminated the sky. Slick and viscous, *aa* lava could be seen rising within the dilating cleft, bubbling and boiling, ready to pour down the mountainside and roar through Lahaina, incinerating and inevitably burying everything in its path.

"The *Manai ikalani*!" Hau shouted. "Quickly, Amos Malone!"

"I've got 'er!" Malone was fumbling with the saddlebags.

"The line," the *ali'i* yelled, "what about the line? Do you think it will be strong enough?"

"I reckon!" Malone hollered back. "Figured since you said we were liable to be dealin' with some serious heat, we'd want something that wouldn't burn too easy!"

A mountain man must be self-reliant in everything, must know how to cook as well as shoot, repair leather as well as hunt, even has to know how to fix his own clothing when there's nary a tailor within a thousand miles. So Malone had no trouble threading the line through the fishhook . . . though drawing one of the iron links through his teeth in order to make it thin enough to fit through the eye did set his mouth on edge.

With the hook securely fastened to the line, he began to twirl one end of it over his head, the sacred *Manai* thundering through the air like a hog-tied earthquake. What he was about to try was not unlike roping steers down in Texas, except that his target this time was at once larger and more difficult to hold down and the line itself was just a tad heavier than your ordinary lariat.

Not knowing if he'd have an opportunity for a second chance, he did his best to fling the hook straight and true. It soared across the expanding seam in the ground, trailing the spare anchor chain from the *Pernod* behind it. The iron links clanked above the roar of the superheated earth as they landed on the far side of the widening chasm.

The fishhook struck the earth . . . and stuck. With a sharp tug Malone set the hook. Making sure the other end was secured to the pommel of Worthless's saddle, he swung himself up and slapped his mount on the side of his scruffy neck.

"Ready there, Worthless? Back, boy! Back 'er up now!"

As Hau looked on in awe and Kanaloaiki in aghast fury, the muscular quadruped slowly began to back to the south, digging his hooves into the ground and pulling the anchor chain with him. The crack stopped expanding and began to contract as Malone drew it shut, binding up the wound in the earth as neat and clean as any surgeon would stitch up a wound. A few dollops of lava boiled out of the ground before the rift was sealed completely. By the time Malone called a halt, the lava near the top of the vent had cooled sufficiently to seal the opening.

No ordinary horse could have managed it, or even an ordinary unicorn, but Worthless, for all his equine peccadilloes, was special indeed.

"Atta boy. Now stand!" Malone patted his steed on its neck as he dismounted. Worthless snorted and fell to cropping the nearest bush, breathing no harder than if he'd just pulled a wagon from a muddy-bottomed creek.

Avoiding the site of the vent, where the ground was still too hot to walk on, Malone joined Hau in approaching the stymied sorcerer. The frustrated *kahuna 'ana'ana* did not try to contest their approach, did not even lift an arm to defend himself as Hau raised his formidable club.

Malone put out an arm to forestall the blow. "Easy there, Hau."

The *ali'i* looked at him. "But if we let him live, he may try again."

Malone shook his head. "I don't think so. Take a good look at him. Can't you see he's done for?"

It was clear that the excruciating effort had used up the old sorcerer utterly. As he lay back, his breath came in increasingly difficult gasps. A grim-faced Hau stepped aside, satisfied.

"Evil can be exhausting," Malone expounded.

At that the old man turned to face him. "You are a great kahuna. I did not know there was such among the haoles."

"Not many," Malone told him. "Say, how come you can speak good English?"

"I, too, went to the haole school." With obvious difficulty, the old man sucked air. "It is not haole learning I was trying to kill. Only haole culture. It overruns the land like a big wave. It is overrunning *this* land."

Hau stepped forward. "I do not know about that, old man, but I do know that it is wrong to kill innocent people. I will have a *kapu* put on this spot so that none will come here and see what you have tried to do. No one will disturb the metal rope, and this ground will stay peaceful."

"You will see," the old man wheezed. "One day you will see. Or your children will." His head fell back as he gazed into the star-flecked black crystal of night. "I hear the Marchers. They could not protect me, and now they come for me. Life is never just; death always is."

With that he went away, eyes open to the darkness and unfulfilled.

"Reckon that's that." Malone began to secure both ends of the anchor chain, choosing volcanic spurs that were firmly a part of the solid rock of the mountainside. Hau tried his best to help, but though he was accounted a strong man among his own people, he could not move any part of the heavy chain, which Malone handled with apparent ease.

"You have done a good thing this night, Amos Malone. Give me the *Manai*." Without word or objection, Malone handed it over.

"What'll you do with that?"

"It is too dangerous to keep where others might find it. I will take paddlers and a canoe far south of here, to the southeast even of the big island, where the sea is very deep. There I will throw it into the ocean. It will fall to the depths and not raise any more land until it is safe." A sudden thought made him look closely at the massive haole. "What will you tell your friend about our cattle lands?"

"That he'd better get here fast if he's interested before these espaniolas already working the slopes buy up all the good grazing. And I reckon you might try to buy some for yourself as well now that the king's allowed as how private folks can own their own plots. Me, I'd recommend acquirin' that beach where we met up."

"Beach?" Hau made a face. "What would a man want with empty beach? You cannot grow anything on it or raise any animals. There is no good water there. Such places are worthless." The unicorn pricked up its ears, whinnied querulously, and then returned to its cropping.

"Mebbe they are now." Malone swung himself up into the saddle. "But take my word on it. Your grandchildren'll thank you." So saying, he started downslope toward the flickering lights of Lahaina, its raucous inhabitants blissfully unaware of the fiery death they had barely avoided.

Hau followed at his own pace, thinking hard as he descended the slope. Beach? What would any man want to own beach for? He decided that his new haole kahuna friend was joking with him. There was beach all around the island, most of it even more desolate, white, and sunstruck than the place where they had met. No one owned it because it was not worth a single American dollar.

And surely never would be.

MID-FLINX

You are one page away from a glimpse into one of the most imaginative, exciting sci-fi series around, from the story-telling master,

ALAN DEAN FOSTER.

Explore Midworld, and meet its charmingly funny star, Flinx, as well as his minidrag, Pip. Discover for yourself why this is one of today's most popular fantasy series.

MID-FLINX

From Del Rey Books.
Available in bookstores everywhere.

If everyone's going to chase me, Flinx thought, I should've been born with eyes in the back of my head. Of course, in a sense, he had been.

He couldn't *see* behind himself. Not in the commonly accepted meaning of the term. Not visually. But he could "sense" behind him. Most sentient creatures generated patterns on the emotional level that Flinx could, from time to time, detect, descry, or perceive. Depending on the wildly variable sensitivity of his special talent, he could feel anger, fear, love, sorrow, pain, happiness, or simple contentment in others the way ordinary folk could feel heat or cold, slipperiness or stickiness, that which was sharp and that which was soft.

The emotional states of other beings prodded him with little jabs, twitches, icy notions in his brain. Sometimes they arrived on the doorstep of his mind as a gentle knock or comforting greeting, more often as a violent hammering he was unable, despite his most ardent efforts, to ignore.

For years he believed that any refining of his talent would be an improvement. He was no longer so sure. Increased sensitivity only exposed him to more and more personal distress and private upsets. He had discovered that the emotional spectrum was aroiling, violent, crowded, generally unpleasant place. When he was especially receptive, it washed over him in remorseless waves, battering and pounding at his own psyche, leaving scant room for feelings of his own. None of this was apparent to others. Years of practice enabled him to keep the turmoil inside his head locked up, hidden away, artfully concealed.

Much to his distress, as he matured it became harder instead of easier to maintain the masquerade.

Used to be that he could distance himself from the emotional projections of others by putting distance between himself and the rest of humankind. Now that he'd grown more sensitive still, that kind of peace came to him only in the depths of interstellar space itself.

His situation wasn't entirely hopeless. With advancing maturity had come the ability to shut out the majority of background low-level emotional emanations. Spousal ire directed silently at mates, the petty squabbles of children, silent internalized hatreds, secret loves: he'd managed to reduce them all to a kind of perceptual static in the back of his mind. He couldn't completely relax in the company of others, but neither was his mind in constant turmoil. Where and when possible, he favored town over city, hamlet over town, country over hamlet, and wilderness over all.

Still, as his erratic control of his fickle talent improved, his worries only expanded, and he found himself plagued by new fears and uncertainties.

As he watched Pip slither silently across the oval glassine tabletop, hunting for fallen crumbs of salt and sugar, Flinx found himself wondering not for the first time where it would all stop. As he grew older and taller he continued to grow more sensitive. Would he someday be privy to the emotional state of insects? Per-haps a couple of distraught bacteria would eventually be all that was necessary to incite one of his recurring headaches.

He knew that would never happen. Not because it wasn't theoretically possible—he was such a genetic anomaly that where his nervous system was concerned, *anything* was theoretically possible—but because long before he could ever attain that degree of sensitivity he would certainly go mad. If the pain of his head-aches didn't overwhelm him, an excess of knowledge would.

He sat alone in the southwest corner of the restaurant, but for all it distanced him from the emotional outpourings of his fellow patrons, he might as well have been sitting square in their midst. His isolation arose not from personal choice but because the other diners preferred it that way. They shunned him, and not the other way around.

It had nothing to do with his appearance. Tall, slim but well-proportioned, with his red hair and green eyes he was a pleasant-looking, even attractive young man. Much to his personal relief, he'd also lost nearly all the freckling that had plagued him since his youth.

The most likely explanation for his isolation was that the other diners had clustered at the opposite end of the dining room in hopes of avoiding the attentions of the small, pleat-winged, brightly-colored flying snake which was presently foraging across her master's table in search of spice and sustenance. While the combined specific xenozoological knowledge of the other patrons peaked not far above zero, several dutifully recalled that contrasting bright colors in many primitive creatures constituted a warning sign to potential predators. Rather than chance confirmation of this theory, all preferred to order their midday meal as far from the minidrag as possible.

Pip's pointed tongue flicked across the tabletop to evaluate a fragment of turbinado sugar. Delighted by the discovery, she pounced on the energy-rich morsel with a languid thrust of her upper body.

Credit was due the restaurant's host. When Flinx had appeared at the entrance with the flying snake coiled decorously about his left arm and shoulder, the older man had stiffened instinctively while listening to Flinx's explanation that the minidrag was a longtime pet fully under control who would threaten no one. Accepting the tall young guest at his word, the unflinching host had led him to a small, isolated table which partook fully of the establishment's excellent view.

Samstead was a peaceful world. Its three large continents were veined by many rivers which drained into oceans congenial of coast and clime. Its weather was consistent if not entirely benign, its settlers hardworking and generally content. They raised up light industries and cut down dense forests, planted thousands of fields and drew forth from the seas a copious harvest of savory alien protein. In dehydrated, freeze-dried, and otherwise commercially profitable compacted forms, this bounty found its way packed, labeled, and shipped to less fruitful systems.

It was a world of wide-open spaces buttoned together by innumerable small towns and modest, rurally attuned metropolises. While air transport was widely available, citizens preferred where possible to travel by means of the many rivers and connecting canals. Working together, humans and thranx had over the years woven a relatively pleasant fabric of life out of the natural threads supplied by their planet, which lay on the fringes of the Commonwealth. It was a pleasant place to call home.

Perhaps the most remarkable thing about Samstead was that there was nothing remarkable about it. It had been a long time since Flinx had come across so docile an outpost of civilization. Since his arrival he'd given serious thought to extending his visit beyond his original intent, perhaps even settling down—if such a thing were possible for him.

It was a world where a new colonist might be able to lose himself in villatic contentment. A world where even he might no longer need to continually employ those figurative eyes in the back of his head. Flinx wasn't paranoid, but bitter experience had taught him caution. This was the inevitable consequence of an adolescence that had been, well, something other than normal.

DEL REY ONLINE!

The Del Rey Internet Newsletter...

A monthly electronic publication, posted on the Internet, GEnie, CompuServe, BIX, various BBSs, and the Panix gopher (gopher.panix.com). It features hype-free descriptions of books that are new in the stores, a list of our upcoming books, special announcements, a signing/reading/convention-attendance schedule for Del Rey authors, "In Depth" essays in which professionals in the field (authors, artists, designers, sales people, etc.) talk about their jobs in science fiction, a question-and-answer section, behind-the-scenes looks at sf publishing, and more!

Online editorial presence: Many of the Del Rey editors are online, on the Internet, GEnie, CompuServe, America Online, and Delphi. There is a Del Rey topic on GEnie and a Del Rey folder on America Online.

Our official e-mail address for Del Rey Books is delrey@randomhouse.com

Internet information source!

A lot of Del Rey material is available to the Internet on a gopher server: all back issues and the current issue of the Del Rey Internet Newsletter, a description of the DRIN and summaries of all the issues' contents, sample chapters of upcoming or current books (readable or downloadable for free), submission requirements, mail-order information, and much more. We will be adding more items of all sorts (mostly new DRINs and sample chapters) regularly. The address of the gopher is gopher.panix.com

Why? We at Del Rey realize that the networks are the medium of the future. That's where you'll find us promoting our books, socializing with others in the sf field, and—most importantly—making contact and sharing information with sf readers.

For more information, e-mail ekh@panix.com